WEDDING BELLS ON MADISON AVENUE

BOOK 3 IN THE NEW YORK EVER AFTER SERIES

HELEN ROLFE

(24 hours)

B

First published in 2018. This edition first published in Great Britain in 2022 by Boldwood Books Ltd.

Copyright © Helen Rolfe, 2018

Cover Design by CC Book Design

Cover Photography: Shutterstock

The moral right of Helen Rolfe to be identified as the author of this work has been asserted in accordance with the Copyright, Designs and Patents Act 1988.

This book is a work of fiction and, except in the case of historical fact, any resemblance to actual persons, living or dead, is purely coincidental.

Every effort has been made to obtain the necessary permissions with reference to copyright material, both illustrative and quoted. We apologise for any omissions in this respect and will be pleased to make the appropriate acknowledgements in any future edition.

A CIP catalogue record for this book is available from the British Library.

Paperback ISBN 978-1-80415-623-0

Large Print ISBN 978-1-80415-622-3

Hardback ISBN 978-1-80415-624-7

Ebook ISBN 978-1-80415-621-6

Kindle ISBN 978-1-80415-620-9

Audio CD ISBN 978-1-80415-629-2

MP3 CD ISBN 978-1-80415-628-5

Digital audio download ISBN 978-1-80415-627-8

Boldwood Books Ltd
23 Bowerdean Street
London SW6 3TN

For my amazing husband and children... the biggest support team ever!

1

DARCY

'To the happy couple!' Holly raised her glass and the others around the table followed suit. 'If anyone can make a marriage work, it's you two. Congratulations.'

Darcy's hand hadn't left Myles's lap since the minute they'd sat down at The Plaza with their closest friends to celebrate their engagement. Cleo and Dylan had come in to the city from Inglenook Falls, Holly had zipped over to The Plaza from her office, and now, as they all sipped champagne at the circular table in The Champagne Bar next to the long window that stretched almost from floor to ceiling, with Fifth Avenue views, Darcy hoped Holly was right with her words. She'd fallen in love, no doubt about it, but their relationship had moved as fast as the Manhattan rush hour, and she was starting to panic that they didn't know one another well enough at all.

'Show me the ring again?' Holly grabbed Darcy's hand the second she put down her glass.

'It's gorgeous.' Cleo leaned forward for a second, better, look. 'I can't stop staring at it. I'm so pleased for you, Darcy.'

'Thank you.' She hugged her friends in turn. She couldn't help but agree with their appraisal, extending her fingers on her left hand so the timeless, rose gold engagement ring with its solitaire diamond on her fourth finger sparkled beneath the lights. As soon as Myles had proposed, they'd gone straight to Tiffany & Co., excited, their future shining brightly in front of them. He'd insisted on being extravagant when it came to the ring and this time she'd let him have his way. And Darcy was glad they hadn't waited either. They hadn't let themselves get back to their busy lives, their careers, and put their relationship on the backburner.

'So come on,' said Cleo, desperate for more information. 'Tell us how it all happened. You guys have only been together for five minutes.'

Darcy pushed the worries out of her mind. 'It was very romantic.'

'I couldn't wait any longer.' Myles beamed at his fiancée, his chocolate-brown eyes barely able to leave her face for a second.

'I think I'm going to need another drink,' Dylan chimed, 'if it's all going to get too soppy.' He earned himself a nudge from Cleo, and Darcy could tell he didn't mean it at all. From what she'd heard, Dylan could be a hopeless romantic when he wanted to be. Only last month he'd made his wife chocolate-dipped strawberries to cheer her up after a crazy day at the store she owned and ran.

'Come on,' Holly huffed, 'proper details. Did he even get down on one knee?'

'Sofia was home from Switzerland so I had a half day at the Inn. It had been days since we'd spent some quality time together, so we walked up to Central Park and had lunch at Tavern on the Green.' Darcy watched the man she'd agreed to marry. Funny how they'd known each other for such a short time, yet she hadn't even hesitated.

'Oh, I love it there,' Holly gushed. 'Is that where it happened? Did he ask you there?'

'Let them tell us the story!' Cleo urged.

Myles took the floor. 'I'd only intended on taking her for lunch. Proposing was the last thing on my mind, but as we sat and talked and laughed, I wondered why I was even waiting to make things more permanent. We left the restaurant and my mind was working hard to think of when and how I could possibly ask her. We went to the Shakespeare Garden, walked up to Belvedere Castle, and as we were making our way back towards the lake we saw a caricaturist.'

'I thought it would be fun,' Darcy grinned, fingers splayed on the stem of her champagne glass, her ring a glistening reminder of that perfect day. 'I thought a picture could be a really nice keepsake.'

'The caricaturist drew Darcy first,' said Myles, 'and it gave me a chance to think. Before he started to draw me I told her to go and grab a couple of cold drinks from the vendor nearby, and it allowed me enough time to put my plan into action.'

Cleo and Holly clasped one another in typical female fashion, on tenterhooks for the next bit, while Dylan was slightly more reserved and enjoying his champagne.

'I gave the caricaturist some instructions and as soon as Darcy sat down next to me again, he got to work. When he'd finished I paid him, kept the picture hidden – not easy when Darcy was desperate to see it – and then as soon as we reached the top of the Bow Bridge I got down on one knee and showed her. The caricaturist had drawn me on one knee, with a speech bubble coming from my mouth that said, "Will you marry me?"' He kissed his fiancée. 'I'm so glad you said yes.'

'Me too.'

'That is so romantic,' Cleo and Holly said in unison.

'Does anyone have a tissue?' Dylan sniffed and pretended to wipe his eyes until Holly shoved him on the arm to berate him. 'No, seriously guys, congratulations. I think it's great news. So when's the big day?'

'You'd better all put it in your calendars,' Myles declared, 'because it's in August.'

'August next year? That's not long, it'll fly by.' Holly finished her champagne.

'August this year,' said Darcy.

'Are you serious?' Cleo shook her head. 'But that's only five months away. How on earth will you be ready in time? Can you even get a venue?'

'That's the only thing we've really sorted so far. We're not having a big elaborate ceremony so that made it easier, plus we're flexible about the day, so we're having it at the Moonlight Loft & Terrace.'

'The rooftop bar that just opened up on Madison?' Dylan ordered a beer for both him and Myles, making Darcy smile. Couldn't keep a man's man down for long; she'd wondered how long before they exchanged the girlie champagne for something different.

'That's right,' said Myles. 'Darcy has a whole vision of what it'll look like. They've done a couple of weddings there already but, being new, they're not booked up.'

'Wow.' Holly was completely in the moment. 'Getting married beneath the moonlight, out in the open air, it's perfect.'

'What happens if it rains?' Cleo asked, earning a frown from Holly. 'What? You need to plan for these things.'

'There's a lovely area inside,' said Darcy, 'but we won't need it. It'll be gloriously sunny by August and not quite as humid as July. It'll be the perfect day. I just know it.'

Talk turned to what she had planned for the wedding ceremony, although she hadn't thought about it in great detail yet, and the men showed as much enthusiasm as they could before their talk turned to hockey and they left the women talking dresses, cakes, and bonbonniere.

'You could have mini preserves,' Holly suggested, 'or a couple I know who got married in the country last year had little pots of honey each with a tiny dipper attached to the side.'

'That's a great idea,' Cleo approved.

Darcy hadn't got down to the finer details yet. 'I actually need to ask you both something.' She grinned as Cleo clasped her hands together, pre-empting what was coming. 'Holly, Cleo, would you like to be my bridesmaids?'

Both women squealed and even the men laughed after they knew what had gone down. 'Oh Darcy, I can't wait!' Cleo could barely sit still.

'I am truly honoured,' said Holly more demurely. An editor with a top publication in the city, she was more reserved than Cleo although Darcy suspected she was maintaining some decorum and that before long, especially when they had dress fittings and saw the venue, her enthusiasm would unleash. 'I haven't known you all that long, are you sure?'

'Of course I am. It doesn't matter how long we've known one another, I consider you a very good friend. So there'll be you two plus my good friends, Isabella and Gabriella, plus my sister, Sarah. I can't imagine doing this without every single one of you by my side.'

Cleo put a hand on her arm. 'It'll be our pleasure.'

'It sure will.' Holly smiled. 'Talking of Isabella, where is she?'

'She couldn't make today, she's away in Vermont with her other half. But because I knew she was heading out of town, I told her right after we got back from choosing the ring. We Skyped Gabriella in Switzerland too.'

'With champagne I hope.' Holly finished the last of her bubbles and they ordered another bottle.

'Why of course.'

'This is all moving so fast, Darcy.' Cleo had a headache she blamed on drinking during the day and opted for a large glass of freshly squeezed orange juice. 'I don't know how you manage everything with work and now a wedding to organise. But I guess, when you know, you know.'

'Never been in that situation myself.' Holly's red hair danced and her white gold chandelier earrings swayed when she moved her head. 'But you two are so right together.'

Darcy looked across at Myles, who winked when he saw her. She had no doubts in her mind that Myles Cunningham was The One. The only doubt she did have was whether both of them could actually find time to build a life together. Ever since they'd started their relationship, it had been a whirlwind of excitement and the pace of getting engaged and married before they'd been together a year was really a representation of how their lives operated all round: breakneck speed, no pausing or deliberating, all go, go, go.

When they emerged from The Plaza, merrier from the champagne and chatting away so much that Cleo almost walked into the doorman, they made their way down the front steps of the building. Horses and carts lined up across the street ready to take tourists on unforgettable tours around Central Park, an iconic yellow taxi pulled up and dropped a new guest at the hotel, a cyclist cut across the sidewalk and back onto the street. Cars tooted their horns at a nearby intersection and a businessman scooted by in talks on his cell phone. This was the Manhattan Darcy loved, with its mayhem and character, but sometimes she knew it would be better if her personal life didn't move at quite the same pace.

She looped her ice-blue infinity scarf over her head so it settled around her neck, and scooped her chestnut-brown hair free from beneath it.

'You liked the scarf?' Cleo didn't miss a thing as they loitered in front of the building, ready to go their separate ways. 'Ruby insisted you would. She picked out the yarn and said it matched your eyes.' Ruby was Dylan's daughter from his first marriage and both she and her brother, Jacob, had a good relationship with Cleo, who'd gone on to have another baby, Tabitha, who had just turned one.

'Then Ruby has excellent taste. She's turning into quite the little lady.' Darcy hugged the woman who'd gone from a casual acquaintance to a really good friend. 'Thank you for making it for me.'

'It's what I do best.'

'Well it's no wonder the Little Knitting Box is booming, it's gorgeous.'

'Do you take requests?' Holly asked.

Cleo grinned. 'Of course! Come out to the store in Inglenook Falls and we'll sort something out.'

'You're on.' Holly pulled on a pair of leather gloves. 'I need some fancier things than these. They're very...'

'City,' Cleo finished for her. 'I'll kit you out in something a lot more fun, don't you worry.'

'Sounds good to me,' said Holly. 'Although I'll be happy to lose the gloves altogether for a while. I can't wait for spring to really get going.' She looked up at the sky, the clouds shielding much of the sun and insisting that this early on in the season they were very much the boss. She kissed each person on the cheek in turn, including the men, and hopped into a cab back to work as Cleo and Dylan went off to the Guggenheim Museum to make the most of a childfree afternoon.

Myles hugged Darcy to him and kissed the top of her head. The five of them had settled into a really strong friendship, as though all their lives had been hovering on the sidelines waiting to be slotted together. 'Shall we take advantage of our rare afternoon off?'

'What did you have in mind?' She snuggled against him as they walked along towards the subway station. The wind whipped around them as a reminder that spring hadn't really sprung at all even though it was the middle of March. Only last week there'd been ice on the sidewalk and down the steps of the Inn and by now Darcy had had enough of the extra work the season brought with it.

When he grinned she knew exactly what Myles was thinking and hand in hand they took the subway which shuttled them up the west side of the park. They hurried back to the Upper West Side apartment, took the stairs quickly, laughing and racing each other in a cardio workout to get to the fourth floor, and barely inside the door, they tugged at one another's clothes before tumbling into the bedroom.

* * *

Myles ran his fingers lazily up Darcy's arm. 'I could get used to afternoon meetings like this.'

In the last hour she'd thought about nothing but him and her. There'd been no room for thoughts of the Inn, advertising, and preparation for guests' arrivals or departures, and it was stolen time they rarely got. When he'd proposed, Darcy had thought Myles impulsive and panicked they weren't doing the right thing, but she couldn't ever imagine feeling this way about another man, and so she'd grabbed her chance with both hands.

'My parents have invited us up at the weekend.' Darcy shivered beneath his caress as it hit a delicate spot and he planted light kisses along her shoulder, moving the wavy chestnut tresses out of his way. Her brother, Tate, lived close to their parents so he'd be there but her sister, who lived in San Francisco, would have to wait to admire her engagement ring and give her fiancé the once-over.

'I'll look forward to it,' Myles mumbled, although he was distracted kissing the nape of her neck.

'You can definitely make it?' she breathed.

'I wouldn't miss it for the world.' He flipped her onto her back and she giggled as the muscles in his arms pinned her down. And then he kissed her until she begged to be released.

'I know work is full on for you.'

'It's always busy, and so is yours. But this is more important.'

Music to her ears. 'I'll tell them it's on then. Sofia flies back to Switzerland on Monday morning so I've got the whole weekend free.'

'You two seem to have a good partnership going.'

'It's working out well.'

'But...? Come on, I sense the hesitation.'

'I love co-running the Inn, you know I do. And the profits are soaring lately, but... I hate that it's not *my* home. I never ended up getting my own place, there never seemed a lot of point and Sofia insisted her apartment was big enough for the both of us, especially when she's away so much, but... well, she's my friend's mom. And although I love her to bits, I need my independence too.' One of her only regrets at getting together with Myles so quickly was that she hadn't had the chance to re-establish herself in Manhattan, rent an apartment, and find her feet before everything changed again. But love had found her, and for that she'd never be sorry.

'You do realise there's no point in you looking for a place now,' said Myles. 'You can move in here whenever you like. Unless you want to look for a place we choose together rather than somewhere that was renovated for me.'

She looked around. 'Luckily you have good taste, suits me just fine. I'll bring everything over from the Inn and from where it's being stored in my parents' garage and move in properly once we're married.'

'Why not before?'

'Sofia will be away a lot over the next few months but I think she'll be back in New York more come the summer. Which means I won't need to stay there so much and I'll have some time to shift all my belongings.'

Myles grinned. 'I think I got things a bit out of step.' Jokingly he tapped his palm against his forehead. 'First, date a girl... second, ask her to move in with you... then, propose.' He propped himself up on his forearm and with his other hand tucked her hair behind her ears. 'I missed out phase two.'

'At least you impressed my dad.'

'How so?'

'You're doing the honourable thing. We dated, you proposed, there'll be no living in sin. At least...' She eyed his naked body. '... not to his knowledge.'

'Maybe I should take a selfie and send it to him.' He put an arm around her and held her close before reaching for his cell phone.

'Don't you dare.' She wrestled away. 'But seriously, Myles, where do we go from here? I work long and erratic hours and am away from this apartment, you often work silly hours too. It won't be much of a home if neither of us is here or, when we are, we're not together.'

'We'll work it out, now would you come back here?' He watched as Darcy grabbed his discarded shirt and tugged it on, protecting her modesty.

The shirt sleeves hung way past her hands and she rolled them up after she'd buttoned the shirt. 'Do you have a pen and paper?'

'Are you wanting to draw diagrams to decide what we're doing next?' he teased.

'Stop joking around for a second. Do you have one or not?' Hands on hips, she scoured the area.

'On the dresser next to the mirror.'

She padded over the wooden floor, grabbed both items, and returned to the bed, brushing away his suggestion she take the shirt off again. They might be engaged but they were very much in the early, can't-keep-your-hands-off-each-other stage of their relationship, and sometimes it was far too distracting.

'What are you up to?' He accepted defeat, reached out for his jeans and tugged them on.

'We have just five months to plan the wedding.' She tapped the pen against the paper. 'We have a venue, but that's it.' Darcy began scribbling away.

'We have a ring too.' He ran a hand up her thigh. 'You know, I remember you making another list once upon a time.'

She stilled his hand but couldn't help smiling at his mischievous expression. 'I remember.' He'd been just a guest back then, but a man with a dilemma, trying to decide whether to take an escort to a work function. Between them they'd put together a pro and con list and he'd ended up asking her to go with him instead.

He peered more closely at the paper. 'Just checking you're not putting a column for "con" on the list when it comes to our wedding.'

She picked up a discarded cushion that had been knocked off during their lovemaking and chucked it at his head as he made his way to the bathroom. 'Careful, or I might think about it,' she called after him.

Lists were Darcy's friend. They helped her to sort through the jumble in her mind and know what she needed to do, the crossing off of items a form of catharsis. But as she looked down at the ten major items she'd already made a note of by the time Myles emerged from the bathroom when he heard his cell phone ringing, she wondered how on earth they could possibly get it all done.

She was about to go through the list with Myles and expand it in more detail when he said, 'I have to go in to the office.'

'What, now?'

'I'm sorry.' He leaned over and kissed her, looked at the shirt and said with a grin, 'It's okay, I'll grab a fresh one.'

'How long will you be?'

He fastened the cuffs on the shirt he'd pulled from the wardrobe. 'As long as it takes, I guess. The shit has hit the fan in a big way so I don't have much choice.'

And just like that, their perfect afternoon was gone. Darcy's visions of taking a bubble bath while listening to music, pouring a big glass of full-bodied red wine each, and snuggling up on the sofa, a rarity in their lives that had only been intersecting for a whirlwind few months, had disappeared.

Had they both leapt into this without thinking?

Their love was new and exciting; it was all the good bits, and they were only just starting to face the practicalities. They'd only been together since Christmas but as the New Year had dawned, both of them had thrown their focus into their separate work commitments. Darcy had been running the Inglenook Inn independently whenever Sofia was out of the country spending time with her daughter, Gabriella, who had been Darcy's closest friend since they were at school. And when Sofia had returned, they'd got straight down to formalities. Darcy was now in a more formal arrangement and paid a decent salary for her efforts, working hard to boost profits and establish herself as one of the finest hoteliers in the industry. She and Sofia had discussed the long-term outlook too, which perhaps involved Darcy taking part ownership of the Inn if that was the route they chose, but for now they were managing it between them and it was working. And the high level of responsibility was a huge step forwards in Darcy's career. The only worry she had was that this would come at a price, especially when Myles's career on Wall Street was also going from strength to strength.

Since the day Myles had kissed her beneath the mistletoe on the steps of the Inglenook Inn in December, Darcy's feet had barely touched the ground. But she had a sneaky suspicion the next few months, as they planned their wedding in a ridiculously short timescale, would test their resolve.

Only two people who were really meant to be would come out the other side.

2

MYLES

Myles was beginning to think he worked with a bunch of incompetents in his job as an investment banker. He was in charge of a team of six, including one troublemaker in particular. Rufus. The guy brought with him a degree and a high level of arrogance he didn't have the right to unless he'd been in the game at least as long as the rest of them. Right now, Myles should've been at his apartment with Darcy in his arms, not in the thronging depths of the Financial District making his way towards the firm's headquarters, where he'd need to execute damage control and babysit a member of his team who needed some further education, better known as Life Skills.

By the time Myles reached the office he was already cranky – at having been taken away from home, at having a problem to sort out that he'd played no part in creating, at the way faces rushed at him as soon as he got there telling him what had gone wrong. Rufus had arrived at the firm two months ago with the same bags of energy that were seen in most, if not all, junior investment bankers. But he'd made the same mistake that so many others did and put his hand up for everything. And it was one thing being seen to be keen, but totally another when things had gone belly-up and it all went wrong.

'You should've flagged this sooner,' Myles told him the second he'd seen the mess Rufus had made with the financial projections. Even at first glance they looked haphazard and meaningless and were no preparation for an important client meeting that Myles's boss thought was all in hand. 'Perhaps I shouldn't have assumed you could do it.' Myles slumped at his desk and tried to summon the energy to get back into work mode after managing to completely switch off with Darcy and their friends. It was rare that Myles took any time off, but today he'd arranged everything down to a tee so that he'd have the special time with his fiancée. Goodness knows they needed it. His father had offered one piece of advice to Myles when he came to New York last year to sort out the mess that was his family, and that was to prioritise and value his personal relationships. His father didn't want him making the same mistakes he had, and Myles was determined not to either. Although when people made his job ten times harder, and demanded more of his time, he began to doubt his ability to see his intentions through.

Rufus scratched at his head, the sweat beading on his brow despite the cool temperature outside and the not particularly warm office. And Myles had no choice but to step up now and spent the next few hours trawling through figures, macros, spreadsheets, calculations, and help Rufus pull together a reasonable presentation ready for the client meeting tomorrow. Myles could've done it himself – easier than if he'd been hand holding – but he did his best to cast his mind back to his first years as an investment banker, remembering the steep learning curve, the punishing hours, and attempted a modicum of sympathy.

When they were almost finished, Rufus sat back in his chair and interlocked his hands behind his head. The leather groaned beneath him but he looked as though he'd got to the end of a taxing day and come out on top. And now it was time for Myles to tell him how it really was. Otherwise the man was going to keep going the same way, like an out-of-control freight train.

'You're all ready for the client meeting?' Myles asked his question but really he was waiting for Rufus to thank him profusely for saving his arse.

'Yep, very confident. We've got this.'

Myles took a deep breath. The office had quietened apart from them. People had gone home to their loved ones, or out in the city that never slept. 'You didn't have it when you called in a panic.'

'Sorry about that.'

'That's not why you should be apologising.' The poor guy looked confused. 'You volunteer for everything. Yes, it's enthusiastic and perhaps proactive, but sticking your hand up for extra projects when you already have too much work on is only asking for mistakes. And that's what happened here.'

'I... I...' he stammered. 'I didn't see it that way. I've always thought it good to get out my comfort zone and push myself.'

Myles's voice softened. A lot of managers would tear a piece off their employee for making them come into the office on a rare afternoon off to sort out a mess they'd created, but he'd go easy this time. 'I've been there myself. I've made plenty of mistakes along the way. What you need to remember is that you can take on the work and push yourself, but make sure you deliver. No cutting corners. It only makes for extra work for the team and a very tetchy manager.' Who'd been quite happy at home with his fiancée, he wanted to add, although just thinking about Darcy made him a bit hot under the collar.

When his cell phone rang he told Rufus to go and start putting together the PowerPoint presentation.

'Darcy, I'm sorry, I'm still here at the office.' He sighed, looking out at the lights across Manhattan and picturing her sitting in his apartment waiting. He wondered if she was still in his shirt, her long legs leading all the way up, teasing at what might be beneath the material.

'How long will you be? I could order Chinese food.'

'That sounds wonderful. How about you order it for eight thirty? I should be home by then.'

'I miss you.'

'I miss you too.' Did he ever? 'Keep the bed warm for me.'

'No chance, I'm lounging on the sofa with a big glass of red and the only place I'll be going is to the door to collect the food when it arrives.'

'I hope you're wearing more than you were when I left.'

'Well...'

He was about to say more when Rufus appeared, looking even more frazzled than he had when Myles first arrived. Myles cleared his throat and sat up straighter in his chair. 'Order the usual, Darcy, and I'll text you when I'm on my way.'

After he reluctantly hung up, Myles turned his attention to Rufus. 'Tell me what's happening.' He was starting to resent the man even more now he'd heard Darcy's voice, teasing him, wanting him to come to her. He had a picture in his mind, of her on his sofa, with a glass of wine, feet tucked beneath her and that soft hair tumbling around her shoulders.

'I can't find the updated financial statements from the client. And when I tried to access the files, I've been locked out.'

Couldn't the man do anything? Myles pinched the skin at the top of his nose between his eyes. 'You get on to the systems administrator and I'll find the files on my own computer so you can work from them in the meantime.'

Systems services sorted the access issue quickly enough but

Myles had already found the files for Rufus to work from, his patience now starting to wane, and between them they finished the entire preparation for the presentation, ready for tomorrow morning.

'Shit.' Myles saw the time. Quarter past bloody ten. He checked his cell but nothing from Darcy.

'Thank you.' Rufus sheepishly poked his head around the corner of Myles's office. 'For tonight, I mean.'

'Don't let it happen again,' said Myles, and his look told Rufus to scarper.

Outside, the temperature had plummeted further and it was almost as though winter was too scared to leave and let spring take its place. Myles navigated the subway until he was on the Upper West Side and walked the final few blocks towards his apartment. When he turned his key and pushed open the door the place was quiet, with low lighting coming from the lounge. He hung his coat on the hook in the hallway, removed his shoes, and padded along the wooden floorboards. Darcy wasn't in the bedroom off to the right, or the bathroom, and he found her in the lounge, curled up asleep on the sofa.

Myles leaned against the doorjamb. He rarely had moments like this where he could just enjoy her, watch her, and wonder how in the world he'd ever been so lucky to meet someone as special as Darcy Spencer. He looked at the empty wine glass on the coffee table, a tiny pool of red at the bottom where the dregs had gathered. He took in the discarded cartons, chopsticks poking out of one of them. He knew what they'd contain: chicken in black bean sauce in one, prawn dumplings in another, and a portion of mushroom rice in the third. He already knew Darcy would've put his half of the rice and the dumplings into the fridge along with his regular order of beef teriyaki. There were so many little things they already knew about each other, the minutiae of everyday life, yet he couldn't help but wonder whether the bigger picture hadn't yet been fully painted and was going to trip them up somewhere along the way, just when they thought they knew what was what. His father had warned him not to lose sight of his personal life under the weight of his ambition and, looking at Darcy now, Myles knew how easy it would be to do just that.

He scooped her up from the sofa and when she stirred in his arms, he put a kiss to her forehead and carried her through to the bedroom.

'My handsome prince is home,' she joked, her voice croaky at having been woken up.

'Goodnight, Cinderella.' He tucked her in and her head nestled into the pillow as she began to fall back to sleep. He took off his shirt, his jeans, his socks, and pulled on some sweats and an old T-shirt. He kissed Darcy once more, moved her hair away from her face, and looked up at the framed caricature picture that would forever remind them both of the day in Central Park when their lives had taken on a whole new direction.

Too wired to sleep after the afternoon he'd had, and unbelievably hungry, Myles shut the door behind him and went back to the lounge, took out his food from the refrigerator and tipped it into bowls. He punched the time counter on the digital display of the microwave and listened to the hum as the machine reheated his dinner, watched the turntable reliably move around to heat the food evenly.

Of one thing he was certain, and that was that he wanted Darcy. It was why he'd proposed in the first place. But he had his career to think about too, and it was important to him.

The problem, or the answer, had to be about balance. But he had no clue how to achieve the ideal. Career had been ingrained in him since he was a boy and, coupled with a powerful work ethic that couldn't be taught, he wasn't sure how to be in this relationship and let the important stuff shine through more than the job he'd worked so hard to get.

How did anyone ever get it right?

3

DARCY

When Darcy woke the next morning, Myles was out for the count, his bare arm slung across her body. She prised it off and climbed slowly out of bed, still wearing the shirt she'd grabbed yesterday when she'd started making the list about the wedding. She could vaguely remember watching a movie last night after she'd finally given up waiting for Myles and eaten her dinner, and she recalled him carrying her to bed when he eventually came home.

It was chilly in the apartment at this early hour. She touched a hand to the radiator by the window to find it still stone cold. She pulled on a pair of jeans from the drawer she had in his apartment. Half of her clothes were here, half at the Inn, so without many choices given that some of her things were waiting by the washing machine in a basket to be dealt with, she grabbed Myles's sweat-shirt and pulled it over her head before trudging to the kitchen to make a much-needed cup of coffee.

With the iPad resting on her knees, which were tucked up against her on the sofa, she looked again at the website for the Moonlight Loft & Terrace. Nestled on the magnificent Madison

Avenue, a street she'd walked a thousand times before, it would mark a turning point in her life. The venue was perfect and she still couldn't believe they'd been able to book their wedding in such a brilliant location. She'd had drinks there when it first opened in the fall and the place had stuck in her mind ever since as being classy yet rustic, lively yet not too showy. When lists of what needed to be done for the wedding began to form in her mind the second Myles proposed, the Moonlight Loft & Terrace had been the first place she thought of. And crossing off the search for a venue was a major worry out of the way.

Her cell bleeped and she picked up a message from Isabella asking if they were still on for 9 a.m. She typed back that of course they were and then fired off a text to Cleo to check again that she could make it. Sofia had the Inn under control and wasn't leaving for Switzerland until early afternoon, so this was Darcy's chance to sort out her dress. Isabella, the friend that she was, had already phoned round – given their ridiculous timescale – and made appointments at three separate stores. Darcy had researched dresses online to know what style she preferred, or at least thought she wanted, compiled them in a document, and had forwarded this to the stores so that the assistants knew what she was after.

'Morning.' Myles had one hand against his bare chest, the other rubbing his eyes as he stood in sweats at the corner of the lounge room.

Darcy smiled over at him. He was gorgeous. Sometimes she wanted to pinch herself that he was hers. 'Did I wake you?'

'No, and I'm sorry about last night.' He looked as though he was waiting to be reprimanded.

'Come here.' When he'd sat next to her on the sofa she put her arms around him. 'You're doing your job, I get that.'

'I don't deserve you.'

'True.'

He made a half-hearted attempt to tickle her but he was still too sleepy. He looked at the iPad. 'What are you up to?'

With a gasp she snatched it away. She'd had a picture up of the wedding gown style she was going for. 'You mustn't see the dress.'

'I thought you weren't choosing one until today.'

'I'm not, but I've done my research. You know I like to be prepared.' She clicked on another window on the iPad. 'And here, this is the venue. I've got all sorts of ideas on how to decorate. I was thinking we string white lights, you know, with the big bulbs like you have on your terrace here, and then flowers – haven't thought about what type yet – and a big long table for the meal. Which reminds me, we need to make a guest list. I know we talked about it, but we need to finalise it so I can get the invites out. There's a place four blocks from here that does them. We could go for cream, white, gold, silver...'

He put a finger to her lips. 'Darcy. It's not even 6 a.m. and you're throwing way too much information at me.'

She was, but what choice did they have? They'd agreed they didn't want a long engagement. He'd suggested they elope or go down to City Hall, but as soon as he'd seen Darcy's face he'd realised that wasn't an option. They'd agreed on a small, intimate ceremony, as long as she could have her five bridesmaids. They both wanted somewhere in Manhattan, and Myles had been enthusiastic, chatting away about where they could go, what it would be like, how happy he was. But somehow work had very quickly taken over for both of them and when Darcy managed to get her own mind back to the wedding, it was hard to get him to do the same.

He kissed her on the lips, then moved to her neck. 'You're so organised, I love that about you.'

'I know you do, but you need to join in so we can get things moving. We don't have long until the wedding. I love doing as much as I can, but it should be something we enjoy doing together.' She giggled when she saw his face. 'Okay, so maybe enjoy is a bit of a stretch. But it should be something we at least *do* together. How about tonight? You could come to the Inn after seven when things have quietened for me and we can at least finalise the guest list.'

'I'm not sure I can do tonight. Can it wait until the weekend?'

'Not really.' She lost concentration when he began to move his kisses lower. 'Myles, you need to get to work. We don't have time for this.' His kisses went lower still. 'And I need to get back to the Inn, shower, and go find myself a dress.' Her words faltered as the warm feeling spread through her body. 'Myles...'

But he wasn't listening. It was a case of actions speaking louder than words, for both of them.

* * *

'You make me sick, you know,' was the first thing Isabella said when Darcy trotted down the steps of the Inglenook Inn. 'Eurgh... you just look obscenely happy.'

'It'll be your turn soon.' She hugged her friend.

'No chance. Jake and I need to get used to living with each other first. I have to make sure he's house trained.'

'How was Vermont?'

'Wonderful, very romantic.'

'It sounds as though everything is still going well for you guys.' They sauntered away from the Inn. The sun was out for once but the biting cold meant sweaters, coats, and gloves today.

'Apart from a little bit of education about doing chores before the woman of the house does, yes. I mean, he always did his own laundry just fine before we moved in.' She rolled her eyes and looped an arm through Darcy's. 'I wonder what annoying habits Myles will show once you're living together full time.'

'I think I'll live in ignorant bliss until then.' It had crossed Darcy's mind that they hadn't had long enough to be irritated by one another's little ways, but today wasn't the day to try and predict Myles's bad points. Today it was wedding gown shopping all the way.

'I thought you'd changed your mind.' Cleo hugged each of them hello when they met her at the first bridal boutique in the East Village. They were starting with the farthest one away and had four stores on their itinerary, with the final one being closest to the Inn. That way, if they were running late, Darcy would be ready to take the reins from Sofia before she left for the airport and they'd juggle her appointment around that.

Darcy took a deep breath and looked up at the storefront signage. Thanks to a feature Holly ran last year in the major New York magazine, *Contemporary Edge*, where she worked as one of their top editors, she'd been able to point Darcy to some of the lesser-known places when it came to wedding gown shopping. 'Well, girls, this is it.'

'Can Holly make it?' Cleo asked as they pushed open the door to the store.

'Not today, she's snowed under with work so says she's relying on you two to choose something perfect for me.'

'Mission accepted,' said Isabella as they stepped around a cluster of women laughing away at the front of the store, one clutching a dress as the excitement got so much their voices reached a pitch Darcy was sure only dogs would be able to hear.

'Please slap me if I ever get that bad,' she whispered to Cleo.

'Deal.'

The assistant appeared and welcomed them warmly. 'You must be Darcy. It's wonderful to meet you.' Her make-up stayed obediently put with rouge that matched her lipstick. 'I have six dresses lined up ready for you, and I think you're going to love them.'

Darcy's heart soared. She'd been excited from the moment Myles popped the question, giddy all the way to Tiffany & Co, but this moment was surreal, like nothing she'd ever experienced before.

She came down to earth with an almighty bump as she made her way through the dresses and it became abundantly clear the woman, whose name Darcy couldn't even remember, either hadn't looked at the email she'd sent or had disregarded it completely.

'Lucky number six,' the assistant sighed as Darcy wiggled out of the fifth dress and handed it back to her.

When the woman helped her step into a mermaid-style dress that Darcy hated with a passion even before she'd manoeuvred it over her hips and up to chest level, Darcy couldn't keep quiet any longer. 'I'm wondering, did you have any dresses like the selections I emailed you about?'

'Huh?' The woman wasn't listening; she was trying to pull the material tightly across Darcy's chest so she could do up the zipper, each tug limiting Darcy's ability to breathe and get her words out to voice her concerns.

'The email I sent,' Darcy tried, between sucking in everything she could and wondering whether it was possible to break ribs just by squeezing into a dress that was clearly on the small side. 'It had examples of gowns I'd go for,' she managed before the woman stood up looking victorious that the zipper had gone all the way to the top.

'We don't have a huge variety in off-the-rack dresses – I've pulled most of them from the floor. I tend to have an eye for what suits a bride and, I think, this is the one.' She put a hand on Darcy's shoulder, smiling at their reflection, and Darcy forced up the corners of her own mouth because that was what was expected.

She shuffled out of the changing room into the communal area where Cleo and Isabella were waiting. 'So, what do you think?'

Neither said a word as the woman circled Darcy and brushed imaginary pieces of dust from the fabric or straightened up sections to make them hang better. Darcy wished she'd give them some privacy but she hung around as though she were part of the wedding party entitled to an opinion. Of all the ways today was going to go, Darcy hadn't imagined this one and she wanted to burst into tears.

'Could you help me out of it?' She didn't look at her friends, just went back into the changing room, and the woman seemed to pick up on the vibe because she said nothing else until Darcy was fully dressed, and even then it was a vague, non-committal exchange about getting in touch.

The three girls left the boutique and only when they'd reached the next block did Darcy hear a snigger.

'It's not funny!' she told Cleo. And then Isabella joined in, her eyes swimming with tears of laughter. 'It's not!'

'I'm sorry, but that last one made you look like Ariel from *The Little Mermaid*.' Cleo's voice shook.

'That was awful, I'm never going back there. I only said I'd be in touch because it felt like the polite thing to say. She hadn't paid attention to a damn word of my email. She has no people skills whatsoever, she put me in dresses I wouldn't be seen dead in.' She finished her rant as her friends quietened so as not to upset her but as they crossed the street she took one look at them and burst out laughing too. 'Oh, please let the next place be better.'

They headed uptown towards the Upper East Side, where they went into a store nestled between a café and a dry cleaner, but the second Darcy walked through the pale blue door, she knew they were onto a winner compared to the last place. This time, the assistant had read the email and brought out appropriate choices.

Darcy loved the place so much that she was disappointed nothing jumped out at her, and so it was on to the next venue.

The third store, in Chelsea, they reached by taxi and it was there Darcy found a dress that was near-enough perfect. It was a sample, fitting snugly but not too tight. The ivory material had a beaded sweetheart neckline and lace appliqués, and both Isabella and Cleo were lost for words when Darcy emerged from the changing room in the gown. The only thing that stopped everyone from smiling was the lack of understanding that Darcy was getting married in August of this year, not the next. The dress didn't come as an off-the-rack garment and there was no way another could be made in time for the wedding, and so off they trudged to the fourth and final store.

'I don't think I'm going to find anything today.' Deflated, she almost wanted to head to the Inn right now, admit defeat.

'Don't say that,' Isabella scolded. 'When have you ever been one to give up without a fight?'

'Come on.' Cleo spotted the store ahead of them on Bleecker Street, not far from the previous one. 'And if you don't find anything, we can go to Magnolia Bakery and buy red velvet cupcakes.'

'If I don't find a dress,' said Darcy, 'I think I'll buy more than a cupcake… maybe a huge carrot cake, with all that yummy frosting.'

Isabella sniggered. 'You'll talk yourself out of this in a minute.' They'd reached the door to the store. 'Come on, in you go.'

The quaint boutique, fronted by a curved window and a small step leading down, was run by two very jolly sisters, one with a tape measure hanging around her neck like a doctor would walk around with a stethoscope ready to listen to the internal sounds of the human body, and the other with glasses perched on the end of her nose as though any moment now she'd be sewing exquisite beading onto material. The second Darcy went in they must've read the look of despair on her face because they rallied round all three women, they offered champagne, they chatted with Darcy to put her at ease before they even looked at a single gown.

'I got your email.' Alexis, glamorous even with the tape-measure appendage, was friendly and warm and took control as her sister, Serenity, handed out glasses of champagne. 'You don't know how helpful it is to have a bride who already has an idea of what she wants.'

'Really? It doesn't make your job harder?' It was the impression Darcy had got from all three of the stores so far.

'Not at all. I've picked out gowns that are as close to what you've asked for as I can, but if you're not happy with those, we'll find others. You can try on every single gown in the store if you like, the floor is yours. We're here to make this part of your wedding plans go smoothly, and hopefully make it fun for you.'

Cleo had somehow managed to wangle a cup of herbal tea from Serenity but Isabella was into the champagne. She'd taken the full day off work so had no hesitation in getting into the spirit.

Darcy tried on four gowns, all beautiful but none of them quite getting there. She was sick of taking off all her layers to ward off the March chill on the Manhattan streets, trying on dresses that disappointed, only to have to put everything on once again and traipse somewhere else.

But it was the fifth gown that made Darcy stand stock-still.

Serenity's soft voice floated on the air as she fastened the buttons on the low back of the dress above the silky bow that would tie and flatter Darcy's shape. 'I think we may have found something here.'

Romantic lace motifs over tulle on this ivory, A-line gown were shaped in an off-the-shoulder bodice that hugged Darcy just right. Her eyes glistened. 'It's beautiful.'

Serenity finished the last of the buttons. 'Would you like to try a veil? I can bring in samples and we'll fit one on before you show your friends. Then we can see their reaction.'

Darcy kept her gaze glued on her reflection as she waited for Serenity to bring back three veils, all at different lengths. But the first sample captured her the minute Serenity put it in her hair. There was no need to try the others. 'I'm ready,' she said.

Serenity pulled back the curtain and with Cleo and Isabella gossiping away, they almost didn't see her.

'Oh, Darcy.' Now on her feet, Isabella put a hand across her mouth.

Cleo grinned from ear to ear. 'That's the one. It really is.'

Darcy stood in the designer label dress that made her feel more beautiful than she'd ever felt before as Serenity and Alexis let all three of them take in the vision of the bride Darcy would be in only five short months. While the girls chatted excitedly Serenity and Alexis jumped on in, bustling around their new client, discussing the minor adjustments that would take this dress from stunning to completely out of this world. They wanted to nip it in at the waist a teeny bit, take half an inch off the hem, pull in the bodice at the back to really accentuate Darcy's shape. Most of it went over Darcy's head, but she trusted them. They worked out a schedule for fittings and booked them in the diary. Cleo and Isabella looked at a few bridesmaid dresses and were all set to make an appointment for a trying-on session but Serenity insisted they do it now. 'You've not got long before the wedding – time is of the essence!' she told them. They tried on gold, red, lavender, bottle green, but when Darcy pulled out a silver lace sequinned dress, with a V-neck that sparkled beneath the lights, she held it up to two nods of approval.

'Holly did tell me no yellow or pink,' said Darcy, urging Isabella to try on the gown. 'But I think she'll be happy with silver. Can I send a photo of this?' she asked Alexis.

'I don't usually allow it, but I trust you girls.'

'We've had people rip off our designs before,' Serenity hollered from the other side of the store where she was rehanging some of the gowns that hadn't been suitable.

'Do people seriously do that?' Isabella asked as Darcy took a photo and sent it to Holly.

'Oh yes.' Alexis explained. 'Wedding gowns and bridesmaid dresses are expensive so people want to cut corners wherever they can.'

'Isabella, you look gorgeous.' Darcy was so pleased it had been easy enough to select bridesmaid dresses, and when Cleo tried on the same dress in her size she looked just as fabulous. 'You're both stunning.'

Alexis fussed around them both talking about slight alterations they would make and when Darcy's cell pinged she pulled it from her bag. 'Wow, that was quick. Holly loves it and wants to know when she can come and try one on.'

With the wedding so close they couldn't waste any time so Serenity set up an appointment for Holly.

'I'll get measurements from my sister and my friend in Switzerland,' Darcy assured Alexis.

'Excellent. We have an assortment of sizes with this new line so you've timed it perfectly. Let me know as soon as you can and I'll put the dresses to one side, then do last-minute alterations once they're in town.'

'Thank you so much, I'm so glad we found this store.'

'It's our pleasure to help,' Serenity chimed in. 'Here...' She passed a business card Darcy's way. 'Give this lady a call; she can do your hair and make-up on the day. Free trial, so no commitment if you don't like her.'

'Thanks, I'll give her a go.' Another thing to tick off her list.

Darcy left the store floating on air. They'd looked at tiaras after the bridesmaid dresses, discussed hairstyles – updo, or loose and floating? – they talked flowers, jewellery, and shoes, and by the time she left the girls and headed to work, she felt as though nothing could stop her now. Everything was moving in the right direction and more smoothly than she'd ever have imagined.

In five short months she was set to be Mrs Darcy Cunningham. And she couldn't wait.

* * *

Darcy had had a grand total of twenty-four hours off from the Inn, but now it was as though that break had never happened. After their success in project find-a-dress, Isabella had gone off to meet her boyfriend, Jake, Cleo had gone to meet her former employee, Kaisha, at Magnolia Bakery – apparently the mere mention of cupcakes earlier had been enough for Cleo to develop a craving that couldn't be ignored – and when Darcy had got back to work there'd only just been enough time to do a handover before Sofia hopped in a cab to go to the airport.

Back in January Holly had arranged for *Contemporary Edge* to give the Inglenook Inn generous coverage, with photographs showing readers a stunning Christmas at the boutique hotel. Holly had also arranged a second article about the Inn, featuring its versatility for corporate bookings as well family breaks or romantic getaways, and the official photographer would be here at 3 p.m. today, which meant Darcy needed to make up the bed in the apartment on the top floor, their best suite, make certain the windows were clean to give the ultimate city views, and ensure fresh flowers were on display all around the Inn. This time she'd chosen daffodils for a bit of colour and a spring lift with their gentle, sweet scent, and once she'd set the vase on the table in the hall, she went through the new menu items with Rupert, the chef.

Before plonking herself at the desk in the lounge to tackle the admin side of things, she booked a trial with Susan, the bridal hair and make-up stylist recommended by Alexis and Serenity, then ducked out to the café nearby and grabbed a caramel macchiato, welcome sustenance as she responded to emails and comments on the Inn's social media, of which they were getting more and more since they'd been proactive with promotion and following Dylan's revamp of the website to bring more hits than ever before. They'd had a steady wave of corporate clients thanks to a contact she'd made through Myles, and word was beginning to get around that this inn was the place to be for Christmas. Every time Darcy received any enquiry about the festive period she thought back to that day, standing on the steps of the Inn, kissing Myles beneath the mistletoe.

She allowed herself a small smile. The Inn was organised and ready for the photographer, and, equally important, she had a wedding gown. She'd texted Myles as she negotiated the sidewalks back to the Inn and his reply came through now with a funny GIF of a bride doing a happy dance. Excited, she pulled out her diary from her bag, into which she'd tucked the big list she'd made last night at Myles's apartment, and put a big tick beside *Find Dress*. Because she'd found the wedding gown of her dreams, she had all the fittings lined up and it was a major part sorted.

When Cleo bustled in through the door of the Inn as Darcy slung her empty takeaway cup into the trash, she took her by surprise. 'What are you doing here? I thought you were meeting your friend and scoffing yourselves silly at the Magnolia Bakery.'

'I did.' Cleo slumped down on the sofa. She didn't look well at all. 'I did that and Kaisha left, but then I came over all funny. I was right near here so rather than try to make it to the station, I thought it best to stop for a break.'

Darcy put a hand to her friend's forehead. 'You don't have a temperature, but take your layers off, I'll get you a glass of water.'

She scurried off to the kitchen, where Rupert was preparing lunch for some of their guests, and returned to the lounge. 'Do I need to call Dylan?'

Cleo thanked her for the water and shook her head as she downed it in one. 'No need. I'll sit for a bit, then I'll be okay.'

'Mind if I keep going around you?' Darcy didn't want to leave her in distress, but Cleo had already shut her eyes and leant back into the sofa.

Eyes remaining shut, she muttered, 'Go ahead, ignore me. I'll be out of your hair soon.'

Darcy positioned firelighters, logs, and kindling. 'I know it's spring, but it's still cold out and the fireplace really adds ambience.' But she was talking to herself and barely got a grunt from Cleo, who looked shattered. She lit the fire, which was in use most days during the winter because it was a welcoming feature of the Inn but which would soon remain dormant as the weather warmed up and flames were replaced with sprays of colour in a floral arrangement.

When Darcy stood up, happy the fire was taking hold, she turned to find her friend asleep, and when Cleo's cardigan fell open with a will of its own, Darcy smiled. It was a barely-there bump, a roundness in her tummy that Darcy couldn't believe she'd missed when her friend tried on bridesmaid dresses, but along with the extreme tiredness, the lack of champagne consumption at the engagement celebrations and the request for herbal tea at the wedding gown store earlier today, Cleo surely had to be pregnant. And Darcy couldn't help but wonder why Cleo had kept this news to herself – she was usually so full of the joys, especially around her friends.

Darcy got a blanket from the closet in the hallway and put it over Cleo's lap. She was fine there while the Inn was quiet and Darcy got on with her admin. She paid an outstanding bill, glad Sofia had the finances more in hand these days, she reviewed two quotes from builders about possibly turning the top floor into two separate apartments rather than one impressive suite. As the owner of the brownstone, Sofia would make the ultimate decision, but she always valued Darcy's input and they'd established a good working relationship.

When the time approached 3 p.m. Darcy knew she needed to wake Cleo, who had settled against the cushions and showed no signs of shifting. With no guests filing in or out in the last hour, at least she'd managed to get a bit of rest.

Darcy crouched down by her friend and touched a hand lightly to her arm. 'I'm sorry to wake you.'

'Oh, Darcy. I'm so sorry.' Disorientated, she rubbed her eyes as she sat up and adjusted to her surroundings. 'What am I like?'

'Come on, let's go into the dining room. I'll get Rupert to squeeze you a fresh orange juice while I speak with the photographer.'

Darcy settled her in the dining room and spoke with Rupert before excusing herself to welcome Josh from the magazine. Holly, a keen photographer herself, had already taken some shots of the Inglenook Inn in December, when it had snowed for Christmas, but this was the chance for *Contemporary Edge* to get pictures in a more official capacity. As Darcy showed him round the place, he took impressive shots of the entrance hall with the steps leading up to the next floor, the daffodils captured as an effective splash of colour. In their top-floor apartment she'd used white tulips, classy and sophisticated in the opulent lounge area, and Josh snapped away until satisfied he had everything he needed.

After she'd finished her meeting with the photographer and Josh went on his way, Darcy asked Rupert to make herself and Cleo one of his famous bagels with pepperoni sausage and mozzarella cheese. She knew Cleo would insist she was fine but she didn't want to send her off to the station to catch a train if she was still feeling rotten.

She set down the plates with the warm, crunchy bread that asked you to bite into it and discover its soft doughy centre. 'Good book?' she asked when Cleo looked up from her kindle.

'It's rare I get to put my feet up, so I'm making the most of it. I called Dylan and explained what happened. He wanted to drive and pick me up but I'll be fine to get the train later.'

Darcy couldn't stop smiling. She bit into her bagel. 'Oh, this is so good. I didn't make any lunch, just had a takeaway coffee.'

Cleo bit into hers, her reaction the same. 'How have I not tried these before?'

Darcy enjoyed half the bagel before she gave up trying to respect her friend's privacy and asked outright. 'Cleo, are you pregnant?'

About to bite into the second half of her own bagel, Cleo put it down on the plate. 'How did you... you know, it doesn't matter. But yes, I am.' And then she resumed eating.

Darcy let the conversation simmer and only carried it on after Rupert cleared the plates and brought out a bottle of sparkling mineral water for them to share. 'It's great news, a little brother or sister for Tabitha.'

'Uh-huh,' Cleo nodded, quickly gulping more of her water.

'What's going on, Cleo? Why did you keep it to yourself?' They both kept schtum when Rupert came out of the kitchen to say he was off and would be back for 5 p.m.

'I'm scared,' said Cleo once they were on their own again. Her eyes were glued to the bubbles fizzing from the bottom of her glass to the top.

'Of what? You've done it before, given birth. I mean, I can't say I know what it's like, it must be quite frightening, but you'll be fine.'

'It's not that.'

'Then what?'

Cleo looked at Darcy now. 'There are things you don't know about me.'

'Sounds ominous.'

'I told you I never got on with my stepmother, Theresa, when I lived in England. It was one of the reasons I left the UK and moved so far away.'

'I remember you telling me. It must've been bad to leave the country where you grew up. But you get on now?'

'I do, but at the start I resented her. Mum was dead, I wanted her back, and I couldn't stand anyone else being there and trying to take her place.' Darcy bit her tongue. She didn't want to interrupt, she wanted to see where this was going. 'What I've never told you is how my mum died.'

'Cleo, you don't have to share if you're uncomfortable. I understand.' She reached across the table and touched her friend's hand.

'I want to.' Cleo took a deep breath and launched into the full story. 'Mum drowned, but it was no accident. She took her own life. She had postnatal depression that started when I was a baby and never went away. Who knows, she may have been depressed in her pregnancy but never told anyone. For a long time I never wanted to have children. I couldn't bear the thought of having miscarriages like my mum did, the hope built up every time the stick turned blue and then the devastation when the baby disappeared just like that. I told myself that I didn't want to go through the same, and I didn't want to bring children into the world and have them endure what I did as a child. Seeing Mum like that is something I can never forget.'

'You know, if you weren't pregnant, I'd go and get a bottle of gin right now.' It worked; Cleo relaxed and carried on.

'I think I got lucky with Tabitha. Dylan and I were well aware of my mum's history and I saw a doctor from early on, to manage the pregnancy.'

'So what makes you think this time will be any different?'

'We didn't plan this pregnancy. I mean, I feel like I've only just given birth and here we are doing it all over again. We have three children between us and it's amazing, I'm incredibly grateful. I mean every day. I literally stand there sometimes and can't believe how happy we all are. I rested a lot when I was pregnant with Tabitha, but life is so much busier now, for all of us. When Tabitha was seven months old, it all started to feel a bit too much. The physical and mental demands of having another child all came into play, but somehow I got through it. I've barely had time to enjoy her and here I am again, making another life.'

'And you will manage it all again.'

'But I'm predisposed to postnatal depression.' She took a deep breath and shrugged as if to say, this is me, this is my lot in life. 'I'm terrified my luck will run out. Nobody can be that lucky a second time, surely.'

'Why not? You've got Dylan by your side, you have three beautiful children, and a successful booming business.'

'A business that is wearing me thin, Darcy.'

'That bad?'

'I love my job, I love having the store. I love my family too, but I wonder, will something break if I carry on being as crazy busy as I am now?'

'You know what I think?'

'Any thoughts gratefully received.'

'I think you need to get a bit selfish, think about what *you* need. I know how good a mom you are to all three of your children but when you fall asleep on a trip around Manhattan, it's time to make changes.'

'I could ask Kaisha to put in more hours at the store.'

'Is she available to do that?'

'After seeing her today, I think she'd love it. We always worked really well together. And the transport cost from Manhattan out to Inglenook Falls would be a bit of a pain, but I could cover that.'

'Or she could rent the apartment above the store, couldn't she?'

'Now there's an idea.' Cleo looked brighter than she had done since she'd arrived at the Inn. 'I wouldn't even charge her rent because the place is empty anyway. I only use it for extra storage for the Little Knitting Box or when I want to duck upstairs for a lie-down in the quieter periods. Dylan has more projects on the go than ever before so we're doing well financially, even with extra mouths to feed. Mainly mine by the way – I feel as though I'm eating for five not two.'

'Make the most of it.'

Cleo clasped a hand across her mouth. 'I'm going to have to pull out of being your bridesmaid.'

'Why?'

'You don't want a heifer in the wedding party do you?'

Darcy burst out laughing. 'No, I stick to the humans of New York, thanks. And don't you worry about it, we'll discuss it at the first appointment and we'll have you looking beautiful. When are you due?'

'Two weeks after your wedding.'

Darcy's face gave away her concern but she quickly righted it. 'It'll be very close, but I'd hate it if you weren't in my wedding party, Cleo.'

'I want to be.'

Darcy wondered if focusing Cleo's attention on the wedding as they led up to it could also be a way of her stepping back from the ever-increasing stress of having a new baby and wondering whether she was going to succumb to postnatal depression. It could work the other way and stress her out more, but Darcy doubted it.

'Then let's go ahead, get you fitted for your dress, and hope that little one stays inside until he or she is meant to come out.'

'Tabitha was late, so I'm kind of expecting the same. But you might want to ensure they use plenty of elastic in my dress.'

'I'm sure that can be arranged. And, Cleo...' Her friend looked straight at her. 'Congratulations.'

'Thanks.'

'I just know everything is going to be fine. Well, it could all go horribly wrong for you if you don't do something.'

Cleo sat forwards. 'What's that?'

'Promise me you'll let me buy *all* your kids a Christmas present this year. You didn't let me buy for Tabitha last time and when they're older, if she finds out, you could be accused of favouritism.'

Cleo laughed. 'Tabitha was tiny last year and we had so much stuff for her. Okay, you're on. This Christmas you can buy her two presents to make up for last year. We'd better not add any more to our brood or you'll be bankrupt.'

'It's a deal.'

'Talking of babies,' Cleo ventured, 'are you and Myles planning on a whole bunch of them?'

Darcy grinned. 'I'd love to have kids.'

'Oh, do it soon! Then our babies could be friends.'

'I think we need to let life settle a bit first.'

'You have kind of rushed into it with Myles, haven't you?' She stopped herself. 'That sounds terrible. I don't mean it in a negative way, I mean when you know, you know. It's just, well, I can barely keep up with the pair of you.'

Once Darcy was happy Cleo was feeling relatively normal, she waved her off to the train station with strict instructions to text her when she got back to Inglenook Falls, and as she shut the door against the cold Manhattan March air, Darcy thought more about the big picture. She and Myles were equally dedicated to their jobs, they were blissfully in love. But somewhere in that larger ideal of which direction she wanted their lives to go long term was family.

And how were they ever going to fit children into their lives when they barely even had the time to collaborate on wedding arrangements?

4

MYLES

He knew he shouldn't have looked at his cell phone, but it was a message from Darcy before the sun had even dared to come up, reminding him she needed his final guest list so that they could go and sort out the invites later today. She also reminded him that he'd promised to get some names of photographers who specialised in weddings. He'd suggested Holly do it as she was a keen amateur photographer with plenty of talent, but Darcy wanted her friend to come to the wedding as a guest and be allowed to share in the day. Fair enough. But Myles still cursed out loud that he'd forgotten to do either of the things Darcy asked for. What sort of potential husband was he?

It didn't take him long to write a guest list and he emailed Darcy before he'd even got out of bed. His parents were arriving in an hour's time, to stay with him – something he would've been dreading this time last year – and it would be good to show that they were on top of things when it came to the wedding. It's how he wanted it to be, he was just having a little trouble achieving the goal.

The second part of Darcy's request set him a new challenge so he fired off an email to his secretary, Rhonda, asking her to find him some names. He apologised profusely that this wasn't work related and hoped she wasn't too peeved when he got to the office later, but he was running out of time and needed all the outside help he could get. He messaged Darcy to say that he'd have the names of some photographers by the time they met up to sort out the invitations later and she replied back saying she'd had a successful practice run with the hair and make-up lady last night. She added a series of emoticons including hearts, so he assumed they were all good and she was happy he'd been working hard with arrangements too.

That sorted, he started his day with a run in Central Park. It was early April now and this was his favourite time of the day, before sunrise, with the scent of cherry blossom filling the air. It was a spectacular sight to behold during a run as the sky changed colour as if by magic, and it cleared his mind like nothing else. The bone-chilling temperatures of winter had been scared away with increasingly long days and milder weather, but it was still easy to be caught out by thinking that spring meant warmth, so Myles had on a long-sleeved top and full-length running pants as he followed the Park Drive on the west. He cut across the park using one of the transverses, mixing up his route along the way.

Since he'd left London behind and moved to Manhattan, Myles hadn't thought much about his long-term plans. In his line of work, flexibility to relocate was key to getting ahead and so he'd always gone with the flow. But falling in love with Darcy had changed things. He had a new apartment that suited them both down to the ground, if they could ever schedule time to be in it together, and he was beginning to see what drew people to this city with its impressive green spaces that were such a welcome escape from the chaos of the city. His life was heading in an unforeseen direction, and it felt right. All that worried him was whether he could keep it that way – could he manage both his career and his personal life like his brother, Winston, seemed to do so well? He had a successful business, a wife and beautiful family, and Myles had always assumed it was something he'd never have. But, now, it appeared to be there for the taking.

It was still dark when he'd left his apartment this morning but, as Myles followed the transverse road, streaks of pink and orange began to overcome the dark purple of the night sky. The backdrop of city buildings was in the shadows, indigo and violet stood out above and created a photographer's heaven with the odd cherry blossom petal skittering across his path. And with every step he ran Myles felt the tension slide off of him so that by the time the sky turned a delicate blue with the sun causing a shimmering effect across the lake and he headed for home, he felt positive that he and Darcy could get their act together and get this wedding under way. From his professional experience, if you were both working towards the same goal with maximum determination, you stood every chance of making it in the long run.

* * *

'I'm sorry I can't take the day off.' Once upon a time Myles wouldn't have been sorry at all, but nowadays, he and his parents were getting on so much better.

'Don't you apologise.' Martha kissed her son on the cheek and hugged him again as she and her husband, Ian, nursed their cups of tea in the kitchen. 'I'm just happy to be here.'

It was the first time his parents had ever been guests in his home, and they were at least beginning to relax.

'It's a wonderful apartment, Myles,' said Ian, taking in the exposed brick wall to one side of the lounge, walking over to the doors that opened up onto a terrace where he and Darcy already planned to sit and enjoy a glass of wine as the weather got warmer.

Myles turned down Martha's second offer of a cup of tea. He'd grab a coffee on his way to the office. 'How was the flight over? Did you cope?'

'It was fine. A bit dull, but that's normal,' Ian replied with a grin.

'I wished I could knit,' said Martha. 'That would've passed the time.'

'I assume you've packed your needles in your suitcase?' Myles probed.

Ian rolled his eyes. 'Of course she has, she's addicted to the craft. There's no stopping her. Careful or she'll have you kitted out head to toe in woollen garments.'

Martha slapped her husband's arm jovially. It was good to see them so together and getting on so well.

'Do you need to sleep?' Myles asked. 'The bed's made up and it's pretty quiet here.'

Ian shook his head. 'Best we don't. We need to get on New York time as soon as we can. Your mother's off to check out the knitting store we found out about at the Inn's Christmas party.'

'The Little Knitting Box?'

'I'm looking forward to it.' Martha smiled. 'I've got the most wonderful pattern to make a jumper so I thought I'd treat myself to some new wool, or yarn as they say here. Maybe see what buttons they have. I was so taken when Cleo told me about the store on our last visit that I've been desperate to see it.'

'Well I'm sure Cleo will look after you, she's a charming girl.' And he loved how passionate his mum was about something, anything. There was a time when she'd lost interest in the world around her and, now, it was as though she'd woken up from a really long sleep.

'I'm looking forward to being independent and catching the

train on my own.' Martha's eyes were filled with a sense of adventure and it still marvelled Myles at how far they'd both come in their relationship to be able to talk about trivial matters rather than everything that had gone wrong in the past.

'How about lunch, son?' Ian clasped his hands together, planning. 'I can come to you. It'll be good to be surrounded by the rat-race vibe again.'

'If we can make it a quick one, then you're on.' Myles picked up his cell phone, his keys, his wallet.

'Perfect. About one o'clock?'

'Suits me. I'm meeting Darcy at four thirty to choose invitations but maybe we could all have dinner tonight? I'll book somewhere.'

'Great.' Martha kissed and hugged her son again.

'Now, Mum, I'm not six years old and going off to school. You know you don't need to keep doing that every five minutes.'

'Oh, indulge me, it's been a long time coming.'

His eyes met hers and he put a hand on her arm. 'I'll see you later.'

* * *

'This place is crazy.' Ian looked around him and Myles almost started to laugh. For a retired businessman, he'd quickly forgotten that the rat race operated at full speed in the office as well as the streets outside, which had a knock-on effect in any venue when it came to lunch.

They'd found a small café around the corner from Myles's office, rattled off their orders to the waitress who'd appeared at their side in milliseconds, and as they waited for their food it gave them a chance to chat.

'Mum seems really happy.'

'She is. We both are. She's even on her way to getting a new job.'

Myles waited for the waitress to move along after she'd set down a bottle of tap water for the table. 'She hasn't mentioned it.'

'I think she feels awkward.'

'Why?'

'She's training to be a counsellor and wants to work for the same group that helped her through her problems.' His dad rarely said 'alcoholism' even though they both knew that was what it was.

'That's great, I think.'

'Do you doubt she can manage?'

Myles shook his head. 'It's not that. It's... well, I guess I'm worried that her time around other people who may still be drinking could lead her down that path again.'

It was Ian's turn to shake his head. 'I truly believe it won't. She's got a focus I've never seen before. You know – with the knitting, the training she's doing for the counselling. It's like having a brand new wife.'

Myles couldn't help but smile. 'Well then I'm happy for her and I won't mention it unless she says anything. I'll let her tell me in her own time.'

'Talking of brand new wives...' Ian paused when the waitress set down scrambled eggs on rye in front of him and Myles's poached eggs on wholegrain. 'How's the lovely Darcy? Still taking the hotel industry by storm?'

'She's doing brilliantly.' He briefly outlined Darcy and Sofia's arrangement, the progress with corporate clients. 'You know, I never thought I'd ever meet anyone with the same passion for their career as me.'

'Me neither. But you two seem to be perfect together and you understand one another. That's half the battle in my book.'

'I wonder how Mum's going at the Little Knitting Box.'

Ian grinned and took out his phone to show it to Myles. 'She sent me this picture an hour ago.'

It was a photograph of Martha sitting on a stool, surrounded by hanks of yarn all colours of the rainbow on a table behind. She was grinning from ear to ear. Cleo must've taken the photo. 'Do you think she'll even come back tonight, now she's found her dream place?'

Ian's laugh rumbled out of him. 'We can only hope.'

Myles tucked into his lunch hungrily, having not eaten since his snatched bowl of cereal before his parents arrived from the airport this morning. Talk turned to business as Myles knew it would. His father may be retired, but his drive couldn't lie dormant all of the time and he wanted to know about Myles's daily dealings, how he spent his hours up there in his office on the eleventh floor, and Myles was happy to recount the details he knew would hold his dad's interest.

They moved from business to family talk, discussing Winston and his kids. His dad told him all about the garden he and Martha were having landscaped back in England, with a pond and a veggie patch. And as they talked Myles realised how normal they were now, when once upon a time the strain had been unbearable.

A text message pinged through from Darcy and Myles grinned. 'Another reminder from my better half,' he explained as they finished up their coffees. 'Telling me to organise a suit, reminding me to pick up the wedding bands we've already chosen.'

Ian patted him on the shoulder as they left the café. 'Word to the wise, son. If she says get it done, get it done. Keep her happy. Who's your best man?'

Myles grinned. 'Do you really need to ask?'

'Your brother will be thrilled.'

They parted ways and Myles headed back to the office. He'd already asked Winston to be his best man and his brother had leapt at the chance, asking him when he'd need his measurements by. Myles had shrugged it off at the time, not wanting to act like a total woman, but he texted his brother en route now to say he might need them soon as Darcy wanted things organised. The first thing he did when he got to his desk was go online and book a favourite Italian restaurant for tonight, requesting a table for four beside the window, and by the time Rhonda came in with a list of photographers he felt as though he was finally staying on top of things.

He was starting to believe he really could have it all.

* * *

Darcy frowned when Myles admitted he'd got Rhonda to draw up the list. Maybe he should've settled with the lingering cuddle and kiss on the lips instead of being too informative when they met outside the stationer's later that afternoon.

'I don't think it's something your secretary should decide.'

He stopped her before she pushed open the door to the store. 'Darcy, she's not making the decision, she merely drew up a list. I heard her helping her best friend with her wedding in February, so I thought she might have insider knowledge. The final say will always be ours.' He put his fingers beneath her chin and lifted it towards him before planting a kiss on her lips. 'You look stressed.'

'I have some difficult guests at the moment.'

'Why? What's happening?'

'They don't eat pork or shellfish, because of their religious beliefs.'

'You're very good at catering for different people. What did you do, force-feed them a bacon sandwich?' They hovered on the sidewalk in front of the store.

'It's not funny, Myles.'

'Sorry, it's not. I was just trying to make you smile.' It worked. 'That's better. So... tell me what's going on.'

'Pork belly was on the menu, as was shellfish, but plenty of other choices too. This couple took exception to being able to smell the pork belly and then voiced their concern, extremely loudly and rudely might I add, that they saw it carried to the table for another person.'

'You can hardly hide everything beneath cloches.'

'Don't even get me started. I explained to them that whilst I respect their choices, I do have other guests who are entitled to choose items off the menu as they see fit. I gave them a list of restaurants nearby that were inexpensive and lovely. But they made a big fuss that they should be able to eat at the Inn, and that this was intolerable. They demanded a refund on their room right there and then, at dinnertime.'

'What happened then?'

'I said that I wouldn't be able to refund their stay – they'd already been there two nights and had been very happy – and, I don't know, as they made more and more fuss I wondered if they were trying to think of anything they could to get a full refund, get a free stay. Who knows, maybe they go all around New York City doing it. Maybe they're one of *those* couples.'

'You're too amenable, that's your problem.'

'I pride myself on keeping guests happy. These are the first disgruntled ones in a long time.'

'And they won't be the last.' He pulled her close. 'It's part of the industry.'

With a big sigh, she finally began to smile. 'Come on, let's get inside. I'll de-stress when I can tick another thing off my never-ending wedding organisation list.'

'You and your lists,' he teased as they pushed open the door.

For the next hour they were bombarded with styles, themes, and colours. Myles hadn't realised there were so many things to consider. He'd thought today's visit would be quick – an invite was a piece of card pushed into an envelope wasn't it? But he sat there as a flamboyant assistant with questionable streaks in his hair took them through styles – elegant, traditional, romantic, and whimsical, whatever that was. He almost thought the worst was over until the assistant launched into a discussion about theme and they were shown sample after sample of watercolour, beaches, flowers, lace, stripes, swirls, and something else called fleur-de-lis. Talk then turned to something called a gate-fold invite, which made Myles want to tune out completely and start thinking about work instead. His mind turned to a company they'd recently taken on as a client. They were looking for advice on potential industries to invest in and Myles already had a few ideas ready to discuss with his boss.

'Myles... Myles...' Darcy nudged him in the end.

'Sorry, what?'

'Silver, or gold, or ecru?'

I don't know, just pick one!' He hadn't meant to sound so exasperated, but he'd already switched to thinking about the structure of a presentation for their new client. 'Darcy, they all look fine.' Okay, not the answer to give. She looked even more annoyed now. 'How about gold?' His thoughts went to Rufus and whether he might mess up again when it came to this new client or whether the lecture the other day had had any effect.

'I'm not sure. But I do like these.' She pulled forwards an example of an entirely different invitation to the ones he'd heard them discussing, the ins and outs of which had sent his mind wandering.

Myles did his best to focus and took the invite from Darcy's hand. He nodded. 'It's perfect.'

Correct answer.

They locked in the wood-coloured invite – apparently in a style known as rustic – which had lights strung across the top of the card and reminded Darcy of the lights on Myles's terrace back at the apartment, the lights she hoped to emulate at the Moonlight Loft &

Terrace when their wedding celebrations continued long into the evening.

'I'm glad that's sorted,' said Darcy after they'd given the number of guests to the assistant and placed the order.

'Another thing to check off your list.' He took her hand as they left the store. 'And I picked up the wedding bands earlier.'

'Thank you.' She put her other hand to his arm. 'Not long now and I'll be Mrs Cunningham.' She laughed at her reference to a *Happy Days* character. 'Is that why your mum kept some things in her maiden name, because she didn't want to be a Mrs Cunningham?'

'Don't be silly. I'm not sure she even knows about *Happy Days*. Do you want to keep your name?'

'I suppose it might be better for work. Then again, the more I say Darcy Cunningham the more I like it.'

He leaned down and kissed her cheek, as far as he could reach as they navigated the sidewalk and made their way towards the restaurant. They'd been in the stationery store for well over an hour – although it felt like more – but at least the days were getting longer now and sunset was still a way off. Soon the evenings would stretch gloriously out in front of them with balmy nights and days spent making the most of the outside.

'Aren't they beautiful?' Darcy indicated the snowdrops sparsely populating the bed of earth surrounding a tree nestled in a patch on the sidewalk. 'I love New York in the spring.'

Sometimes Myles forgot he'd yet to experience all four seasons in Manhattan. He hadn't been here all that long and already he was settling down – something he'd never thought would happen.

'Talking of flowers,' Darcy continued. 'I had some ideas for the ceremony.'

'Go on then, tell me.'

His face must've given him away because she said, 'I will...

unless you think invites plus flowers is too much of a dent in your masculinity.'

'Darcy, tell me, please.' He put his hands together as though praying.

'You're mocking me now.'

Arm around her, he pulled her close. 'Just a little.'

She wasn't deterred. 'Well, I was thinking, white freesias with some baby's breath.' When he sniggered she said, 'See, I told you it could be too much.'

'Oh, Darcy, I do love you.' He turned her round so she was looking up at him. 'I have no idea what either of those flowers is like.'

'They're elegant, they're—'

He put a finger on her lips. 'I trust your judgement. I'm sure they'll be beautiful.'

They could see his parents seated inside the Italian restaurant and went in to join them. The flowers were yet another wedding detail to be addressed, but Myles was feeling increasingly out of his depth. And when talk turned to knitting soon after they sat down, it was almost a relief to focus on a topic that wasn't related to their upcoming nuptials.

5

DARCY

'You didn't have to come with me,' Martha insisted when she arrived at Penn Station on Sunday afternoon to meet up with Darcy. 'I know how busy you are. You and Myles work hard and you barely get any time for yourselves as it is.'

Darcy bought her ticket to Inglenook Falls, Connecticut, where they were heading for the Little Knitting Box. Martha was desperate to go one more time before she and Ian flew back to England tomorrow. 'To be honest, Martha, I'm really looking forward to doing something totally different and something that has nothing to do with the wedding.'

'You're not having second thoughts are you?'

'What? No!' She shook her head vehemently when she caught her future mother-in-law's stricken face. 'It's just all been a bit much. And also I wanted to spend some time with you before I see you again in August. Myles is unfortunately having a crazy time at work with some young up-and-coming guy who keeps making mistakes. Myles saves him every time, but I'm not sure that'll last much longer.'

They made their way to the platform to wait for the train that would take them out through Stamford and eventually to the leafy suburb of Inglenook Falls.

'Myles is nothing but fair,' said Martha.

Of all the women she could get as a mother-in-law, Darcy was pretty happy with Martha. 'Anyway, I thought it would be nice to get to know you better, he'll meet up with his dad again and that way everyone is happy.' She didn't need to tell Martha that she and Myles had argued about it this morning when Darcy pointed out that his parents had seen little of him this week and that he needed to prioritise. His answer was that they totally understood, and he couldn't be expected to drop everything when work was so busy, and for the sake of peace Darcy had let it go.

'Ian is addicted to being in the Financial District,' Martha confessed. 'We went along Wall Street the other day. Once was enough for me, but I saw the way his eyes lit up. I guess it's hard to leave something behind when it was such a big part of your life.'

Darcy stood as the train approached. 'Myles definitely has the same drive when it comes to business.'

Once settled in their seats and having both removed the layers of clothing still required in early spring when the day could very well catch you out, Darcy popped open a can of drink while Martha sipped on a bottle of water. The journey would take just over an hour, and they soon relaxed into conversation about the Inn, the upcoming article that would be in the press next week, and Darcy had a captive audience when it came to discussing the wedding flowers.

'Baby's breath sounds wonderful and, with the white freesias, it's classically beautiful,' Martha smiled. 'I doubt Myles would have a clue about anything to do with floral varieties. He's never been one to show an interest in horticulture.'

'Since I started at the Inn I've become more familiar,' said Darcy. 'I made it my personal stamp, if you like, to always have fresh flowers dotted around, so, depending on the season and which colour I fancy, I've slowly got to know various different species. I did suggest to Myles that we put some pots on the terrace.'

'That'll be lovely, add a bit of colour. Don't tell me, he left it up to you.'

'You know your son well. But I have a contact at a florist near here so hopefully I can find something neither of us has to pay too much attention to. I can nurture anything I buy for the Inn because I'm there all the time, but I need something very easy to care for at home given our work schedules.'

'Are you still enjoying your work at the Inn?'

'I'm loving having so much responsibility, but there's always that nagging feeling in the back of my mind about having my own place one day, being the person completely in charge.'

'You must feel very loyal to Sofia.'

Darcy shrugged and took her sunglasses from her bag as the sun made a beeline for the carriage they were seated in. 'It's not that. I mean, yes, I feel loyal, but there are other things to think about.'

'Darcy, I don't want to pry – goodness knows I still feel as though I'm stepping on egg shells when it comes to doling out any advice about my son's life – but you can confide in me if you need to.'

After hesitating just a moment longer, Darcy revealed, 'I hope you don't mind, but Myles told me everything, back when we first got together.'

Martha seemed to take it well. 'You mean our history and the family that almost broke?'

'I'm sorry, that was rude of me. Please tell me to mind my own business.'

'I won't,' she said matter-of-factly. 'Because I like things to be out in the open. I'm done with secrets and not saying things I should, keeping everything bottled up.'

Darcy felt a sense of ease as the train trundled along the tracks, clickety-clack, clickety-clack, and found herself making an admission she'd kept to herself until now. 'I'm worried that Myles's ambition alongside mine will be a recipe for disaster.'

'In what way? You're a match made in heaven. Anyone can see that.'

'We're both ridiculously busy. Neither of us works a traditional nine-to-five job. I have shift work, I often stay away from the apartment, and Myles works long hours. Then even when we're both together we spend a lot of time answering emails or phone calls, sorting out problems or catching up on things we didn't manage to get to during the day.'

'But you're doing okay. On top of everything, you're organising a wedding, don't forget. And from what I remember back when Winston was getting married, there are a million and one things to do.'

Darcy smiled back at Martha. 'There certainly are.'

'You'll enjoy your day and things will settle down.' When Darcy gazed out of the window at the tops of the trees, blurring as the train sped past, Martha added, 'But that's not what you're worried about, is it?'

Darcy shook her head. 'One day I'd like to start a family.' She didn't miss the lift in Martha's gaze, the upturn of the corners of her mouth at the exciting news that wasn't even a definite. She turned to face the woman who might one day be the grandmother of her children. 'But what will happen when we do? We barely have time for each other, let alone a child. And then it'll be a competition over who's the busiest, who has time to do this, that and the other for baby Cunningham.'

'Baby Cunningham. That has a wonderful ring to it.' Martha

smiled and at last made Darcy laugh. 'Darcy, I can see where your thinking is going. Myles's dad keeps telling him to make time for a personal life as well as his work, and even I can see my son is doing his best, but I guess no one can siphon the drive out of either of you. It's the way you're both wired.' She leaned forwards and took Darcy's hand, the first physical gesture aside from a kiss on the cheek that the pair had shared. 'I think you're worrying about something prematurely. You and Myles have your whole lives ahead of you and you're in love. That's what counts.'

But as the train rumbled on and talk turned to Martha's knitting project, Darcy wondered whether they should've lived some of that life together before jumping in at the deep end and committing to marriage.

* * *

'This town is wonderful.' Before they went to the Little Knitting Box, Darcy took Martha across the street to grab hot chocolates and they took a good look at their surroundings. She'd been here before, but not for a while, and bathed in spring sunshine Inglenook Falls looked even more welcoming. Sometimes she could understand why people wanted to get away from the big city. It was an escape like no other. They'd walked the short distance from the train station and stood on Main Street taking in the oval of green space with a bandstand in the centre and a handful of retail outlets lining the sidewalk, including a bakery, the café they'd been to, its name now displayed on their takeaway cups, a hardware store, and a clothing place that seemed to sell a vast array of outdoor gear.

'It's hard to believe you were ever anywhere else,' Darcy told Cleo when they stepped into the store that looked as though it had been in position forever. 'Do you ever miss the bright lights of Manhattan?'

'I actually haven't had a chance to miss it,' said Cleo. 'I've been there often enough since I left.'

Darcy smiled. 'And it's always lovely to see you.'

'This place is busier than I ever expected. I have knitting groups four nights a week – when I moved out here the local group of knitters came in on opening day and that was it – customers float in frequently and sales are ticking over nicely, online does well too, and then of course there are the Christmas markets.'

'I need to come to those this year.'

'You do.' Cleo excused herself to serve a customer who'd selected some gorgeous pale pink yarn and Darcy wondered if it was to knit something for a newborn baby girl. It looked perfect for that.

Martha had already selected more yarn to take back to England with her and Cleo insisted she and Darcy hang around out back in the space where she usually ran the workshops.

'Are you sure we're not in the way?' Martha tentatively sat down.

'Of course not. My regulars are always popping in. The social side of knitting is a big draw, let me tell you. Sometimes I can't get rid of them.'

'Well, it's lovely to be here once more,' said Martha. 'And I need to visit again around Christmas. Check out the markets for myself.' She leaned closer to Cleo who had led them into the back room. 'That's if I don't turn out to be a monster-in-law.'

Darcy grinned. 'You haven't yet, but give it time.'

'Christmas in New York is the best.' It was Cleo's colourful assistant, Kaisha, emerging from the store room, where she'd been unpacking boxes, with a bag slung over her shoulder. 'And we have a huge market stall this year so book your flight.'

'I'll see what I can do,' said Martha.

Cleo chatted with Kaisha, who was heading out to grab lunch from the café, and then it was back to the task in hand.

'So Kaisha is up for helping you out?' Darcy probed. 'Did you ask her?'

'I did. And I can't tell you how much better I feel.'

When Martha looked at them quizzically Cleo spilled the beans that she was pregnant and their talk turned to babies until she had to go off and serve a customer.

'You've chosen a beautiful yarn,' Cleo told Martha when she returned out back.

Darcy had thought she might join in and do some knitting herself but right now the hot chocolate she'd grabbed from the café on her way here was all she needed, plus the faint scent of lavender in the air that she'd come to associate with her friend's store. The scent was thanks to the sachets Cleo left around, on shelves, tucked on window sills or behind displays, and was a technique passed down to her from her grandma Eliza, who had once owned the Little Knitting Box in the West Village.

Martha showed Cleo the tension square she'd knitted to check which needle she should be using. The fawn yarn she'd selected was soft to the touch and incredibly flattering against Martha's skin. She was spoiling herself, she said, with a new jumper for autumn in England.

'Oh no.' Martha's brows pulled together in the same way Myles's did when he was facing a crisis at work. He'd even worn the same expression when they were at the stationery store the other day and the assistant had bombarded him with all sorts of fancy terms.

'What's wrong?'

'I think I've dropped a stitch.'

Cleo looked at the yarn. 'I'm afraid you have. Don't panic.' She pulled out a stool after she'd found an implement that Darcy learned was called a crochet hook and with her prowess she manoeuvred the hook from one side of the yarn to the other, back and forth a few times, until she said, 'Sorted.'

Relieved, Martha took the knitting back. 'Thanks. We might need to do FaceTime if I get stuck when I'm at home.'

'You need to find a knitting group near you,' said Darcy as she sipped her hot chocolate, its thick velvety liquid going down a treat. Next month things would really start to warm up and she'd probably be looking for iced chocolate as an alternative.

'I should do,' Martha agreed. 'I've been a bit busy of late.'

'It sounds as though you have something interesting going on,' said Cleo, and Darcy's ears pricked up.

Martha put down her needles and rubbed her palms against her knees. She looked at Darcy. 'I haven't mentioned this to Myles, but I'm training for a new job.'

'Well, unless it's to be a pole dancer then I'm pretty sure he'll be happy for you.' Darcy grinned.

'A pole dancer... can you imagine? No, it's not that.' She paused briefly, clearly deciding whether to go for it or not. 'It's to be a counsellor, for people with alcoholism.'

Darcy couldn't deny she was shocked. 'Martha, that's... honestly, it's awesome. I'm really pleased for you.'

'Really?'

Cleo discreetly went out to the store to give them some time.

'I really do. You've come a long way. And you'll know better than anyone what those people are going through. It's a good thing and Myles will be pleased.'

'Do me a favour and don't tell him yet?' She sipped her hot chocolate. 'I don't want him worrying. I'll tell him once I've finished training and I'm doing it.'

'I won't say anything. I'll let you share the news.' Darcy doubted she'd even have time to tell him, given that whenever they were together they were either ironing out wedding details or hurtling along parallel tracks as they sorted out their individual work crises.

Darcy watched Martha's needles clicking away, the action

almost mesmerising. And when Kaisha arrived back at the store, colourful in a Fair Isle knitted cardigan with a bright red base and a white, green and blue pattern, finished with novelty navy blue flower buttons, Darcy and Cleo left her talking with Martha out back while they went through to the store.

Darcy helped her friend unload a cardboard box and between them they restocked an assortment of coloured yarns in the basket nearest the door.

'This is quite popular,' Cleo explained, repositioning the label that read Icelandic Yarn so it was easily visible.

'Have you used it yet?' Darcy wasn't an avid enough knitter to really know the difference between types of yarn and what their uses were, but Cleo oozed a passion for this business.

'Of course. I try everything we buy in at the store. It might be terrible and then I'd be doing a disservice to my customers if I sold it.'

'What have you made?' Darcy pushed in the sides of the cardboard box to flatten it as Cleo dragged another box next to the shelf stack against the wall. An island in the middle of the store housed an assortment of haberdashery items, more yarn, and on top was the cash register.

'I knitted Ruby a beautiful poncho.' Back over at the Icelandic yarn basket she plucked a wine-coloured hank. 'Beautiful, isn't it?'

'It's gorgeous. And just her colour, I can imagine.'

'She's certainly all about the bold colours now she's turned nine.' Cleo grinned. It was easy to forget she was stepmother to Ruby and Jacob because the kids treated her like their mum and she treated them no differently to baby Tabitha. It was a family match made in heaven.

'And what's this yarn?' Darcy bent down to the second box they needed to unload. 'It's got to be cashmere, surely.'

'Spot on. You should grab some, knit something.'

With a sigh, Darcy ran her fingers across a hank of the pale pink cashmere and laughed when she saw the label. 'This one's called piglet.'

'There are some interesting names, but it's so beautiful, isn't it?'

'It sure is. I might put in a request to have something made,' she added cheekily.

Cleo pushed all of the piglet hanks onto the same shelf then another load of something called meadow onto the shelf above. 'Maybe when the kids have left home I'll have a bit of time, and then, of course, I'd love to knit you something.'

'Nonsense. You can't keep away from your knitting, you need it to relax. This could help you.' She'd been worried about Cleo ever since she'd turned up at the Inn that day. Watching her now, Darcy thought she appeared calm and collected and it would be easy to assume nothing much bothered her at all.

'And maybe it's you who should knit more, to help *you* to relax,' Cleo suggested. 'I worry about you too, you know. It works both ways.' She squeezed Darcy's arm reassuringly before she went off to serve the customer who had only popped in for new row counter.

Darcy folded down the second box, checked Martha was still gossiping with Kaisha as Cleo's assistant ate a snack out the back, and then joined Cleo, who had said goodbye to the customer and was unwrapping another lavender sachet from the pile lying beside the cash register.

'You know me and my lavender,' Cleo grinned.

'I most certainly do. Where's that one going?'

'I'll tuck it beside the sewing machine.'

Cleo's grandmother's Singer sewing machine sat proudly on a shelf up high at the rear of the store. A sturdy, black, 1930s piece, the machine shone and stood out, next to its brown, hardwood case, with gold, embossed writing. Stretching up on tiptoes, Cleo, with a grunt, just about reached high enough to slot the sachet in next to the machine.

'You be careful doing that, in your condition,' Darcy said as her friend got her breath back. 'You'll wear yourself out doing too much.'

'I don't think replenishing a spent air freshener is pushing it, do you?'

'Did you tell Kaisha your news?' Darcy kept her voice low.

'I did, but I've asked her not to talk about it in front of others until I'm a bit further along.'

'You don't think anything will go wrong, do you?'

Cleo shook her head. 'No.'

'Then what? Are you worried about what we discussed the other day?'

'I can't help myself. Common sense tells me I'll be fine, I'm thinking enough ahead to keep it under control, but that's the scary thing about depression. It can creep up on you and before you know it, it's the boss of you, not the other way round.'

Darcy urged Cleo to sit down while she could. 'This is what you should do, whenever the store is empty.' She frowned because Cleo might be sitting down but she'd picked up a notepad and pen she must've got from beneath the cash register and was making a list. 'What are you up to now?'

'I'm a bit forgetful of late, just making a list of things I need to do after closing.'

'That's it.' Darcy took the pad and pen and put both on the counter. 'You can give me ten minutes before I try to extricate Martha from your beautiful store.' She whispered, 'Our train isn't for a while but I think it'll take a bit of time to persuade her to leave.'

Darcy checked on her future mother-in-law again and returned to Cleo to find her sitting on the stool, except this time she'd done as she was told and had put down the notepad and pen.

'How are the wedding plans going?' Cleo asked. 'Any more progress?'

Darcy leaned against the cash register. 'We're getting there, slowly. We've talked about flowers and we chose invitations, which were prepared quickly. I mailed them all this morning after making Myles sit with me and write them all out. I think he's off looking for his testicles today.'

'I heard that!' came a voice from out back.

'Sorry, Martha.' Darcy smothered a giggle with the back of her hand and beckoned Cleo to the front where they wouldn't be heard.

Darcy picked up the stool and put it down by the window display as they both looked out of the store. Tucked around the corner from Main Street, the Little Knitting Box provided a view of fields across the way, trees huddled together in groups, their rich green a sign that spring was establishing itself yet again. 'I'm in awe of you and Dylan.'

'Us? Why?' Cleo toyed with a hank of yarn, feeling its soft fibres beneath her fingers. Darcy guessed that was allowed.

'You've both got crazy busy lives, but you work well together. You're managing a family as well as jobs, you have a great relationship.'

'Ah. You're worried you can't have your cake and eat it?' Cleo asked. 'Oh, cake. I think I might need a slice.'

'I'll run around the corner and get you some if you like, keep your blood sugars up,' Darcy grinned.

'I'll ask Kaisha when you leave, or I might go myself, I could use some fresh air.'

'Sounds like a good idea to me.'

'So, is that what it is? You don't think you can ever have it all?' Cleo got back to the point in question and when she rubbed her tummy Darcy wondered whether she was aware she did it so often or whether her protective motherly instincts made it second nature. 'I never thought I could have both. And look at me now. But Dylan and I have our problems too, everyone does, you just don't always see them and it can make life so much harder if you constantly compare yourself, thinking of others as perfect.'

'You're right,' Darcy sighed. She let Cleo serve the next customer and Kaisha reappeared to see to the gentleman who'd been browsing in the baskets at the front for a while and was obviously a bit lost. She went out back. 'How's it going?' Martha was concentrating on her knitting, her bottom lip pulled in as her teeth kept it in place while she concentrated.

Martha did one more wrap around with yarn, pushed the needle through, and said, 'There. I'm on my way. It's so much better with a few tips from the professionals. Did you know Kaisha knitted that cardigan she's wearing?'

'It's impressive.'

'It's something to aim for.' Martha smiled as she pushed everything into her knitting bag. She'd told Darcy she ordered it off the internet and took it almost everywhere with her now. Ian had joked that she was like one of those celebrities who carried a designer bag around with them and it was at the forefront of every paparazzi photograph captured, whether they were walking down a street, on the school run, or at the park. 'I'd love to knit Myles something special.'

Darcy didn't laugh, because it was incredibly sweet. 'Myles is a bit hard to please when it comes to clothing.'

It was Martha who laughed instead. 'I rather think you're right. I expect he'd only wear something I made in case it upset me if he didn't, but I wouldn't do that to him. Maybe only if he ever annoys me too much.'

'Good idea.'

'I can't believe we're flying home tomorrow.'

'Myles and I have enjoyed having you here.'

'I'm glad. And we can't wait for the wedding.'

'Me too.' Just mentioning the W word threatened to send Darcy into a spin when she thought about everything they still had left to do: sort the bridesmaid dresses, order flowers, choose food for the day, select music – and that was only a snippet of the to-do list.

'I'm making us Lancashire hotpot tonight, will you be able to make dinner?'

'I can be at the apartment by eight o'clock, but please don't wait for me.'

'Nonsense, of course we will. It's our last night so it'll be a wonderful meal for the family.'

Darcy didn't miss the note of pride when Martha referred to family. This woman had been through a lot and she was still trying so hard to do things right. 'I couldn't have asked for a better mother-in-law, you know.'

'Oh, you'll have me getting soppy in a minute.' Her British stiff upper lip didn't hide the little smile at the corners of her mouth as they thanked Cleo and Kaisha for their hospitality. Martha picked up some more accessories until Darcy ushered her out before she bought the entire store, and they left the Little Knitting Box beneath a glowing April sun.

As Martha had knitted today, she'd chatted, unabashed, sharing segments of her life with Darcy. Given the history of the Cunningham family, Darcy could imagine how difficult it would be for Martha to relax and entirely be herself around Myles. She seemed nervous when they were together as though she was holding back, probably scared, and Darcy got that. It was how she'd felt before she'd got involved with someone, keeping a little bit of herself to herself, maintaining her independence so nobody else could damage it or take it away.

'Inglenook Falls is going down as one of my favourite places,' said Martha. They were sitting on the train that would whisk them all the way back to Manhattan.

'It's beautiful, isn't it?'

'A little slice of heaven with the shops, the little school at the end of the road, and as for the Little Knitting Box, I'm a fan for life.'

Darcy grinned, pulling down her shades as the sun streamed through the window. Before long the leaves on the trees would flourish, the cherry blossom would thrive and the temperatures would go up a notch, promising summer was on its way. She thought back to what Cleo had said about everyone having their problems, and she hoped her friend and Dylan would manage this crazy time of their lives in the same way they'd coped up until now, letting their love and support for one another work its magic.

'Do you think you two will ever tire of the city?' Martha clutched her tapestry knitting bag on her lap.

'I'm not sure Myles will ever tire of his career.'

'I suspect neither will you.'

Darcy smiled. 'You're probably right.' She thought about Dylan and Cleo, the crazy family life they managed, just about, the life they'd chosen away from the mayhem of Manhattan. Maybe someday it could be the solution for her and Myles, but not right now. They both loved the city, their jobs were there, and somehow she had to believe they could make it work.

6

MYLES

'Mum, this smells delicious.' Myles was leaning over the Le Creuset Dutch oven his mum had used to cook dinner tonight. His stomach rumbled at the promise of a home-cooked meal and it had been torture with the waft of fried onions, rich lamb, and the Worcestershire sauce as she'd put the dish together and slotted it into the oven. They'd passed the time chatting, something they were slowly getting better at.

'Step away, Myles.' She came over to the bench top in the compact apartment kitchen, armed with some butter and what looked like a paint brush, except it was to be used for food. 'I need to brush the potatoes on top with more butter, pop it under the grill and wait for it to brown some more and crisp up.' She expertly did as described and then turned her attention to the cooker.

'Do you need some help?' He'd watched her fiddling with the dials.

'It's always hard, cooking in a kitchen that isn't yours. Where's the grill function on this thing?'

Myles did the honours and before Martha had a chance, slipped the oven gloves on ready to put the pot back into the oven. 'It's so heavy.' Surprised at its weight, he slotted it onto the shelf.

'It's good quality, Darcy will approve,' said Martha. 'I thought I'd treat you.'

He put a hand on her shoulder. 'You do know that it isn't likely to get used much by me, don't you.'

'Oh, come on, you need to be able to cook some basics.'

'And I can, but my basics are just that. No fancy dishes, no brushing things on top of ingredients.' He grinned. 'Would you mind if I grabbed a beer while I wait?'

'It's your apartment, Myles, you don't need to ask me.' She dropped the brush into a bowl of hot, soapy water.

'You know why I do.'

She didn't look round. 'Go ahead, relax. You've earned it. And hopefully' – she looked up at the clock, which had just ticked round to seven o'clock – 'Darcy will join us soon.'

'Let's hope so.'

'Actually, I do have a small favour to ask.'

'And what's that?'

'Could you fix me a mojito? A non-alcoholic mojito,' she added before he could ask the obvious.

'I don't think my kitchen skills extend that far.'

'Open the top drawer.' She nodded to it and he did as told. 'There, pick up the wooden muddler.'

'The wooden what?'

She laughed. 'It's what the professionals use to make cocktails. Bit like a pestle and mortar, I guess.'

'You know your way around this kitchen better than I do.' He took out the wooden implement with the rounded end. 'Now what?'

'Now you need some fresh mint leaves, half a lime and some sparkling water. The ingredients are all in the fridge, I picked them up.'

He took them out, plus a glass to make the drink. 'Next?' He was enjoying this, being together, doing normal things most families probably took for granted.

She told him to pick up the pan over by the window sill, in which was a syrup she'd made out of sugar and water before leaving it to cool. She instructed him to tear off a few leaves of mint and, along with the slices of lime, put them in the glass, and use the muddler to press down gently. 'It releases the flavours. Now mix in the syrup. That's it. Now pour it into a nice glass and add some ice.' She waited for him to follow the instruction. 'And finish by topping up with the fizzy water.'

'It almost looks better than my beer.' He finished making the drink before handing it to his mum.

She clinked her glass against his beer bottle. 'Cheers.'

'Cheers, Mum.'

Back to her task, she asked, 'What should I serve with the hotpot? Broccoli? Cauliflower?'

Myles grinned. 'I'm assuming you've bought both of those.' He took another beer from the fridge and handed it to Ian, who was sitting on the sofa flipping his way through the *New York Times*.

'I didn't think you'd have any. You really should look after yourself, Myles.'

'I do,' he countered, taking a welcome sip of the beer. He set it down, then took out a saucepan, filled it with water and as it came to the boil, snipped the corner of each bag of frozen vegetables and took out enough for four.

Martha kept an eye on the hotpot and when it was even more golden and possibly smelled more mouth-watering than before, Myles lifted out the dish and set it on the marble trivet. He strained the vegetables and divvied them out between the four plates that had warmed at the bottom of the oven, and when Darcy still wasn't back, Martha covered hers with foil and set it aside.

'I feel bad eating without her,' said Martha. Myles had ushered them to the neat little table at the side of the lounge room joined to the open-plan kitchen.

'She won't mind. This is pretty run-of-the-mill for us. We don't often get our timings right.' His mum looked as though she had something to say, but Myles's cell phone pinged with a message from Darcy and his attention went elsewhere as he read on. 'She's held up for a while longer,' he explained. 'Three last-minute guests and she's running around like a blue-bottomed fly.' He was used to it although it was a shame it had happened on his parents' last night.

'Blue-bottomed?' Martha enquired, sipping her virgin mojito.

'I'm trying to be on my best behaviour. Now dig in,' Myles smiled. 'She'll be another hour at least.'

The hearty home-cooking was delicious and Myles was beginning to realise how much he'd miss his parents when they left. Over the years he'd got so used to tolerating their presence, dealing with it the best he could, that it was a totally different concept, actually relishing the time they spent together.

They enjoyed their dinner, chatting more about Manhattan, the sights, the restaurants, the expanse of the arts from galleries to theatres and street performers, they covered culture, traffic, the cityscape and parks. They talked knitting and Martha's experience of Inglenook Falls, and by the time Darcy got home and came through the door soaked head to toe from a surprise spring shower, they were ensconced on the sofas and Myles was enjoying a glass of red wine.

'You're drenched.' He grabbed a towel from the laundry cupboard so she could at least dry her hair, which was gathered in clumps around her face.

'Oh, Darcy.' Martha put down her knitting that she'd picked up and carried on with almost without thinking about it, and went into mum mode. She immediately ushered Darcy towards the bathroom. 'Pour her a glass of wine, Myles. She needs it,' she called over her shoulder.

Myles did as he was told as his mum took over what he'd been about to do himself, although rather than resent it, he just let it happen. He'd heard enough horror stories of spouses who fought with their in-laws to know how lucky he was that Darcy and his mum seemed to have hit it off. She got on with Ian, too – even back in the early days at the Inn when Ian was a guest and Myles had resented his presence, Darcy had welcomed Ian and ended up being someone for his father to confide in.

The rain continued to hammer against the window pane. Myles left Darcy's wine on the table and, while she had a long shower, listened to his parents' plans for a cruise around the Mediterranean next year. It sounded as though they fully intended to make the most of their reconciliation and every time he spoke to them they'd planned something else. It was a good sign.

When Darcy emerged, Myles popped her plate of Lancashire hotpot into the microwave. 'I'll warm that first and do the vegetables separately or they'll turn to mush.' He planted a kiss on top of her head, her hair warm and dry from the hairdryer and smelling of the meadowy shampoo that she used and which sat in two white-and-purple bottles in his shower. She had a toothbrush here, some extra clothes, even pyjamas. But with her staying at the Inn so frequently it still felt as though it were a token effort, like she was almost afraid to make the full transition.

'I'm so sorry I missed dinner.' Darcy kept her voice low as they huddled in the kitchen and his parents talked between themselves in the lounge area. 'I was literally just packing up for the day when three little old ladies turned up wanting accommodation for a couple of nights.' She giggled, reminding Myles of the less stressed Darcy he'd fallen in love with, not the one who had taken on far too much. 'They were so sweet: Rose, Lynnie and Ellen. They're native New Yorkers, their kids have all grown up and moved on and they met when Lynnie put a note in her local convenience store for a mothers' group with a difference. She wanted a social life after her husband died. Rose saw the ad twenty minutes later, and Ellen saw Lynnie ripping the ad down, embarrassed at what she termed "begging for friends".'

'It sounds like it worked,' said Myles.

'They seem really close, as though they've known one another years. Ellen lives on the Upper East Side, Lynnie in Brooklyn, and Rose in Chelsea.'

'So how did Rose and Ellen see the ad if the store was local to Lynnie?'

Darcy took cutlery from the drawer as Myles added the vegetables to her plate of steaming food and put it on a tray to carry to the table.

'Ellen's son lives in Brooklyn so she was over there minding the grandkids for the morning, and Rose was on an adventure, she said, trying not to give in to old age, getting out and about to see the city she loved.'

'Wow, you learned a lot about your new guests. No wonder you were so late.'

Darcy pinched his butt as he took her tray over to the dining table. 'You know I like to make people feel welcome.'

'You're very generous with your time,' Ian piped up. Myles hoped he hadn't seen Darcy's mischievous behaviour. 'It sets you above the rest, makes you stand out: the inn with a difference.'

Myles whispered in her ear. 'You certainly gave me a lot of time and attention.'

'Behave!' Darcy teased. She sat as Martha put down her knitting and she and Ian came over to them at the table. 'Oh, now I feel really bad, you've all eaten and you have to sit and watch me.'

'Don't worry, there's still dessert to go,' Martha assured her, 'we can share that.'

Darcy covered her mouth after her first forkful. 'Martha, this is amazing.'

'She's a good cook,' said Myles, Ian agreeing wholeheartedly. How was Cleo today? Mum said you hung around in Inglenook Falls for a while.'

'She seems well and it was good to see her. I love it out there. When I was younger it was all about the bright lights of Manhattan, but I can see the attraction of being where they are: the sense of space, the community feel.'

'It works well for them,' said Myles. 'Dylan certainly hasn't looked back.'

They talked more about the Little Knitting Box and Darcy bored Myles with talk of different yarns. Martha made it worse by going into detail about knitting techniques until he and Ian got their revenge by talking about the English football league.

By the time they were on to the dessert – apple crumble with creamy vanilla ice-cream – talk had turned to the wedding and once they'd finished eating and Myles had told his parents and Darcy to leave all the dishes for him to do later, they squeezed in around the iPad looking at pictures of the venue, flower choices, and potential outfits for him. Darcy took the iPad into the bedroom so she could show Martha the dress she'd chosen and when his mum returned to the lounge room, if Myles wasn't mistaken, she had a tear in the corner of her eye. He hoped it was happiness for him rather than relief that he'd actually managed to hold down a relationship. Because his track record had never been that good. Then again, he'd never met anyone quite like Darcy before.

'You're a lucky boy.' Martha hugged her son to her, making him feel like a schoolboy all over again, anxious for parental approval. She'd even used the word boy rather than man, but he didn't mind.

They had a lot of ground to make up for and he'd take the affection in whatever way he could.

'Why don't you get a wedding planner involved?' Ian suggested when Darcy yawned for the umpteenth time and Myles wasn't far behind, rubbing tired eyes and slouching so far back on the sofa that he looked as though he might fall asleep.

'Darcy doesn't want to outsource the wedding to someone else.' She'd dug her heels in pretty firmly with Myles on that one.

'I think it would still very much be your wedding,' said Martha, 'but you'll exhaust yourself otherwise. If someone else took over a few of the details it might make you both feel better.'

Darcy shook her head. 'Myles did suggest at the outset that we had a wedding planner. But I've always wanted to organise my own special day, right from when I was a little girl.'

Myles sat up straighter, her comment another reminder of how short a time he'd known this woman.

'I always dreamed I'd get married beneath a huge archway, with flowers creeping up the sides. I'd plan all the food, the invitations, the guest list. I never wanted anything too elaborate. I didn't want hundreds of people, a sea of faces I barely knew.' She looked fondly at Myles. 'I wanted the really special people in my life to all come together, a relaxed affair, with lots of talking and dancing. And I think, between us, we'll be able to put a good plan together.'

'A wedding planner would listen to all your needs, it would still be about what you want,' Martha assured her.

Darcy shook her head again. 'I've always been organised and I want to do it.'

'Then that's settled,' said Ian from his position on the sofa. 'Now leave the girl alone, pour her another glass of wine, and let's talk about where you're going on honeymoon.'

Myles and Darcy looked at one another.

'Tell me you're having a honeymoon,' said Martha.

Darcy pulled a face. 'We will, but not right after the wedding. We're both too busy at work. Myles could arrange the time off but it'll be busy at the Inn and Sofia will need me in the summer months. We're planning to do something in October.'

'Where are you off to?' Ian asked. 'Overseas, somewhere in the US?'

Myles shrugged. 'We haven't decided yet.' The truth was, when they'd discussed postponing it he'd put it to the back of his mind. But maybe the honeymoon was something he could sort out for the both of them, surprise Darcy with it.

Martha groaned. 'I can't believe we're leaving you both tomorrow.'

'It's been great having you here,' Myles said, and Darcy nodded in agreement.

'Well it won't be long before we're back.'

'How's the packing going?' Myles asked as Ian took the empty wine glasses to the kitchen and his mum picked up the knitting she'd left on the coffee table. It seemed she rarely wanted to be parted with it these days. Perhaps it helped for her to have something to do with her hands when everyone else had an alcoholic drink. His father had never suggested they abstain in front of her – he'd once said it would make Martha more awkward to know she was putting people out – but it had to be hard for her sometimes.

There he went again. Seeing it from her point of view, at last. For years he'd been in turmoil, feeling she'd wronged him. And, by her own admission, she had, but it hadn't been done maliciously. Life had finally taken hold of Martha again and she'd been able to find a way forwards.

'We're getting there slowly.' Martha pushed yarn in the top of her knitting bag before zipping it together. 'I wish I could take this on the plane.'

'At least the flight isn't crazy long,' said Darcy. 'Those ones to

Australia used to take it out of me, cramped up in a seat for twenty-odd hours.'

'True.' Martha smiled at her younger son. 'But it's plenty far enough away for me.'

'The time until the wedding will fly by,' Myles reassured her. 'You'll be back before you know it. And spring's lovely in England, all those daffodils in the park near your house will be out by now.'

'They were before we left. It's my favourite place to walk,' Martha admitted.

Walking was another thing that bonded his parents these days. They'd been on trips to the Jurassic Coast, up to the Lake District, even to Scotland.

'Right.' Myles clapped his hands together. 'You women chat away while I clear up.' He wouldn't hear their protests. 'And then in the morning I know a great little café for breakfast before you go.'

Even Myles thought his eyes might have misted over at the thought of them leaving, and he realised how much he'd valued having them here to talk about his wedding, to show off his bride to be.

He looked over at Darcy chatting away to his mum and when she saw him, Darcy winked at him and he knew they'd be just fine.

* * *

'I'll bet it's nice to have your apartment back,' said Dylan as they finished their run by making their way along the High Line, hopefully early enough to avoid most of the crowds.

Myles's parents had left yesterday and, this morning, with Darcy staying over at the Inn again, and having arranged to meet her and her parents later for taste testing at the Moonlight Loft & Terrace – which he felt sure his stomach would thank him for after the exercise – he needed some headspace.

'It is, but it was good to have their input.' Myles had told Dylan about his history with his parents. Unlike women, they didn't have too many deep and meaningful conversations – although, then again, maybe they did, but they didn't think of them that way. Myles saw it more as being open and honest with a mate. 'Mum is looking well and they're... well, they're just happy.'

'Then that's all they need.'

They swerved to avoid a couple with a selfie stick who had stepped back just at the wrong time. They ran on some more and took the steps down to the street and headed towards the crowds of the Meatpacking District where they stopped and Dylan ducked into a small Italian place.

'Something smells good. What did you get?' Myles had stayed outside to absorb some of the spring sunshine and the breeze as he cooled down.

'I promised Cleo I'd take back her favourite.' He held up the package he'd bought. 'Puttanesca spaghetti.'

'Pregnancy craving?'

'Yep. Same as last time. It's the rich tomato sauce, she says, and apparently she can't make it the same at home.' He grinned sheepishly. 'She'd kill me if she knew I told anyone but yesterday she tried to whip up a batch and the pasta was soggy – she forgot about it and didn't have any more to cook. And then she sat in a heap on the kitchen floor and just cried.'

'Sounds terrifying.'

Dylan laughed. 'It is when you don't know what's coming. One minute she's up, the next she's down. Then her emotions come to the surface. But she's doing okay.'

'I'm glad. You know, that food smells so good I'm tempted to hijack it for myself.'

'Don't you dare! Cleo would string me up by my you-know-whats.'

'Time for a coffee?' Myles checked his watch.

'Too right. We've earned it.'

They found a café nearby and sat beside the window, Myles with a latte, Dylan with a cappuccino, and a large jug of water that they demolished in a few short minutes.

'That was a good run.' Myles set his empty glass onto the table and turned his attention to his coffee. 'These are a work of art.' He almost didn't want to plunge his spoon in to stir the liquid and spoil the circular floral pattern that had been made out of cocoa powder on top.

'It sure was. The furthest I've run in a while, and nice to take a different route.'

They'd met at Myles's apartment and gone from there, over to Riverside Park, continuing along past the Hudson, past the piers, and coming off at East 34th to take the High Line. 'It feels like a getaway from the city when I see water.'

'Know the feeling.' Dylan took an appreciative gulp of coffee but winced at the heat of it.

'I wish I could be more like you and want out of the rat race…' Myles looked out onto the street, listened to taxis honk their horns, watched people dart between parked cars, bustle along the pavements. '…but I'm addicted to the Manhattan mayhem right now.'

'Addicted to the city, or to work?'

'It's kind of one in the same thing for me. I guess the pace of the city fuels the adrenaline for work and vice versa.'

'It's called ambition, buddy. There's nothing wrong with that. And you wouldn't be you if didn't think that way.'

'I guess I wouldn't.'

'Jeez, it was good for me to get out of the house today though.'

Myles grinned. 'Working from home not all it's cracked up to be?'

'I wouldn't have it any other way, but sometimes I do get bored of my own company. Most weeks I have clients to meet and discuss requirements with, but this week has been like being in a box. And when Cleo comes home she's not really up for talking. The kids keep us both busy and she falls asleep as soon as we've cleared up after dinner and got them all to bed.'

'Is Tabitha sleeping through?'

'She is now, at least most of the time. But at the start it was exhausting.'

'I'll bet.'

'Cleo and I did shifts and one of us slept on a mattress in the nursery so we'd be there when Tabitha woke up, usually screaming for a bottle – that way it didn't wake the entire household. Jacob doesn't get back to sleep very easily if he's woken. Ruby wants to come in and help out, which isn't good when she needs to wake up for school in the morning.'

'I take my hat off to you.' Myles sipped his coffee, which was by now the perfect temperature. 'I don't know how you do it.'

'I don't think even *we* know how we do it, but there are plenty of people who do the same.'

'Has Cleo had much morning sickness? I'm thinking no if she's on the puttanesca.' He eyed the plastic carrier bag with the afore-mentioned dish tucked safely inside.

'I almost wish she did, so maybe she'd slow down. She has Kaisha helping her out now.'

'Darcy said Kaisha used to work for Cleo when the store was in the West Village.'

'That's right. And she's a lovely girl, a friend as much as anything, and she's a hard worker. I feel better knowing she's there with Cleo.'

'But you're still worried.'

'Cleo is almost herself when she's at the store or when she's with other people, but when we're at home on our own and I watch her, I can see her mind has gone somewhere else.' He briefly filled Myles in on Cleo's family history. 'I don't want to bring up what happened to her mom because she's worried enough already, that the same could happen to her. She was paranoid the first time around; it's the reason she never wanted to have a baby before we got together. It's a big thing for her.'

'I can understand why, but isn't she at least a bit reassured by how well she coped with Tabitha?'

'It doesn't seem to help her. Logically, it should. But I can tell she's terrified. And because she's terrified she can't relax, and when she can't relax she gets stressed out, and it's one big vicious circle. I'm grateful at how she holds it together for the kids, but I've asked my ex, Prue, to have Ruby and Jacob a bit more than she already does.'

'Did your ex mind?'

'For Prue she was surprisingly accommodating.' Dylan smiled, stirring the remains of his coffee. 'Once upon a time she would've been as awkward as possible, but she's more settled now, she seems to have grown up a bit. She's having them all day tomorrow, too, even though it's not her scheduled day with them.'

'Well at least that's something. Have you spoken with your family doctor?'

'I talked to the counsellor who saw Cleo when she was pregnant last time and his advice was to ensure she eats well, rests, and gets some daily exercise. Basic, but at this stage the best way forwards apparently. So' – he gestured to the takeaway pasta – 'the first part of the advice is done, the second will be when I let her lie in tomorrow morning, the third will be when we go out walking in Inglenook Falls.'

Myles couldn't believe he was about to say this but the words were out before he really considered their full impact. 'Why don't you really have some time off? Come to the city, drop Tabitha with me and Darcy, and go off, just the two of you. Walk through Central Park, take Cleo to Tavern on the Green, or maybe Ess-a-Bagel – I heard her talking about that place with Darcy a while back.' He was thinking about it, Myles could tell. 'I can't offer to come to Inglenook Falls because Darcy will want to be nearby for the Inn, but it'll be a day out for you and an easy one with just the baby, especially when we take her off your hands.'

'Are you sure you know what you're letting yourself in for?'

Nope. 'We'd love to.' He'd better text Darcy and hope she felt the same way.

'In that case, you're on.'

7

DARCY

Spring season was in full swing today as though all of a sudden the weather had decided it should get its act together. The sun beat down from above as Darcy hurried to the subway station beside Madison Square Park. She looked at her watch for the umpteenth time. She was late, very late, for their tasting at the wedding venue and already her cell phone had pinged with two messages from Myles asking where she was. She'd replied to both, saying she was on her way, and now, as she rushed down the steps to the underground world of Manhattan, she was stressed. And she so hadn't wanted to feel that way for such a key moment in the planning of their wedding.

The subway played its part and whizzed her all the way from Midtown to the Upper East Side, and when she emerged to ground level she dodged the crowds, ran through a side street to Madison Avenue, and finally, with no time to enjoy the splendour of the upscale jewellers, boutiques and hair salons en route, she was at the Moonlight Loft & Terrace with a peeved-looking Myles standing out front next to her parents, Paul and Sandy.

'I'm sorry,' she panted, 'I know I'm late.' She kissed her mum and then her dad, who squeezed her into a tight hug she hadn't realised she needed until now.

'You look stressed,' he said. 'Are you looking after yourself?'

'Paul, she's not little any more.' Her mum smiled. 'But are you?'

Darcy was glad they were both here, if only to dilute the tension between her and Myles. 'I'm fine, we both are.' She reached for Myles's hand and the skin-on-skin contact seemed to placate him. 'I'm really sorry I've kept you all waiting.'

Myles asked, 'More little old ladies?' She couldn't tell if he was pissed or trying to lighten the mood.

'A guest checking out late.' She held the door for her parents and they all filed into the building and over to the elevator. 'He managed to get himself lost in Manhattan this morning. He'd only gone for a last-minute walk before he headed to the airport. I didn't have the heart to reprimand him as he was already freaking out that he'd miss his flight.'

Myles shook his head as they stepped into the elevator that whisked them up to rooftop level. The door pinged and they stepped out to a foyer with double glass doors directly ahead, the words 'Moonlight Loft & Terrace' emblazoned across them, and a bustling bar scene on the other side.

'Then my cleaner, Jill, had to rush off,' Darcy carried on, 'so I ended up tackling the room myself.'

Myles's back was to her now and he was striding towards the doors. Her parents must've picked up on the strained atmosphere because they excused themselves to use the restrooms before they met the events manager.

She put a hand on his arm, stopped him before he went in.

'I'm sorry, Darcy, but right now we have the wedding to focus on.'

'You think I should've made a fuss and charged him for not checking out on time?'

'I'm not thinking about your business right now.' His demeanour softened. 'Let's enjoy this; it's for our big day.'

She nodded, calming a little. When she and Myles had first got together they'd found it therapeutic to discuss business problems on both sides, iron out concerns. But now it felt as though this mutually supportive part of their relationship was already disappearing when they were less than five months in.

When her parents re-joined them they went inside and Darcy instantly relaxed as they were introduced to Lisa, events manager of the Moonlight Loft & Terrace. Darcy desperately wished she could freshen up, gather herself for a minute before they dived in to the taste testing, but she wouldn't push it. Myles was putting on a brave front with her parents here, she knew, and she'd never seen him so annoyed, at least not since the day they'd first met in London when he'd been the victim of a practical joke gone wrong and he'd complained so much that it had resulted in Darcy getting fired. She'd just have to sit here, put up with it, and hope she didn't smell.

'Come through. I've a table set up outside,' said Lisa as they walked across the middle of the expansive room with the wooden-topped bar in the centre and stools lined up beside it. 'I thought it would give you a chance to be in the exact place your wedding will be. It'll help you visualise the day better.'

Darcy was confident that today would be successful. Lisa seemed to be in control, and she was right – this wasn't just about the food tasting but was an opportunity to get a feel for the venue and how their day would work. Although, as they sat discussing table settings, Myles let Darcy and her parents do most of the talking and if she tried to pull him into the conversation he was prickly and disinterested. Darcy wondered if he'd thought they'd just be eating, nodding yes to some options, no to others, and then they could be on their way.

When Lisa went to give the go-ahead for food to start coming out, Darcy took Myles's hand beneath the table. 'I'm sorry I was late.'

'I don't know about you but I'm parched,' said Paul. 'Come on, Sandy, we'll go get a jug of water.' Darcy wasn't sure but she thought she heard him mutter, 'or something a bit stronger,' under his breath as they escaped the mounting awkwardness.

Myles rubbed a hand across the back of his neck. 'I've made them uncomfortable. I'm sorry.'

Darcy gripped his fingers. 'I'm sure they understand. Dad'll use any excuse for a cold beer.'

That got Myles smiling. 'I'm being an arse, I'm sorry.' He kissed her gently on the lips.

'Careful, or we'll look like sickly lovebirds and people might gag on their drinks.'

'Let them.' Shades on as the sun streaked across the outside area that stretched all the way along the front of the building and wrapped around the corner, he kissed her full on the lips, lingering a moment until Lisa coughed to announce her return along with Darcy's parents.

'The food is on its way,' Lisa reported, 'and it all smells delicious. I think you'll be happy.' She ran off a few extra details about what they'd be trying today, beginning with entrees, and as they waited they talked more about the set-up for the ceremony itself.

'Where will we put the long table if it rains?' Sandy asked.

Lisa pointed to the inside. 'The bar area will fit everyone just fine, and we can have the flowers arranged so it looks just as special.'

'Do we need to contact you if the weather is bad?' Myles asked, his irritable mood now replaced by his full attention. 'Or will you make the decision?'

'We usually make the decision a couple of hours before as it takes a while to move everything into place,' Lisa replied. 'But we will consult you on the day of course.'

They moved on to talk about the specifics and Paul handed Myles a beer as the women led the discussion about an archway covered in flowers, positioning of the aisle, the arrangement of chairs for the ceremony itself before the less-formal celebrations that would follow.

'It's all beginning to come together,' Paul assured his future son-in-law.

Darcy noticed Myles's shoulders relax, whether from the comment or the beer she wasn't entirely sure. And when Lisa reminded them all that she would need the final headcount for the guest list as soon as possible, she caught his eye and they both added a reminder to the calendars in their cell phones. The RSVPs had come in thick and fast, with only a couple of people who couldn't make the day.

She was going to marry this man no matter how complicated it got. When something was meant to be, it was meant to be.

'And here come the entrees.' Lisa put down her pen next to a clipboard that looked to have a list of everything they'd be trying today.

'You know, Darcy,' her dad began, 'if you like I could always cook up a turkey and do my famous sourdough leftover dish.'

Lisa grinned. 'That sounds good. What is it exactly?'

The waiters laid out dishes and napkins as Paul detailed the way he scooped out the insides of a round loaf, filled it with chopped turkey, garlic, onion and chives, and melted cheese on the top.

Darcy leaned in and whispered to her dad, 'I love that dish, but I'd rather keep it in the family.'

'I've seen her devour it,' said Myles, 'after last Christmas, and it wasn't a pretty sight.' He earned himself a playful slap on the arm. 'Not the behaviour becoming of a bride.'

Amongst chatter and laughter, Darcy, her parents and Myles made their way through an assortment of canapes that they could serve guests upon arrival, three different entrees, and three different mains. They tried miniature beef Wellingtons, crab cakes, vegetarian spring rolls, roast loin of pork with a tomato ragout, bourbon-glazed beef – which the men had declared, without a doubt, had to be one choice – seared tuna, and lobster and crab en croute.

'Any allergies in the wedding party, or on the guest list?' Pen poised, Lisa was ready to take note.

'I don't know of anyone,' said Darcy, looking for confirmation from the others who all shook their heads. 'But there are a couple of guests who don't eat meat but love seafood.'

'So how about the bourbon beef,' said Myles, 'then we can choose between the tuna and the lobster?'

Darcy conferred with her mum.

'They were both delicious,' said Sandy. 'But the lobster and crab was different.'

'That's settled then.' Darcy was triumphant. Today would be another tick on that exhaustive to-do list as their wedding date crept closer and closer.

'Happy?' Lisa asked after Darcy reeled off the final choices and she read them back to confirm.

Darcy and Myles shared a moment until Darcy turned and said, 'Very.'

'We didn't do dessert,' Myles pointed out.

'Dessert is up next,' Lisa explained, smiling, 'but I thought you might like a bit of a breather first.'

'Oh, thank God.' Paul stood up, rubbing his stomach. 'I don't think I could fit another thing in.'

'Sit here,' said Lisa, 'enjoy the atmosphere. I'll bring you some nice cold drinks, and then we'll do the dessert choices in half an hour. How does that sound?'

'Perfect.' Darcy finally escaped to the restroom to freshen up, although she felt a damn sight less flustered than she had when she'd arrived. It could've been the full stomach of food or the gin and tonic she'd had after Lisa ordered drinks on the house – apparently Paul had got in there too quick with his beer order before she could make the suggestion.

As she was coming out of the restroom, her cell pinged with a text message from Holly to say she couldn't wait to see Darcy on Wednesday afternoon for her dress fitting. She also told Darcy to look out on newsstands as of Tuesday morning because the summer edition of the *Contemporary Edge* would be on the shelves then and she'd be able to see the Inglenook Inn in all its glory. Apparently the photographer had got a brilliant shot of the courtyard garden beyond the balcony doors from the dining room, with the curtains billowing on either side.

Holly was good with her words, her articles shone, and Darcy went back to her parents and Myles with a smile on her face. Her professional and personal life appeared to be running on an even par today and she couldn't be happier.

'You're looking pleased,' said Myles. When Darcy didn't comment he said, 'Out with it.'

'No, this is about the wedding.'

'And you're smiling about something else?' His voice was teasing and she knew she could tell him.

She shared the details of the upcoming article. 'I'm so pleased we're getting coverage. I swear it works.'

'Never hold back information from me, Darcy.' He spoke into her ear as he pulled her closer. 'I get stressed just like you, but I want you to share your highs and your lows, about magazine articles and having to clean the Inn making you late to meet me.' It was his way of apologising for being so moody when she arrived and Darcy was almost disappointed when her attention was needed elsewhere.

'Ready for dessert?' It was Lisa, followed closely by Darcy's parents who'd taken a break and gone for a quick walk.

First up was something different: a dessert shot, served in the glass with the same name and filled with pastry, cream and butter-scotch. Next up was a light, summery raspberry mousse, which was a refreshing finish to the meal. Third came profiteroles filled with fluffy cream lighter than air and finished with a chocolate sauce. But it was when Lisa took them inside to taste the fourth option that Darcy and Myles exchanged a knowing smile.

Inside, lined up on a table at the far end of the room, were candles, then a tray filled with skewers, a bowl of marshmallows and another tray with a row of Graham crackers, plus squares of chocolate.

Lisa stopped and turned to her four attentive guests. 'This is our s'mores bar. It's something new we're trying and I've set it up inside for now, but we can position it out on the rooftop on your actual wedding day.

Darcy and Myles couldn't stop grinning.

'Do you remember trying your first one?' She took his hand and whispered in his ear.

His look answered her question. 'When I saw you making them at the Inn I knew then and there that you were the woman I wanted to spend the rest of my life with.'

She patted his stomach. 'So all it took was crackers, marshmal-lows and chocolate?'

'And New Year's together, remember.'

They'd spent New Year's Eve at the Inn, guests out doing their own thing right past the stroke of midnight. Darcy had taught Myles how to make s'mores over the open fire and they'd seen the

New Year in with the delectable treats and a bottle of champagne, vowing to never ever spend a major holiday apart.

'Come on, get stuck in,' Lisa encouraged.

'This is very naughty,' Sandy giggled, picking up a skewer.

Darcy nudged her dad. 'Remember Christmas Eve when us kids were little?'

'Do I ever?' He took a skewer and pushed a fluffy, white marshmallow onto it before holding it over the flickering flame. 'You'd all fight over the best toasting position in front of the fire.'

'Don't let him fool you,' Sandy told Myles, 'he was worse than they were.'

'Only because I wasn't allowed them too often. And, Darcy, if you have these at your wedding, I'd get the dressmaker to kit you out with a bib if I were you.'

'I can handle a s'more,' she grinned. 'I've had enough practice. They were a big tradition in our family,' she explained to Lisa. 'Every Christmas Eve we'd all sit around the fire and make them, and Dad would usually tell us a story that Mom would have to finish off because... well, he was a bit rubbish at storytelling unless it was from a book.' She'd lowered her voice but he still heard.

'I may be older, but there's nothing wrong with my hearing. And she's right,' he told Myles, 'I was terrible. I'd start by telling a story with three princesses and by the middle I'd start talking about magical fairies as I'd totally forgotten the thread.'

'Can you remember how?' Darcy watched Myles putting the marshmallow onto the Graham cracker and square of chocolate.

'I learned from the best.' He put the other half of the cracker on top, waited a bit, then gently manoeuvred the skewer out so the s'more was intact.

They gathered on the deep-burgundy sofa next to the table and as they ate they laughed and joked as though the food selection encouraged it. They raked up other childhood memories as well as the toasting of s'mores, and Darcy was pleased Myles joined in and talked about what he and his brother, Winston, had got up to when they were younger. There were still scars from a less-than-ideal home life as the years went on, but over the last few months, as Darcy had got to know Myles more, he'd been able to dig deeper and remember some of the better times.

Her dad leaned back against the sofa. 'Don't ever let me eat again. At least until the wedding.'

'Don't let me either,' Sandy implored.

Darcy and Myles joined Lisa, who'd left them alone to enjoy the sampling of the s'mores bar and discuss whether they wanted this or one of the other desserts.

'I knew when I saw your faces,' said Lisa with a big grin, 'that s'mores were the winner. It sounds as though they bring back powerful memories for you and that's what your day is all about.'

The look Darcy shared with Myles made her feel as though everything was on the right track now. They were getting organised, this wedding was going to happen in August, and she couldn't wait.

By the time they left the Moonlight Loft & Terrace – walking gingerly on account of how full they both were – Darcy couldn't let go of Myles's hand. Today had gone from stressful to pleasant, ending up being absolutely amazing, and gone now was all the worry that they may have rushed into this.

After they'd waved goodbye to her parents who headed towards the station to meet their train, Myles and Darcy walked along Madison Avenue, bathed in spring sunshine. Darcy was never more sure that this was the man she wanted to spend the rest of her life with. 'Spring is in the air, everything is coming together.' When he sniggered she asked, 'What's so funny?'

'Nothing, it's just there's something I need to tell you. I've kind of volunteered us for a little job tomorrow afternoon.'

'Oh?'

'It's only for a few hours.' He was still grinning.

'Myles, what is it?'

'I'm not sure you'll be so relaxed when you find out what it is.'

She dug her fingers into his ribs to tickle it out of him. 'Just tell me.'

He pulled her in tight with his arm around her shoulder. 'We're about to experience parenthood, that's all.'

8

DARCY

Yesterday, filled to the brim with wedding fare and not to mention the s'mores that had won them over from the moment they saw the preparation table, Darcy had felt less anxious than she had in a long time. Her mood didn't even waver when Myles told her they'd be on babysitting duty the following day. She and Myles had enjoyed some time together. They'd gone to see the photographer, viewed sample pictures, and paid a deposit to secure their booking. And they'd gone over to Madison Square Park where they sipped from cold cans of soda as they flipped through cake designs on Darcy's cell phone. 'I'll ask Mom to taste test, but I think given our work schedule and everything else, we'll have to outsource this part,' Darcy had said. Myles had agreed, although he'd teased her at letting even a smidgen of the wedding out from under her control, and they'd both decided guests would have a field day with the s'mores as it was, so they'd get wedding-slice gift boxes and guests would be able to take the cake away. They'd discussed not having a cake at all, but when Darcy had thought of the photographs they'd seen of happy couples, the groom's hand on his bride's as they performed the first joint task as husband and wife, she decided the cake was non-negotiable.

At the Inn now, Darcy sneaked another peek at the photograph of the red velvet cake with its white fondant icing and the delicate beading around the base of the bottom tier, the red, crafted fondant petals on top and cascading down one side. It was simple, elegant and beautiful. When she'd called her mum to explain about the cake and their busy schedule, Sandy Spencer had leapt into full mother-of-the-bride mode. Her outfit and hat were sorted – along with enough pins that it wouldn't blow away from the rooftop venue – and she was delighted to take on the responsibility for this part of her daughter's wedding.

With Rupert at the Inn to field any emergencies that fingers crossed wouldn't arise this morning, Darcy left work after breakfast. The sun was shining in the sky, there was no sign of spring showers, and, setting off to meet their friends in Central Park, Darcy felt lighter than she had in a long while. Even the prospect of looking after baby Tabitha wasn't as daunting as she would've once imagined.

She caught the subway from Madison Square Park, whizzed all the way up to 72nd, cut across Fifth and met the others in the East 72nd Street playground of the park to do the changeover.

'I think Tabitha's a bit little for most of these things,' said Darcy, hugging Dylan hello and then Cleo before giving Myles a kiss on the lips. He handed her a takeout caramel macchiato. 'Thank you. Is this to calm me before we take charge of a baby? We're novices, I hope you trust us,' she said to their friends.

'Of course we do,' they both answered. They were holding hands and Darcy was glad she and Myles could do this for them both. Cleo could use the break and perhaps as much as anything they just needed time to wander together, aimlessly.

'Drink up.' Myles nodded to the takeout coffee cup Darcy was holding. 'It'll be cold soon enough.'

'I'm not late.' She checked her watch.

'I didn't mean that. It's just that I bought it en route and I was early.' She and Myles both looked again at their charge, smiling away as she sat in her stroller.

'Hello, Tabitha.' Darcy crouched down to the little girl's level. She had the same dark blonde hair as her mum, green eyes like her dad – a perfect mixture of them both – and the look of the devil on her face as Cleo and Dylan suddenly seemed as though they couldn't get away quick enough.

'You are coming to pick her up, right?' Myles laughed before they made their sharp exit.

'I don't know,' Dylan shrugged, an arm around Cleo's shoulders. 'Could be kind of fun seeing you two manage.'

Cleo gave her other half a shove. 'Take no notice of him. We really appreciate this, guys. We don't get much time just to ourselves, so we're planning a leisurely afternoon beneath the sunshine.'

'It sounds wonderful.' Darcy extricated her fingers from Tabitha's clutch although Tabitha didn't seem too impressed and started to squirm and want out of the harness keeping her put.

'Diaper bag is here.' Cleo put her hand on it, hanging from the back of the stroller. 'There are diapers, wipes, cream, hand sanitiser, disposal bags, and two changes of outfit should she need it. Oh, and sunblock. I've already put a layer on her, but you might want to top up if you're on the lawns without any shade.'

'Right.' Darcy took it all in.

Cleo crouched down and tapped a Tupperware box in the netted basket beneath the stroller. 'In here are some snacks for Tabitha. There's lunch in the blue containers, there's a bottle with a portable bottle warmer.'

'Is it easy to use?' Myles looked a bit panicky and Darcy couldn't help laughing at his face, although even she thought this was more high tech than either of them had expected as Cleo explained how to use the warmer, wrapping it around, pressing a button, zipping it into a pouch for ten minutes.

'And we thought today would be simple,' said Myles.

Dylan patted him on the back. 'Never simple when kids are involved.'

'I'm beginning to realise.'

Cleo carried on. 'There are some rusks in here.' She patted the side pocket of the diaper bag. 'Tabitha likes to gnaw on them. She doesn't usually get very far before she drops them out of the stroller, but they give her gums a workout and keep her amused for a while.' She picked up a brightly coloured teddy bear. 'This is her favourite toy.' Tabitha's hands reached up and she pulled the bear towards her, burying her face in its fur.

'That's cute,' said Darcy. 'Did you make it?'

Cleo nodded. 'It was my first knitting project after she was born.'

'It's gorgeous, and way too clever.' Darcy nudged her friend. 'Lucky she loves it.'

'She does, but be vigilant. She often drops it out of the stroller, and she won't go to sleep at night without the thing.' She lowered her voice so only Darcy could hear. 'I keep meaning to make another, a spare, but I think we've washed this one so many times she'd know I was trying to trick her.' She kissed her daughter's head. 'I think we've told you everything you need to know for now.'

'Then off you go,' Darcy encouraged. 'And have a wonderful time. We've both got our cell phones if you need to get in touch with us, but otherwise we'll see you in a couple of hours.'

'Bye,' said Cleo, a bit reluctantly Darcy thought as she, Myles and Tabitha all waved her off.

'Thank goodness she's not one of those kids who screams when her parents leave her with someone else,' said Darcy as Myles took control of the stroller so she could finish her coffee, which was just warm enough to enjoy.

Beneath the sunshine and with the scent of daffodils from the flowerbeds nearby, this wasn't as difficult as Darcy had thought it would be. They even enjoyed a relaxed conversation as they sauntered around the pathways, bought an ice-cream for Tabitha at the little truck waiting on a bend inside the park, stopped and watched her waddle around, arms outstretched, chasing a butterfly on the lawn. They took Tabitha to the lake, paranoid she'd fall in when she wanted to dip her fingers in the water, and they all sat to watch a jazz band play to a captive audience while Tabitha ate a revolting snack of something unrecognisable but that Darcy knew Cleo would've made with nutrition in mind.

'I don't know how babies eat that stuff.' Myles dropped the empty container into the basket beneath the stroller.

'They don't have many teeth at this age.' Darcy cuddled Tabitha, who seemed to be feeling the tiredness after all the excitement of being set free at long last. 'They need it all mushy.'

'Come on, admit it, the food looks pretty much like what comes out the other end.' They'd done rock, paper, scissors and Myles had ended up with the joy of changing Tabitha's nappy half an hour ago.

'With any luck we'll hand her back before I have to take my turn at changing her.'

Myles shook his head. He got down on his haunches, stroked Tabitha's head as she snuggled against Darcy. 'She looks sleepy.'

'Shall we heat up the bottle?'

'Good thinking, then we can pop her in the stroller, walk some more and hopefully she'll fall asleep.'

With Darcy's hands full, Myles took out the bottle warmer and the milk and got things moving.

'You're a professional,' said Darcy as Myles put the warmer away and Tabitha leaned back against her, satiated as she glugged down the bottle, her eyes rolling backwards as she fought sleep.

'I could say the same about you.'

A look passed between them and Darcy's tummy flipped. This was what they both wanted. Family. Togetherness. Was it possible that their dream could come true, one day? It was hard to believe it wouldn't, sitting here in the tranquil surrounds of Central Park, which felt a million miles away from the stresses of work or the busyness of arranging a wedding.

Myles sat next to Darcy and put a hand out to let Tabitha clutch his fingers. Tabitha's other hand was on her bottle as though daring anyone to try and take it away.

'How about it one day?' he asked. 'How about we have a Tabitha?'

She looked at him, half reclined on his elbow now, squinting against the sun. 'Maybe.' Her words weren't one hundred per cent sure but the look she gave him told him of course it was what she wanted too.

'Come on.' He took Tabitha from Darcy when the milk ran out. 'Let's get you in your stroller and we'll have another walk. You could fall asleep, it'll be like heaven in the sunshine.' He looked at Darcy as he lowered the little girl into the seat and did up the harness. 'I could do with a snooze myself. Imagine being pushed around in one of these.'

Darcy laughed. 'No chance.' She handed Tabitha her rainbow teddy and then, after a brief check around that they hadn't left any debris, they pushed the stroller off the grass, down to the pathway, and continued on round the park. Darcy battled through a throng of people who seemed to have no qualms about standing in the way. The stroller wheels jammed against a collection of twigs in the gutter and the whole thing almost toppled over when she attempted to hoist it up onto the path again. 'It's so much busier than it was earlier.'

'Imagine what it's like come summer.' Myles took control of the stroller for Darcy whose shoulders were already aching. Tabitha wasn't exactly light and there was enough paraphernalia underneath and hooked on the handles that it made it more difficult to manoeuvre than a cart at the grocery store.

'I can't imagine pushing a child around when it's boiling hot.' Darcy followed him as he managed to jostle his way through a crowd who had gathered to watch a street performer doing some kind of break dancing, spinning, throwing parts of his body down on the floor in a far too athletic way for Darcy's liking. 'Is she asleep?' She peeked in the stroller but Tabitha was wide awake and now she was leaning forward in her harness.

'Sit back, Tabitha,' Myles encouraged. 'We don't want you toppling out.'

Darcy linked Myles's forearm with hers as they walked on and followed the curve of the bend that would take them back towards the playground to meet Dylan and Cleo.

'Where is it?' Myles's stricken face looked in front of the stroller, behind, to each side.

'Where's what?'

'The teddy!'

'What... oh, the rainbow teddy. Oh crap.' She turned round and stepped aside of the crowd to try to see if it was back the way they came, and at the same time Tabitha started to squirm in her seat, scrunching her hands out in front of her in a grabbing motion as though wondering where the bear had got to.

'I don't believe it.' Myles had done an about turn with the stroller. 'How long do we have?'

Darcy checked her watch. 'We're meeting them in less than half an hour.'

He upped his pace and Tabitha upped her fidgeting, adding a wail to it that made Darcy and Myles walk even faster. 'Did we take that path or this one?' Myles pointed to two choices in front of them.

Darcy had no idea. 'You take the one on the left, I'll take this one, meet you back here in ten minutes. Do you want me to take her?' She looked at their charge, snot coming out of her nose then disappearing back up again, her cheeks sodden with tears.

'No, I'll be faster with it. Just run. We can't give her back without that thing.'

The wails increased. 'I think she heard what you said.'

'Don't be ridiculous.' And with a look, he took off.

Darcy took the right-hand path; she ran and ran, knowing she'd have to turn back after five minutes to give her enough time to get back to Myles. And just when she was about to call it a day, her cell pinged: 'Found it.'

She doubled back, ran towards the place they'd parted and ended up there at around the same time as Myles, Tabitha still red-faced and grouchy, covering a dirty rainbow bear with snot. 'Where was he?'

'In a flowerbed, face down.'

Darcy stood on tiptoes and kissed him. 'Well done.'

They didn't waste any time getting towards their meeting point with Dylan and Cleo and managed to make it there first.

'I'm glad we're here before them,' said Myles. 'I need to catch my breath, pretend nothing happened.'

Darcy laughed. 'What, you don't think they'll know she dropped it when they see the state of the bear, and her?' He looked vulnerable when he was concerned and it only made her love him all the more.

'You know what,' she smiled, 'Rupert said if I can go back to the Inn over dinnertime, he'll sleep over tonight so he's there for customers and for breakfast.'

'Are you saying what I think you're saying?'

She put a hand to his chin. 'I'm all yours tonight.'

'Remind me to thank Rupert when I next see him,' he replied, his eyes never leaving hers.

Cleo appeared before they had a chance to share a kiss, but she wasn't interested in them. Arms open wide, she ran towards Tabitha's stroller and didn't seem to care a jot that her daughter now had mud mixed with snot and tears. 'Mummy missed you.' She unclicked the harness, hoisted her daughter into her arms and hugged her close.

Dylan, who'd now caught up with Cleo, planted a kiss on his daughter's head and bent down to retrieve the rainbow teddy that had jumped ship again. 'What happened to this? Did you bury it alive or something?'

'I can explain,' said Myles. 'Rainbow ted may have been MIA for a while.'

'MIA?' Amused, Dylan waited to hear more.

'She kind of dropped him... and we kind of didn't realise and had to retrace our steps.'

'How long was he gone this time?' asked Cleo.

'Must've been at least forty-five minutes.'

Dylan put a hand on Myles's shoulder. 'Buddy, it's not the end of the world.'

'But she got so distressed, look at her.'

Dylan shrugged as they watched his daughter, happy in her mother's arms. 'It happens to the best of us.'

'I don't know about you,' said Myles after Cleo and Dylan had thanked them profusely and relieved them of their responsibility, 'but I could use a very large, very cold beer.'

Darcy cuddled against him as they walked along. 'Hold that thought. I'll go back to the Inn, then how about beers on the terrace at your place later?'

He hugged her closer. 'Now you're talking.'

* * *

Darcy was more than ready to relax by the time she'd been to the Inn, got through dinnertime, and handed over properly to Rupert. He often stayed over in Sofia's apartment, and they all joked they were more like college roommates these days with all their comings and goings. And Darcy appreciated it because she could use a proper night away from it all. He'd even told her to turn her cell onto silent and promise not to check it more frequently than every hour.

She showered at the Inn and changed into a pale-blue, ruffle tea dress with a navy longline cardigan. She took the subway and let it shuttle her all the way to the Upper West Side where she walked to the apartment she longed to spend more time in as part of a couple.

'Myles,' she called as she went through the front door. 'Myles, it's me. Are you here?' No answer, although soft jazz sounds came from the lounge. She set down her bag, slipped off her shoes, and put her keys on the side table in the hall, calling his name along the way and peeking into each room. When she finally reached the end of the corridor she could feel the breeze coming across the lounge from the doors that opened out onto the terrace. The sun had almost set by now and Myles must've strung up the festoon lights they'd chosen a few weeks back. With frosted bulbs, they lit up the terrace plenty, and as they weren't overlooked Myles had already put a weatherproof day bed in place, where he was lying now, asleep, a beer on the ground beside him.

Darcy grabbed the fawn throw from the back of the sofa in the ounge and tiptoed close before draping the material over him. Beads of condensation ran down the half-drunk bottle of beer and she sneaked inside for another.

Back beside him, she nestled herself at the end of the day bed.

'Your legs are freezing,' he said.

'I'm sorry. I didn't mean to wake you, and I was being so careful.'

He shuffled over, took her beer from her hand, and placed it on the ground beside his before pulling her down next to him. 'Don't apologise. This is time for us, I don't want to spend it asleep.'

It was warm with his arms wrapped around her along with the darkness.

'Tabitha wore me out,' Myles whispered in her ear.

Darcy couldn't stop a giggle escaping. 'You and me both. I thought it would be a lot easier than it was.'

'I think losing the teddy bear was what did it.'

'It would've been a lot smoother if that hadn't happened.' She could feel his breath in her hair, the vibrations of his voice as he spoke. She could hear the city in the distance, a closer rumbling as a car passed down their street. Right here, right now, was exactly where she wanted to be.

9

MYLES

The rest of April continued cold and wet and the sunny days that had hinted at spring were exchanged for blustery downpours that made everything more difficult. Moving down the sidewalk amidst a sea of umbrellas was next to impossible, Darcy had told him she was sick and tired of mopping the hallway at the Inn after people brought the weather in with them, the subways were packed for his commute, and the mood was dreary. Energy levels dipped all round. Even early-morning runs weren't much of a consolation when the weather was so bleak.

By the time May arrived it at least brought with it an end to the incessant rain, and instead of casting his eyes downwards from the moment he left his apartment to battle his way to the Financial District, he left beneath bright skies and pleasant temperatures.

This evening, with the sun still shining, he left work at a reasonable time to meet Darcy at the Chelsea Market. In the old industrial building with wooden floors, exposed bricks, and a vibrant collection of businesses, he met her beside the waterfall.

'How was your day?' he asked after kissing her on the lips. He deliberately wanted to steer the conversation away from his work for now, at least until he knew what to do with what they'd just sprung on him.

'Good. But even better now we're here.' She squeezed his hand and led the way into the Lobster Place.

'How long do we have?'

'Over an hour before I need to get back to the Inn.'

He followed her through the crowds selecting from stands of the freshest seafood in town until they reached the back, where they joined the line for lobster.

'How was the handover from Sofia?'

'All good. I'm glad she's been here for the past few weeks, I don't know how I would've got everything done otherwise.'

'I bet your list has a lot of ticks on it,' he teased. The only reason he got away with his comment was because the line had moved super quick.

They decided on the medium-sized lobster to share and hovered near the collection point to pick it up.

Darcy took a notepad from her bag. 'My list is looking a lot healthier.' She'd found shoes, men's clothing was sorted, the cake had been selected, and both of them were relieved to see more items checked off than not. They'd even given the final headcount to the venue after the last couple of RSVPs came through a week ago.

When their name was called, Myles collected their order and they stood at one of the benches, opened the pots of butter and tore into the flesh.

'I haven't had one of these in forever.' Darcy used a small fork to prise some of the lobster from its shell. She bit into it and closed her eyes. 'I'd almost forgotten how good they are.'

'I had my first with work colleagues, right here as it happens.'

'Yeah?'

'A few of the guys had talked about this place and we came here after taking a client on a boat cruise around Manhattan.'

'Were they impressed?'

'Hell yeah!'

She sniggered. 'You sound very American when you say that.'

'Have I lost my British accent?'

'No chance.'

'I'm glad we're here, finally.'

'Me too,' she smiled.

They'd been running on empty for most of March and then April, with Darcy putting in crazy hours, Myles at the office late every night, both falling into bed either alongside each other when they could, which wasn't often, or else him in his apartment and her at the Inn. There'd been little time for anything else. And he had more on his plate at work than he wanted to burden Darcy with. He hadn't decided what to do with regards to the latest development. All he knew was that it would knock Darcy sideways and she didn't need it right now.

Sofia's return to New York from Switzerland had at least given them a bit of respite but things were still full on and Myles had been trying to meet up with Darcy for dinner for weeks. Right here, in this moment, he had everything he'd ever wanted, his desire for this woman as strong as any work ethic he'd ever had. But they'd jumped into getting engaged and although he didn't regret it, part of him longed for the getting-to-know-you phase they'd skipped, the long, lazy days they should've spent together before they reached this point.

But at least they were here now, and for once they weren't juggling the to-do list or making phone calls or confirming arrangements.

'I wonder what the English guests will make of the s'mores,' said Darcy.

'I'm sure they'll go down a treat, especially with my niece and nephew.'

'Just don't let me get any on my dress.'

'I'll do my best.'

'Gabriella says she'll be first in line for them.'

'Not if I get there first,' he winked. 'How are the bridesmaids anyway?'

'Oh, they're so excited.' She dipped a big bit of juicy lobster into the garlic butter. 'Holly especially. She just did a huge spread on weddings for the summer issue of *Contemporary Edge* and it put her in the mood.'

'Is she seeing anyone?'

'She was. That jerk Donovan.'

'Oh, him... didn't like him much.'

'Turned out nor did she.' Darcy sipped from a bottle of water. 'At first it was all exciting but he liked to talk about himself a lot. She can at least have a laugh about it now.'

'I'm trying to think which single friends I have coming to the wedding.'

'Don't. She hates set-ups. I love Holly to bits, and with Isabella I could meddle, but with Holly, she likes to do things her way.'

'Well we won't meddle then.'

'So what's Rufus been up to lately?' Darcy asked.

He didn't really want to discuss work. Not when he had a decision to make. 'He seems to have settled down, not so much of a loose cannon capable of going off at any time. Two calls into the office at the weekend and I had to put my foot down before he made an even bigger mistake that could've cost him his job.'

'Mr Tough Guy. I kind of like it.' She took his hand across the table.

They talked about the buzz of the Financial District and Ian's ease in the area, the way he fitted in even though he'd retired.

'I don't think my dad's head will ever leave the game,' said Myles.

'How's their garden coming along?'

Myles wiped his hands on the napkin and took out his cell phone, bringing up photos. 'Here it is so far. That's where the pond will be, then in the area that's been cleared' – he showed her the photograph of a patch next to a fence where trees and shrubs had been pulled from the ground – 'Mum's having a summerhouse at the bottom to put all the garden furniture in. I suspect it's more for Winston's kids to enjoy. They hinted at a treehouse, which neither Winston nor my parents were keen on so this would be a compromise.'

'Kind of like an outside cubby?' She nodded her approval. 'They'll love it. She'll never get it back though once the kids take over.'

'I suspect you're right.'

'Talking of kids, I spoke to Cleo last night.'

'And how are things? We didn't do any lasting damage with the losing-the-teddy incident did we?'

'No, she didn't even mention it. I think she's struggling.'

'Tired?'

Darcy nodded. 'I think Dylan is too, but Cleo sounds absolutely exhausted. Tabitha cut three teeth at once and has been screaming in the early hours for the last couple of nights.'

'Has Cleo still got help at the store?'

'She has, but I think she needs a proper break.'

'Don't tell me, Cleo won't hear a word of it.'

Darcy smiled. 'Exactly.'

'Sounds like someone else I know.'

'I'm not that bad.' When he raised his eyebrows she added, 'Well, not yet. I just like being in charge of anything to do with me. I like my independence.'

'I know, and I love you for it. How's Dylan holding up?'

'He's tired but Cleo said at least he works from home so can look as scruffy as he likes – her words not mine.'

'I need to get him out for another run.'

'You haven't been much lately.'

'I've got into bad habits with the cold weather hanging around.' Not to mention the turmoil in his head since work had thrown new challenges his way.

'That doesn't sound like you.' She shook her head as they wrapped up the remnants of the lobster, the deep-pink shell that had nothing left inside, their napkins, the little forks they'd used to spear pieces of the delicate flesh. 'You usually get out in all weathers.'

He pushed the remains into the trash can and pulled her close for a hug. 'Something has to give. I just hope it's not my waistband if I don't get out and pound the pavements soon.'

'Well, I think Dylan would appreciate the company,' said Darcy as they passed the waterfall again and made their way towards the exit.

'Did you talk with him?'

'Only briefly when I asked him to make a change to the website, but he sounded just as worn out as Cleo. We only had a couple of hours with Tabitha that weekend they came to the city; imagine three kids, twenty-four hours a day, seven days a week.'

One day, that was exactly what he wanted with Darcy and he knew she wanted it too. They'd talked about it a lot when they first got together, especially when he told her what had gone on in his family over the years. But lately they hadn't had the chance to have one of those talks where they'd stay awake and contemplate the future. He sometimes wished he could put his foot on the brake to give them a moment to simply see each other.

They emerged from the markets and into the Manhattan

evening. By now the sun had gone down and Myles felt Darcy slip her hand into his after she'd done up her coat. 'I'll walk you to the Inn.'

'You don't have to, Myles. I know you've had a long day, don't you want to get home?'

'Not without you.' He stopped her beneath a streetlamp, wishing the moment could last a little longer. 'How about I walk you back, have a nightcap, and then I'll hang around until it's time for you to come home?'

'Okay. It'll be a novelty to both go back to the apartment together.'

They held hands all the way, chatted some more about Cleo and Dylan and their experience looking after Tabitha, and as they met West 14th and joined Greenwich Avenue, Myles asked, 'Is it good having Sofia in town for a while?'

'I feel spoiled,' Darcy admitted. 'I know she likes to spend as much time with Gabriella and her grandkids in Switzerland as she can, and it's nice running the place on my own as it means I make decisions and take on more responsibility, but at the same time, especially with the wedding coming up, it's exhausting.'

'But you love it though. I bet you'd never want to give it up, no matter how hard it got.'

She kept a hold of Myles's hand but turned so she could look up at him. 'Are you asking me to?'

His laughter laced the air. 'What, you think I'm one of these old fashioned types who think once we're married you should stay at home, apron on, barefoot and pregnant? Actually... there's a thought...'

'Myles, I'm serious. I need to know what your expectations are.'

'I'd never expect you to give up what you love, Darcy. It would be easier to have a family if one of us was at home full time, I admit, and I bet Dylan and Cleo would find it easier if one of them only had to focus on the kids and not work, but they don't do that because it doesn't suit them. There's no one-size-fits-all, and it wouldn't work for us.'

'You don't think so?'

'Darcy, I know it wouldn't. It'd be fine for a while, but whoever was the stay-at-home parent would resent the other one. If you were home, you'd resent me for carrying on with my career. You would,' he said again when it looked like she'd protest. 'And if I stayed home, I could end up resenting you. Although sometimes when it's freezing, in the depths of New York winter, it'd be nice not to leave the apartment.'

Darcy grinned. 'It's always a case of wanting what you can't have. Those people at home probably want out, those in an office long for their houses and think it's much easier to be there.'

'You thrive on your independence,' he said. 'And I get that.' It's why she'd always been reluctant to let others into her life. But talking this way made him realise how much they still had to learn about one another.

'I just worry...'

'Because of my history,' he finished for her. Because it worried him too. His family life hadn't worked at all, and that was with one parent at home.

'I know you're anxious to do things right, that's all. Which makes me anxious at the same time.'

'We'll make it work, I promise.'

As they made their way towards the Inglenook Inn he almost told her about the latest development at the office, but he knew enough about Darcy Spencer to know she had already taken on too much and if he added anything else to the mix, her world could come tumbling down around her.

* * *

'I'm sorry.' Darcy put a hand on Myles's shoulder as he sat on the sofa with a glass of bourbon, reading the newspaper in the lounge room at the front of the Inn. 'We've had a huge corporate booking and Sofia just wanted to make sure everything was set up and ready for them. You've been so patient.'

'You carry on.'

She looked at him peculiarly. 'You do look a little bit *too* comfortable there, I must say.'

'Actually, I feel as though I'm a guest again, and it feels good.'

'Well, no hitting on the boss.'

'Sofia?' He shook his head. 'Lovely woman but not my type.'

She ruffled his hair before going towards a guest who'd just come downstairs wanting a cab to head downtown.

Myles watched as Darcy worked away. The Darcy he'd fallen for, hook, line and sinker. He couldn't imagine her not being a career woman. Women like Cleo managed to have both family and a job, so there was no reason they couldn't do it too. He took out his cell phone. Thinking of their friends had reminded him to fire off a text to Dylan and arrange a running session.

'I'm ready.' Darcy finally had her coat in hand.

'About time,' he grinned. 'Hey, Sofia.' Darcy's boss, or almost-partner, had come into the lounge. He'd met her a few times, but like Darcy, she was usually very busy.

'Myles, wonderful to see you.' She kissed him on each cheek. 'I hope me being here gives you both a bit of a break. How are the wedding plans?'

'I've already told you,' said Darcy.

Sofia's sea-blue eyes twinkled with mirth. 'I know *you* have, and now I want to hear it from Myles.'

He laughed and as Darcy put on her coat while she spoke with Rupert, he told Sofia how things were going from his side.

'Well, it sounds as though the two of you have it all sorted,' she said.

'We're getting there.'

'But it's exhausting?'

'It is. We both work long hours and I'm not sure how it'll change once we're married.' He hadn't meant to be quite so open, but Sofia was one of those women you could easily share a problem with.

'You'll both find a way.' Sofia kept her voice low while Darcy was preoccupied at the computer, checking something – or, knowing Darcy, re-checking something that she'd looked at a couple of times already. 'Darcy is a lot more relaxed now the corporate booking is sorted out.'

She'd mentioned something about a huge booking a while ago but, he had to admit, Rufus had been making life hard at the office at the time and Myles hadn't been able to take in anything else. 'She does like to keep everyone happy.'

'And you should know, this client is *very* happy. Darcy was the one who got this for the Inn in the first place. It's a huge account – gosh, it still feels crazy saying that. Up until recently we had individual guests and families, but, thanks to Darcy, we now have a much more lucrative side to the business. She pushed for corporate business by making a proper presentation to me. You'd have been impressed, Myles. Now, if you'll excuse me.' She moved away to help a guest in the hallway who was turning a map this way and that, looking for a landmark.

Myles knew all about the presentation and as he watched Darcy answer the phone at the desk, he thought back to the girl who'd had her guard up when he first showed an interest, the strong, independent business woman he was incredibly proud of.

'What were you and Sofia talking about?' she asked when she finally cut the apron strings of her business to come away with him.

'Just how amazing you are,' he told her as they stepped out into a clear Manhattan evening.

'Well, what can I say?'

'Home?' They stepped off the stoop and made their way along the sidewalk.

'We need to talk about our vows,' she said as they crossed opposite the café and headed for the subway station. 'The phone call I took at the Inn was from the celebrant and she's got one slot free this week, on Thursday at two o'clock.'

'Doesn't someone else tell us what to say?'

'Either that or we can write our own. What do you prefer?'

They crossed at the intersection, running as the lights changed. 'I think my professionalism lies with numbers rather than words.'

'Oh, I don't know about that, Mr Cunningham, you can be a smooth talker when you want to be.'

He had a sudden thought about one of the projects he was dealing with at work and stopped walking. 'Oh no, did you say Thursday?'

She stopped too. 'Myles, I did ask what day was best and you told me Tuesday first thing or any time Thursday afternoon.'

He scraped a hand across his jaw. 'I know. I did.'

'And you're backing out?'

He hesitated, which was enough. He reached out a hand to stop her walking away. 'Darcy—'

'I knew you'd do this.'

'What? Now that's not fair.'

'I did the flowers on my own, sorted out the string quartet, and I didn't moan once that you couldn't make those appointments.' Now she looked more hurt than she had every other time he'd put work first. But the meetings he'd had to attend hadn't been out of choice, he wasn't able to put them off, and he didn't dare tell her what some of the talks had involved because the words 'relocate' and 'promotion' coming in his direction had been pretty much the order of the day and he wasn't sure how *he* should react, let alone how he should tell his bride to be.

They'd reached the subway station and, moving with the crowd down the steps, Myles kept close to Darcy, taking her hand as soon as they were at the bottom, before they even went through the barriers.

'I'm sorry, Darcy. I need to be at this meeting on Thursday. I can get away by five o'clock.'

'I'm busy at five. I have to check in the corporate party and they're our biggest client. This is still a relatively new direction for the Inn and we need to get it right every time.'

'I'm sure Sofia can handle it.'

'She can, but I worked hard to get this client and I want to be here.'

He couldn't argue with that. Promotions and changes came his way from other people's actions and decisions, but Darcy was making her own future happen and she was on the upwards trajectory. She was here, where they'd met, where they'd agreed they both wanted to be. She wasn't the one who'd changed the rules.

Being together and having their careers as well as some kind of married life was starting to look way out of reach and all Myles could see was a messy family life much like his own had been as a kid. And that wasn't what he wanted. It wasn't what he wanted at all.

10

DARCY

'Oh, Darcy, you chose well.' Holly was standing in front of a full-length mirror in the changing area of the wedding gown store in Chelsea and Serenity had just finished pinning the bottom of the dress to the ideal length after noting down an adjustment she needed to make to the waist so it fitted Holly perfectly.

Darcy hooked an arm into her friend's. 'You look amazing. A bit too amazing – you'll upstage me.' Holly looked every inch the feminine beauty with no business edge to her whatsoever in the sparkling silver gown with its flattering V-neckline.

'Don't be ridiculous.' She grinned. 'But I don't want to take it off.'

'August is getting close, scarily close. You'll be wearing it before you know it.'

'I still don't have a plus one for the wedding.'

'There's a pretty hot guy staying at the Inn right now...'

'Single?'

'As far as I know.'

'Straight?'

'Seems to be.' Darcy smiled.

'Now we're talking.' She turned this way and that, admiring her reflection as her auburn hair licked across her shoulders. 'Age?'

'Early forties perhaps.'

'Tall? Short? I mean, I'm five seven, so he needs to be at least five nine, preferably a bit taller.'

'Jeez, fussy. I mean, beggars can't be choosers and all that.'

Holly swiped a hand through Darcy's hair. 'Watch it, lady. You want to stay on the right side of your bridesmaids.'

'I'm only teasing. And I'd say he's about Myles's height.'

Holly's face said she was starting to think about it. 'Sounds promising. Hair colour?'

'Dark, bit of grey.'

'So, like George Clooney.' When it was Darcy's turn to make a face, although a slightly less positive one, Holly said, 'Okay, don't answer that.'

'Good-looking though.'

'Eye colour?'

'I've no idea.' Darcy accepted another glass of champagne from Serenity, who'd been discreetly hanging back.

Holly took a second glass and set it on the side table before she reluctantly let Darcy unzip the back of her dress. 'What's this mystery man's name?'

'Alexander.'

'Nice. Strong. Masculine.' She stepped out of the dress and rehung it and reached for her jeans. She stepped into them, and buttoned them up. 'Hang on a minute. If he's a guest, where is he from?'

'Phoenix.'

Holly made a grunting sound and reached for her drink. She promptly took a nice big gulp. 'You should've led with that.'

'Okay, so maybe not him. I need to find out if Myles has any single friends coming over from England. I'm sure there was one at least.'

'England? Seriously.' She tugged on her top.

'You never know, you could fall in love with a handsome Englishman and he'll move over here to be with you.'

'I think for the sake of my sanity we should stick to the Tri-State area.'

They finished their champagne and left the wedding gown store beneath a beautiful spring sky. 'Sofia's at the Inn and I'm on a break until later,' said Darcy. 'Do you have to go into the office at all today?'

'Thankfully not, or it wouldn't look good. All this champagne in the middle of the day has gone to my head. How long do you have?'

Darcy checked her watch. 'Myles managed to re-jig things at work – although he wasn't happy – and we're meeting the celebrant at three o'clock, so I've got a few hours.'

'Perfect. Alcohol always gives me the munchies and it's gorgeous out here. How about heading over to the Shake Shack in Madison Square Park and we can people watch, see if we can't find me a date for your wedding?'

Darcy giggled. 'You're on.'

* * *

'Him?' Darcy asked, nodding to a man in a crisp, white shirt with faded chinos. They were sitting at one of the green outside tables in the park.

'He's not bad.'

'Or him?' Darcy gestured to another guy, who looked like he'd been sponsored by far too many fashion labels with one on his shirt, another on his sunglasses, and another on the rear pocket of his jeans.

'Great butt,' said Holly, looking in the same direction as her friend. 'But way too much of a fashion follower.'

They both lost all interest when their buzzer sounded and Darcy leapt up to collect their order.

'Best burgers ever,' Darcy declared after taking a few satisfying bites of a cheeseburger topped with smoked bacon and cherry peppers.

'Agreed,' Holly managed to say with her mouth full and a hand covering the evidence.

'I'm really glad you love the dress.'

'So am I. When my auntie got married I wore lemon yellow, with frills. Disgusting. Even now I can't look at the photographs.'

'How old were you?'

'Seven, but that's not the point.'

'Oh, come on, it's a different ball game at that age.'

'I guess.' She licked her fingers after demolishing the burger in record time. 'I'm sorry if I've been awkward with the appointment times and not able to make it at the same time as the others.'

'Don't be silly. I understand everyone is busy. And to be honest, I love going into the store. Rather than stressing me further, I calm down the second I step inside.'

'Serenity and Alexis are pretty cool.'

'I'm so relieved I found them.'

Holly tucked into the fries poking out of a cardboard box. 'You're not still worrying, are you? You seem to have everything planned well.'

'I'm getting there.'

'Is Myles pitching in?'

'He's been really good. I mean, every now and then he suggests getting a wedding planner involved, but it's me who's insisted we don't. It's almost like a challenge.'

'You say that like you're doing something wrong.'

'I am, aren't I?'

Holly's hair danced beneath the sunshine coming through the trees that carried with them a spring breeze. 'Of course you're not.'

'So it doesn't make me a control freak?'

Holly sipped from her water. 'I run articles on weddings and bridal parties, and trust me, wedding coordinator or not, anyone can turn into a monster when it comes to the big day. And you've managed not to do that. You're tackling the wedding in the same way you would a work project for the Inn, with just as much grace and togetherness. Believe me when I say that, Darcy.'

'Thanks.' It was her turn to sit back in her chair and relax. She watched a squirrel scurry from the flowerbed nearby to one beside a deserted table. 'I know Myles is snowed under at work, and I am too, and he'd gladly let someone else take over some of the planning, but I feel... oh, I don't know, I feel as though if we can get through this then we can tackle whatever comes our way. I mean I didn't set out to make it any kind of test or anything, but as time has gone on, it's what I've started thinking in the back of my mind.'

'Well, again, I don't think it's a bad thing. And getting married is supposed to be one of the most stressful things we ever do – apparently – so your brain is working the right way.'

Darcy could only hope her friend was right and that by taking on too much, she wasn't going to mess things up.

They spent a good hour lapping up the spring sunshine and Darcy left Holly reading a good book on a bench as she made the most of the weather, knowing they were in for some rain over the next week. She hurried out of the park, lifted a hand to flag down a taxi but lost out to someone who'd been quicker off the mark. She was about to flag down another when her cell phone started to ring.

Recognising the number, she kept one hand out ready to shout for the next taxi as she put her cell to her ear. 'Sofia, what's up?' She had to drop her hand and use her finger in her opposite ear so she could make out what Sofia was saying. 'What do you mean, they're here early?' The corporate clients had checked in ahead of schedule – which they were allowed to do, but Darcy had wanted to be there to greet them at 5 p.m. as planned.

'I just thought I'd forewarn you,' Sofia explained. 'That way, you can come straight here after your appointment with the celebrant.'

This wasn't how it was meant to be. 'Sofia?' When another voice had Sofia's attention it took a while to get her to carry on with the call. 'What's happening now?' Darcy shifted out of the way of pedestrians all vying to get to their destinations and not one of them happy that she was hogging the section of the sidewalk to answer her cell.

'The hot water system isn't working.'

'What? You mean there's no hot water… anywhere in the inn?' She raised a hand when she saw another taxi about to cruise on past.

'I'm going to have to go, Darcy. I'll make some calls, get them out to fix it as soon as they can. Don't you worry. I'll see you later.'

Her hand worked the magic this time because the taxi stopped. But instead of telling him the Upper East Side address for the celebrant she found herself saying, 'The Inglenook Inn, Greenwich Village, please.'

* * *

An hour and a half later, and things at the Inglenook Inn were decidedly calmer. Darcy had distracted the corporate clients from the mayhem in the basement – and from Sofia's panic-stricken face at the prospect of no hot water for her guests – by having Rupert fix canapes as quickly as he could. She hosted a welcome for her new guests in the lounge area and, with these clients all the way from Dubai on business, she reeled off local information, places to visit, highlights of the city she called home. And she managed to keep them happier still with drinks all round, omitting the charges from their bill. All she wanted was to keep them in the room, keep them happy, until the water was fixed.

Sofia gave her a discreet thumbs-up signal as she talked away to two of the businessmen about their sightseeing itinerary and Darcy heaved a sigh of relief.

'Where did you send them?' Sofia asked when their clients finally used the facilities in their apartments before heading out into the New York metropolis.

Darcy put the cap back on her pen and set it on the desk. 'They're starting at Times Square, then on to a Broadway show before dinner. And tomorrow they're heading to Central Park in the morning, before the rain starts – I've warned them it's going to be torrential – and they're hoping for the Museum of Modern Art. I think Sunday they're being entertained by business associates and Monday, the fun's over.'

'Shame. They seem so interested in the city. It's a pity it's mostly all work.'

'I know, I got the impression a few of them wished it wasn't.'

'Thanks for coming over, Darcy. I hope Myles wasn't too upset with me.'

Darcy had no idea what Myles's take on her standing him up today was. She'd texted him from the taxi on the way over and hadn't dared look at her messages since.

She sneaked a look when Sofia went off to see Rupert in the kitchen, but there was nothing. Hopefully that meant he'd talked to the celebrant about the vows and would come away with some direction. She was happy to write their own, or they could choose something and make small changes to personalise the words.

Disaster averted, and with the hot water back on now, Darcy finished her work at the Inn by forwarding guests' breakfast choice to Rupert, replying to Facebook messages about future bookings, and taking the balance payment over the phone for a guest booked in for early August. Sofia was so grateful she'd stepped in this afternoon that she paid for Darcy to get a cab home rather than take the subway, and as much as Darcy had protested that she was fine, when she was whisked door to door she was relieved Sofia had insisted.

She let herself into the apartment building and in the elevator shut her eyes as it climbed each floor in turn. Her feet ached from rushing around, her head hurt from the champagne at lunch and being so busy this afternoon that she'd barely taken a sip of water since her time with Holly in the park.

'Myles?' Inside the apartment she took off her shoes and left them in the hallway before padding across the wooden boards to find her fiancé. Being here was a relief. She could shut out the rest of the world for a time, at least until she went back to the Inn tomorrow. 'Myles, are you here?' The breeze she felt circulating as she approached the lounge told her he'd be outside. She tugged the pins from her hair and let the chignon unfurl and her hair settle across her shoulders as she stepped out onto the terrace. She'd expected him to be lying on the day bed, eyes shut, beer leaving a ring of water on the ground as the coolness of it faded away, but he was sitting up looking at the darkness, the space between the buildings where nothing else existed.

She bent over and kissed him on the cheek but he didn't turn as he usually would so their lips collided. 'I'm sorry about today.' She assumed he was pissed because he still hadn't said a word. And when he didn't say anything – 'not your fault', or 'couldn't be helped', or perhaps 'don't worry, it's all in hand' – she sighed and went off to pour a very large glass of water, which she took straight through to the bathroom.

If Myles was going to be obstinate, then right now she didn't have the energy to argue with him.

Darcy relaxed in the tub, the scent of orange blossom bath salts enveloping her in a state of relaxation she could never have reached tonight out on the terrace, and when she was done, dried and had refilled her glass with water, she went outside again. This time Myles was lying on his back on the day bed looking up at the sky. He'd got himself a beer and set it down on the ground.

'Room for one more?'

'Sure.' He shuffled over.

'I am sorry, you know. I haven't missed any other appointments, this was the only one.'

He seemed about to say something but changed his mind. 'Don't worry about it.'

She set her glass down, well enough away that she couldn't kick it accidentally. Wrapped in a fluffy bathrobe, she was glad their terrace wasn't in view of anyone else. 'You say that, but I know you're pretty annoyed right now.'

He sat up but still didn't look at her.

'Myles, talk to me.'

'I rearranged my meeting so I could make it to the appointment in time – the appointment you *insisted* couldn't be dealt with by just one of us.'

'It's for our vows, we should both be involved.'

'And, yet, you weren't there.'

'Did you read my text? There was an emergency at the Inn and I had to be there.'

'No, Darcy, you didn't. Sofia could've handled the clients and the fixing of the hot water. Admit it, you went because you wanted to not because she insisted.'

He had her there. 'It's my job, Myles.'

'And it was my job to be in a meeting today.'

'A meeting you rescheduled.' She took a big gulp of water. 'So no big deal.'

'No big deal?' His voice rose at the same time as he did.

'Myles, don't yell at me.' She shuffled back more comfortably on the day bed now he was out of the way.

'I'm not yelling, but I'm pretty angry.'

'Myles, do you know how many things I've done for this wedding that you haven't been there for?'

'I know!'

'You're yelling again!' And now she was doing it back and was even more glad there were no neighbours around.

'Darcy, you tell me time and time again about what I haven't been involved in, but rather than altering appointments you've chosen to take them when it's convenient.'

'But... we'll never fit everything in unless I do that. We're both so busy.'

'Exactly.'

'You know what? It would've been nice if you could've taken the list and maybe done a few things off your own back, without having to have me hold your hand.'

'But you would never let me, Darcy. I would've happily done so if I thought it would work.'

She opened her mouth to argue but she couldn't. Because he was right. 'I'm sorry I missed the appointment today, and that work came first.' She took a deep breath. 'Can you at least tell me how it went?'

He sat down beside her, picked up his beer and took a big swig. 'I've got a whole collection of words we can choose to say, ways they can be changed. And I've told the celebrant you'll confirm the appointment next Thursday, same time.'

'Can you make it then?'

'I can. I've blocked out a space in my diary so nobody can put anything in there.'

Pleased to feel the warmth of his body against hers, Darcy leaned her head against his shoulder. 'I am sorry.'

'Me too. And sorry I snapped at you.'

'It's okay. I really did want to be there, you know. And you're right, Sofia didn't ask me to come, she only told me the clients were early so I could get to the Inn as soon as my appointment was over. But, I don't know... I guess it feels that because I started the ball rolling with the corporate side of the Inn, I should see it through. And, more than that, I wanted to.'

'I guess we took on a lot by deciding to get married so fast.'

She pulled back. 'Do you still want to get married?'

He leaned over and planted a kiss firmly on her lips, lingering for a moment longer than was necessary. 'Like you wouldn't believe.'

'It's not long now.'

'Less than three months. How's the list looking?'

She grinned. 'I can at least check off Holly's final fitting.'

'I forgot you had that as well today. How did it go?'

'She loves the dress, she looks gorgeous, only thing she needs is a date.'

'I'll ask what Rufus is doing for the night.'

'Don't you dare.' She gave him a shove. 'I know for a fact that Holly can't bear men who are disorganised or arrogant, and he sounds a bit like he has both qualities.'

'Oh, come on now, I don't think you're being fair. He's a decent guy, once you get to know him.' Responding to her expression, he said, 'Okay, so he's probably not quite what Holly is looking for, and I haven't forgotten you warned me not to meddle.'

'Promise me, no more fighting about the wedding.' She steered her mind away from anyone else's love life and back to their own.

'I can't guarantee anything.'

'Not even for me?'

'No way.' He stood and held out his hand. 'Because with fighting comes the best part.'

'And what's that?'

'The make-up sex. Now get inside before I have to drag you there myself.'

11

MYLES

He watched Darcy sleeping in his bed next to him. When his alarm had gone off this morning he'd hit snooze with a contented thump. He'd never done it before, but today he was going to baulk tradition.

Darcy's arm across his chest lifted into action a few minutes later and patted him gently. 'You need to get going, Myles.'

'I'm taking the day off.'

He didn't think he'd ever seen Darcy wake up so suddenly. 'What's the matter? Are you sick?' She put a hand to his forehead. 'You don't have a fever or anything.'

He took her hand and kissed it. 'The office can wait today.' And so could the talk with his boss about the new path that had opened up to him and he'd avoided taking so far. 'Making up with you is far more important. That, and meeting Dylan later on. And I've taken the initiative, contacted your mum, and she and I will be sorting the seating plan today. We're meeting in Inglenook Falls.'

Darcy's face was a mixture of shock and desire to leap in and help.

'Are you okay there?' He was teasing because he knew how hard it was for her to not be a part of every detail, but he had to prove he was in this as much as she was. 'It's been on the to-do list for ages and I've heard you putting it off because you're so busy. So I'm here to save the day.'

She smiled. 'It's fine. I'm sure the both of you know what you're doing.'

His laughter bounced off the walls. 'I'll keep you updated, don't worry.'

She lay down and when he moved over her she wrapped her arms around his neck. 'I thought we were done making up.'

'I'm nowhere near done with you, Darcy.'

* * *

Later that morning Myles travelled out of Manhattan and met Dylan at the Little Knitting Box, leaving a change of clothes in the apartment above the store.

'It's nice to be out of the house.' Dylan pulled down his sunglasses as they stepped out onto the sidewalk. 'What time are you meeting Sandy?' He adjusted the laces on his running shoe.

'She'll be at the café on Main Street by midday. I considered heading to their place but they're not far from here so I thought I'd double up so we could have a run. I don't know about you, but I really need the headspace.'

They set off down Main Street, past the station and through the back streets where houses became more spread out, huge elm trees dominated front gardens, enormous porches wrapped around the exteriors of graceful properties.

'How are the wedding plans?' Dylan asked as they pounded the tarmac on the street instead of the sidewalk, which they left to pedestrians.

'Not bad, we're getting there. I'm trying to do as much as Darcy is, but she likes to keep control. You should've seen her face when I told her I was taking charge of the seating plan with her mum.'

'You're a brave man, but Darcy's reasonable. She's not one of those women who turn into a bridezilla. Not yet, anyway.'

Chuckling, they ran up onto the sidewalk now they'd passed the crowds and carried on down and round another bend in the road.

'I still don't know how you and Cleo do it. That one time we looked after Tabitha, we barely managed.'

'What? You guys were awesome. Cleo and I can't thank you enough. We had a great time going around the city, having a bit of time for just the two of us.'

Myles got that. Amidst all this wedding preparation and their busy work schedules, he knew it would be easy to disregard the romantic side of his relationship with Darcy, and he never ever wanted to do that. 'Is Cleo excited about being a part of the wedding?' he asked as they rounded a corner to a much quieter street where they could run side by side without having to dodge anyone.

'She is, although she says she'll look massive compared to the others.'

'I hate to state the obvious, but she's pregnant.'

'She's pregnant, and gorgeous, but she doesn't see it.'

'How is she? Darcy said she sounded exhausted.'

'We're doing okay. But I have to remind myself not to fuss over her too much; she hates it.'

Myles shook his head. 'Women.' He'd never let himself get this close or this serious about a woman. Maybe if he had, he wouldn't feel so out of his depth now.

They took the path around the perimeter of the field that come the end of the year would be transformed into the Inglenook Falls Christmas markets, and finished their run opposite the Little Knitting Box. As they got their breath back, they waved to Cleo who was about to go back into her store with a takeout coffee in hand.

'That better be decaf!' Dylan called out to her.

She rolled her eyes and grinned across at them. 'I'm allowed one coffee a day. Would you tell him, Myles?'

'Oh no, don't go getting me involved in your domestic.'

She laughed and held a hand up to shield her eyes from the sun. 'How's life in the big city going?'

'Great,' Myles answered with a thumbs up, before a car passing by drowned out his words. Cleo went inside the store and he took a seat on the bench next to Dylan. 'She's looking really well. Must be all that caffeine. I'm kidding.'

'She's a lot better since Kaisha started helping out, and I'm glad we didn't have to advertise for someone completely new. Cleo at least trusts Kaisha when it comes to the business. You know, if Kaisha hadn't said yes, I think Cleo would've kept doing it all on her own. I help out when I can, but aside from ringing up orders on the cash register, I can't do much else. I don't know one end of a knitting needle from another.'

Myles tipped his face against the sunshine, making the most of the warmth. 'Good to hear it.'

'She tells me once upon a time Darcy was really getting the knitting bug.'

Myles thought about it. 'She doesn't have a lot of free time. Neither of us does.'

'Hey, it wasn't a criticism.'

'I know.'

'When I was with Prue we got on with life, we muddled along, and when she left it was such a shock. I asked myself what I could've done differently, whether I'd failed her, failed as a husband and as a father.'

'From what you've told me, you two were very different.'

'We were, but now, whenever Cleo snaps at me or I snap at her, because we're both dog-tired, I worry that something between us will break and I won't be able to fix it.'

Myles sat forwards. 'You're doing everything you can.'

'I managed to get a place at day care for Tabitha and the new baby one day a week, which is better than nothing. Then I'll have them for a full day, plus I'll be on hand a lot of the time when it's Cleo for the other three days, depending on my workload. And if Kaisha can take the reins more at the store, we should be able to make it work.'

'You don't sound convinced.'

'I know Cleo too well. She'll have Tabitha and the new baby with her and she'll be in the store every five minutes, probably stressing herself and everyone else. She might not do much when she goes in there, but it's almost like she needs to see it every few hours just to make sure nothing disastrous has happened. I suggested we get a nanny who can be at home with the kids on the days when I don't have them. The nanny could do school pick up too and that way, life would be so much easier.'

'Don't tell me, Cleo wouldn't go for it.'

Dylan harrumphed. 'You'd think I suggested leaving the kids to fend for themselves.'

'Sounds a bit like Darcy.'

Dylan laughed. 'We both chose very strong-willed women.'

'They're very similar, I agree.'

They let the traffic pass on by, Dylan waved to one of the locals who came out of the Little Knitting Box and went on her way.

'You and Cleo will get through this stage, I know you will. And you'll come out the other side happier than ever.'

'Let's hope you're right. We're both looking forward to the wedding, by the way.'

'That's good to hear.'

'Cleo's dad and stepmom are coming over from England to see the grandkids and look after them when the new baby comes along, so we'll have some time to ourselves. It might help keep our sanity.' His smile faded at the undercurrent of how true that statement might be, given Cleo's family history.

'It sounds like you guys have it all mapped out.'

'As do you and Darcy.'

He wasn't so sure about that. 'You know, I'll never once regret proposing. She's the love of my life.'

'But you wish you hadn't rushed into it?'

Myles took a deep breath before admitting, 'We booked the wedding date like both of us do everything in our lives... in a big rush. I wish we'd had some time together first. And then there's work...'

'You're both busy, but you'll find a way to manage it.'

'I've moved around a lot with my job. It's what brought me to Manhattan. Up until now it's what's kept me on top of my game.'

'You don't want to move on from New York, do you?'

'No, I don't at all. But there's been talk of promotion.'

'Well that's good. Job security, more money I'd assume.'

'All true, but also new location.'

'Ah. Where to this time?'

'Boston.'

Dylan whistled. 'I'll bet Darcy is already wondering how that's going to work.'

Myles didn't say anything, but checking his watch he knew he didn't have long before he met her mum.

'Darcy does know about this, doesn't she?' Dylan read the answer on Myles's face. 'You need to tell her. I'm no expert on women, but I find it's best to keep things honest. It'll hurt more if she finds out you kept it from her.'

'How can I tell her? Manhattan and the Inglenook Inn are her whole life. There's no way she'll want to move away.'

'I agree.'

'So what do I do?'

Dylan sighed, leaned back against the bench and put his hands behind his head. 'I think you know the answer to that.'

'When you put it that way it sounds simple.'

'You have a choice to make and I may not have known you that long, but I think you value your relationship above all else. Am I right?'

He thought about the career he'd worked so hard at over the years, the job that had always, always come first when ambition never left his side. It sounded simple, choosing between a job and a relationship, when in reality it wasn't easy at all. He wanted to provide, he wanted a family, and his father had done the same, his grandfather before that. And what happened if he turned down the promotion? Would that be it, would he be one of those employees who was shunted to the back office and gradually phased out of the place? Or one of those workers who went in day after day, no new challenges coming their way, the drudgery of the office something they endured rather than had a passion for?

* * *

Dylan went home to work and after a shower in the apartment above the Little Knitting Box, Myles handed the keys to Cleo and went to meet Sandy at Marlo's café on Main Street. She was already there, relaxed and chatting away to the waitress serving her coffee. She stood when Myles pushed open the door and enveloped him in a hug.

'You look flushed,' she said, 'did you race here?'

His hair was still damp and his face hot from the water. 'I went running with Dylan. But don't worry, I'm clean now so ready to get going with the place-setting plans.' At least it would take his mind off work for a bit. He'd already ignored a phone call once and set his cell phone on silent so they wouldn't be disturbed.

'How are Dylan and the lovely Cleo?' Sandy asked.

'Busy as ever,' he grinned, and they lost themselves in conversation about the kids, the pregnancy and Myles's mum's love of knitting.

'The first thing she'll do when she's next here is go to the Little Knitting Box,' he told Sandy. 'It's almost like her second home. Or third, if you count my apartment.'

'You sound as though you like having her around.'

'Actually, I really do.' More than he'd thought, he was looking forward to them coming back to New York. He'd missed out on a lot with her over the years but his family life had shaped him into the person he was now: hardworking, cautious, and a man who knew what he wanted.

'Right, first things first,' said Sandy. 'Remind me of the exact headcount for the wedding.'

'Fifty in total.'

'Nice round number.'

'Would've been fifty-three but there are a few from the UK who can't make it, what with family commitments.'

She opened out a rolled-up piece of paper and flattened it on the table as Myles ordered a latte and another cappuccino for her. So we have the top table seating eight, and then another six tables each seating up to eight guests. This diagram shows round tables but do you know if that's definitely what the venue has in mind?'

He shrugged. 'Do you want me to check with them?'

'No, it won't make much difference to who we put with whom. Hopefully they'll be round though, it's much more sociable. And more relaxed, I think, which is the atmosphere you're both going for, am I right?'

'That's the idea.' He wished they could carry forward that atmosphere to their day-to-day lives right now.

'The top table will be rectangular, I remember the lady at the Moonlight Loft & Terrace telling me that part,' Sandy continued.

'Who sits on the top table?' Myles had no idea. Thinking back to Winston's wedding, he was definitely sitting there as the best man, but he'd either blocked from his memory who else was sat there with them or else decided it wasn't really important.

'You and Darcy, obviously,' Sandy smiled, 'then both sets of parents, the chief bridesmaid plus the best man.' Using a pencil she wrote in the names. 'Now, I'd suggest we mix the guests up a bit, rather than having all of the groom's guests together and the bride's on their own tables. What do you think?'

If Darcy could only see him now, deep in conversation about the wedding seating chart. He was tempted to take a photo as evidence. 'Sounds like a good idea to me.'

'No skeletons in your closet? People I need to avoid?'

He laughed. 'I think we're safe. What about on your side? I haven't known Darcy long enough to know any deep, dark secrets lurking in her past.'

The waitress set down the coffees and took Sandy's empty cup away. 'No secrets lurking, rest assured.'

They sifted through the list of names he had on his cell phone, putting some guests from his side together with some from Darcy's trying to match people they thought would hit it off.

'At the end of the day,' said Sandy when they were done, 'it's only for the food part of the wedding, then it'll be on to dancing and socialising.' She glanced over at the counter and the menu behind. 'Can I interest you in lunch, Myles, or do you have to rush back to the city?'

He needed to check in with work; he knew they were waiting for an answer. 'I've got time for lunch,' he said before he could change his mind.

Myles settled on the house burger with thick-cut chips and Sandy went for the Caesar salad with extra anchovies, and they chatted away about all things New York and about living out in Connecticut.

'Once upon a time we lived in the city too,' Sandy told him.

'Whereabouts?'

'We were lucky enough to be in the Theatre District. It was great while we were young, especially before we got married. We went out all the time, ate at some fabulous restaurants.'

'It's an amazing city.'

'We moved further out once we knew we wanted kids, and settled down a bit.'

'It's hard to imagine suddenly getting to that stage.' He dunked a chip into the ketchup in the small china bowl on the side of his plate.

'You and Darcy are very similar. You both operate on fast-forward.' She ate a forkful of anchovy but quickly covered her mouth. 'It's not a bad thing, it's the way Darcy's always been and I get the impression the way you have always been too. You'll both find a balance, I know you will.'

Myles wondered how much of that was a mother's wishful thinking. He'd been used to calling the shots in his life. With nobody else to consider, work asked him to jump and all he needed to know was how high. He packed up, moved around, and never had he questioned it until now. But he knew he couldn't avoid confronting the issue for much longer. His boss needed an answer and Darcy deserved to know everything.

'Thanks for sitting down with me today,' said Sandy after Myles picked up the tab and they emerged into the sunshine.

'I enjoyed it.' And actually he had.

'Between you and me, I'm a bit worried about Darcy.'

'You are?'

She hesitated. 'I think she's taking on too much. I'll bet she wasn't entirely comfortable with you coming here to do this without her, was she?'

He pulled a face.

'Don't worry, I know what she's like. She's a determined young lady, it's what's got her so far in life, but I wish she'd take a step back sometimes. I'd hate to see her put her career before everything else.'

'I think we've both been guilty of that in the past.'

'I'm ashamed to say Paul and I talked about trying to persuade her to wait a while before you got married.' She put a hand on his arm.

'She never mentioned anything.'

'That's because we decided to leave it up to the both of you. We have nothing against you at all, Myles – in fact, we couldn't be happier she found you – but we just wanted you to have what we had.'

'The Theatre District, the dinners, the Manhattan life?' He smiled, because they were talking his language. If only he and Darcy could be so honest with each other. It was as though each of them was worried about pushing the other one that step too far by admitting there was anything wrong.

'Exactly.'

'I thought about suggesting we postpone the wedding a year,' he admitted. 'I never once regretted proposing, but I could've done with a bit more time.'

'Why didn't you say anything to Darcy?'

One eyebrow hooked, he said, 'For the same reason you didn't.'

'She'd never listen,' they said at the same time.

'I wouldn't change it now, we're too far into the planning. But I'm not sure either of us will be able to keep up in the race if this is the pace we're going to go at.'

'It'll slow down,' Sandy assured him.

When he caught the train that pulled in moments after he arrived at the station, he texted Darcy with the words: 'Seating Plan Tick!' so she could cross something else off her list. And with the physical exhaustion of the run, coupled with the mental exhaustion that came with any wedding planning, he sat back in his seat and shut his eyes as they trundled all the way back to the metropolis.

12

DARCY

As May rolled into June, New York welcomed spring like an old friend – reliable and just what you expected. On the subway this morning Darcy had stood next to a woman holding the brightest bunch of daffodils poking out the top of their paper wrapping and the smell evoked the season as much as the sunshine warming the city when she emerged onto Seventh Street. She stopped at the florist herself but instead of a bunch of spring flowers, this time she chose a terracotta pot filled with geraniums.

'Let me get the door.' It was Rupert behind her on the stoop when she arrived at the Inn. 'Or give me the pot.' He gave her no choice and took it from her.

'Just pop it in the hallway, I'll find a place for it.' She shook out her arms. 'The pot wasn't heavy at first, but I've walked four blocks.' She did the honours and opened the front door. With the time well before 7 a.m. they were greeted with nothing but a stream of sunlight in the hallway.

Rupert left it at the entrance to the lounge and went back to retrieve his bags of groceries from the stoop.

'What do you think?' she asked once he appeared inside. She'd positioned the terracotta pot in front of the open fireplace and was admiring the heartleaf geraniums with their dark green leaves spilling out of the sides of the pot and their umbel-like clusters of purple flowers.

'Much better than the fire for springtime,' he smiled.

'It's another gorgeous day.' When Rupert went through to the kitchen Darcy took a moment to look out the front window of the Inglenook Inn, onto the street with comings and goings just like any other day. A few weeks ago it had been a sea of umbrellas at this time of the morning – multiple colours shielding the people beneath as they hurried about their business. But now everyone moved more leisurely, reluctant to give up a chance to bathe in the beauty of this city now that spring was in full swing. Last night she and Myles had walked in Central Park, a rarity in their busy lives but necessary for sanity, and the entire park had started its push of colour, awash with fragrant magnolia flowers and a sea of purple, pink and white lilac blossoms on the little path along Sheep Meadow. Temperatures were on the up and, with them, Darcy's spirits. It had been a hectic few months but her wedding to-do list was littered with ticks and it was all coming together.

While she waited for the computer to wake up, Darcy chatted with Rupert about the lunches today. They had a family in the suite upstairs who'd arrived very late last night and had requested a meal before they went off to explore. Darcy had felt for them – they were exhausted after travelling all the way from Tasmania – and she looked forward to making sure they were comfortable and giving them some advice about how to spend their time in the big city.

'I'll collect the fish order mid-morning, once I've done the breakfasts.' Rupert sipped from a very strong looking black coffee. 'Do you need me to pick up anything else in the way of groceries? I've already got fresh bread, bagels, and a selection of fruit.'

'That should do it. Do we have enough milk?'

Rupert checked. 'Almost out here.'

'I'll get some from the fridge in the basement and then we'll probably need to pick some up tomorrow.'

'Happy to do that. Do you need me to stay over tonight?'

'No, I'll stay this time.' With Sofia away, she had to pitch in. She tried not to leave it any longer than three nights before she went back to the apartment, and lately she'd been lucky enough to have had quite a few evenings in a row with Myles. But he'd been weirdly preoccupied, something she'd had to stop worrying about and force herself to put down as just being busy at work.

After talking with Rupert, she made a quick escape over to the café for her favourite caramel macchiato and enjoyed it while she dealt with an online reservation for a guest coming over from Atlanta, another from someone who lived in a studio apartment in Manhattan but needed a room for her mother at the end of September when she was coming to visit all the way from Nova Scotia. Coffee powered her on as she sent an email to a guest who'd checked out yesterday but whose credit card would be charged extra for breakages; after she'd done the inventory on their apartment she'd found two broken wine glasses buried in the back of a cupboard, two plates completely missing and a big crack in the bathroom mirror. They'd left their apartment filthy, with crumbs all over the kitchenette floor and so much hair – not the sort that grew on your head – in the shower that Darcy had had to clean it up herself as she'd felt sorry for Jill and feared she'd leave her cleaning job at the Inn if she'd had to tackle it.

Darcy shuddered at the thought as she pressed send. She didn't expect apartments to be immaculate at checkout but she did expect a little bit less of a shock than what these guests had left them with.

She'd just dropped her takeaway cup into the trash when a call came in on her iPad. She raced back to the desk, clicked on the icon to accept, and beamed when she saw Gabriella's grin all the way from Switzerland.

'Did they really leave it that bad?' Gabriella asked after Darcy told her all about the email she'd just had to send.

'They're lucky I didn't charge more for the cleaning. Anyway, enough of them,' Darcy smiled at the friend she'd known since her schooldays. 'How's it going in babyland? It all seems very quiet over there.'

'Trent exhausted Kyle at the playground this morning and they're both asleep in our bed, and Millie is right here.'

Darcy peered closer. 'Where?'

'Unless you want to see my boob, you'll have to wait. She's feeding.'

'Wow, you're such a professional I didn't even notice.'

'As soon as she woke and I got her started, I knew it was the perfect time to call you. She'll be at least twenty minutes.'

'You look really well, she must be sleeping at night?'

Gabriella gave the biggest smile across the miles. 'Finally, she is, from about 8 p.m. right through until 6 a.m. We're hoping for even longer once she's on solids, which we're starting next week.'

The talk turned to weddings, New York, Gabriella's introduction of s'mores to Trent's family when they visited at New Year's, and Myles's crazy work schedule. And after they'd exhausted most topics it was on to the bridesmaid outfits.

'I'm finally back in my jeans,' Gabriella announced, 'so I'm hoping the dress will look good by the time August comes around.'

'I don't think you'll need any help looking good, the colour will be fabulous on you. I can't wait to see you in it when you come over and have the final fitting.'

'Me neither. Have you had any more fittings for your gown?'

'No, we're almost there. The dress wasn't too far off my size anyway. I was incredibly lucky to find that place.'

'And how are Holly and Isabella? Excited?'

They talked about how Isabella was already dropping humongous hints to Jake about getting married even though not so long ago their friend would've run a mile at such a suggestion.

'He's such a lovely guy too,' said Darcy. 'Really genuine.'

'And how about Holly, does she have a date?'

'Not yet. She's working on it, she says.'

'That sounds promising. Although I'll be on my own with Trent staying in Switzerland with the kids. So it'll be good to have other singles to talk to.' She leaned closer to the iPad at her end. 'Between you and me, I can't wait for some me time, and some girl time with you. It seems like forever since I was anyone other than "mom".'

'It's nothing to be ashamed about.'

'I feel terrible admitting it.'

'Well don't. You'll have a great time and you can return to your husband and kids completely refreshed.'

'That's what I'm hoping.'

When Darcy finished the Facetime call she turned her attentions to some of the laundry waiting in the basement. She'd stripped the beds in the apartment vacated by the McNastys – the name Jill had naughtily given them when Darcy briefed her yesterday after tackling the major clean – and bundled the sheets into the washing machine without looking too closely in case their unhygienic ways had left their mark. Next it was on to checking out the guests from apartment three, who, thankfully, were incredibly clean, and she almost wanted to give them a gold star for not making her cringe when she went in to do her inspection. Satisfied everything was as it should be, she immediately emailed them with her usual farewell email thanking them for staying at the Inn and wishing them a safe trip home, hoping they'll come back again soon.

She chatted with some other of her guests who sat down in the dining room for lunch and discussed how they could fill their time in New York, although she did have to explain how big the city was and that even though a few blocks on the map didn't look that far, it could take a few hours to cover the ground they had in mind. They had children with them and their initial thoughts had been a stroll from Greenwich Village to the Brooklyn Bridge, then a walk to the One World Trade Center, before heading to Macy's, Times Square, Central Park, and The Met. She gave them the low-down on the subway system, explained the difference between a local service and the express so they didn't find themselves whisked all the way to Harlem.

When lunchtime finally came around Darcy was ready for some spring sunshine and walked a few blocks to meet Holly for lunch at one of their favourite cafés, where tables spilled out onto the sidewalk and aromas pulled customers in with no effort at all.

The waiter delivered the mushroom and pepperoni pizza to the table and ground black pepper across its surface. Darcy, sunglasses in place, took a slice at the same time as Holly, separating the stringy cheese from the other pieces on the plate.

Holly devoured her first mouthful. 'I still have a full-on afternoon to go, but I needed a break. I've been editing a feature article and the freelancer who wrote it has got several of her facts wrong.' She shook her head. 'The thing is, I like this writer, I'd like to keep her on but not if it means I'm basically doing her job.'

'Maybe she was having an off day when she wrote it.'

Holly shrugged. 'I suspect it's more to do with the fact she's planning her wedding. The last time I called her, another phone rang in the background and she couldn't get off our call fast enough. She's obsessed with which flower arrangement she should go for, whether to wear a long or short veil, an ivory or white dress, who will sit with whom at the tables when half of the groom's family don't speak to one another...'

'Sounds frighteningly familiar,' said Darcy. 'Not the fighting family part, but everything else.'

'Yeah, but your wedding is in two months, you're entitled to have a lot going on.'

'When's this other wedding?'

'A year in November!'

Darcy took a second slice. 'Now that makes me glad we didn't have a long time between engagement and ceremony.'

Holly helped herself again too. 'You guys have done the right thing. This girl is tying herself in knots with too much time. I say just get it done. I've been invited to hers but already I've heard enough to know I'm not excited about it. But yours I can't wait for.'

'I'm glad. Me neither.'

'How is Myles dealing with everything?'

It was the only thing to dull the spring sunshine. 'He's got something on his mind but I'm not sure what. I try to talk to him about it without piling on the pressure, but I don't know... maybe it's pre wedding jitters.'

'I'd think so. It's a lot for a man to take in. I think most of them feel out of their depth.'

Darcy wasn't really reassured but she couldn't obsess about it any more. She hooked a stringy piece of cheese below another pizza slice as she tore it away from its base. 'How's operation find-a date going?'

Mouth full, Holly still managed a grin and took out her cell phone, scrolling through her photos. When she'd finished chewing she wiped her hands on a napkin. 'Isn't he gorgeous?'

'Who is he?'

'He's just relocated to Manhattan from Chicago and I bumped into him at Ess-a-Bagel. I recognised him from somewhere but couldn't place him. Turns out we went to high school together. And between you and me, he *never* looked that good back then.'

'Is he free on the day of the wedding?'

'Baby steps, Darcy, baby steps. I don't want to scare him off.'

'What's his name?'

'Pierre,' she said with a flourish. 'His parents are French.'

'Ooh la la!'

'No French accent I'm afraid, pure American. He's lived in this country since he was six.'

'And is he as nice as his picture makes out he is?' Darcy couldn't deny the man was handsome.

'He seems to be. And he's asked me to lunch on Saturday.'

'That sounds promising. I can't believe you didn't tell me all this the second we met today.'

'I was going to keep it to myself until I'd been out with him.' It was the most sheepish Darcy had ever seen Holly look. She hadn't known her all that long but they'd hit it off from the moment they'd bonded over flower arrangements in a florist not too far from here, and now it felt as though they'd known one another for years.

'You know there's no shame in coming to the wedding on your own, don't you?'

'I know. But... well, it's more than just a date for the wedding.' She hesitated while the waiter took away the pizza plate they'd cleared. 'I need to get out there a bit more. I've worked my butt off for years, just like you, and I don't see any Myles Cunninghams hanging around anywhere waiting to kiss me under the mistletoe.'

'I think I got the last one,' Darcy grinned.

'I'm only thirty-two but, I don't know, since my friend died last year I've begun to think more and more that life is not just about existing but it's about living too. Am I making any sense?'

Darcy topped up both glasses with water from the carafe chock-full of ice cubes keeping it cool. 'Perfect sense. And I think, had Myles not come along, despite my desperate need to keep my inde-pendence, I'd be thinking along the same lines.'

'I don't particularly want to end up alone, but if I do then that's just one of those things. I know there are other ways to live the best life you can without a man by your side.'

'Too right,' said Darcy. 'Sole possession of the remote control, domination of the bathroom without it being tarnished by man smells, pretty things in your lounge, nobody sprawled out on your side of the bed.'

'I'm thinking I might make some changes at work.'

'But you love your job.' Darcy asked for the cheque when the waiter passed by.

'I really do, but I also love photography, and I'm going to try to branch out a bit. I've been looking into taking a course. Up until now photography has been something I've done myself, continuously practising and self-teaching along the way, but there's an intensive one-day course I could do here in the city, or I could go for a one-on-one session, maybe a weekend workshop.'

'You sound so keen.'

'I really am. I was getting quite down about where my life was heading.'

'I wish you'd said something.'

She didn't hesitate for long. 'Don't get me wrong, I'm so happy for you and Myles, Cleo and Dylan.'

'The smug-marrieds, huh?'

'Not at all.' She slid a couple of extra dollar bills onto the tray to make up her share and handed it to the waiter. 'It just made me so angry with myself.'

'Angry, why?'

'I was getting wound up that I was single, and it's never been something that bothered me much. Men came and went from my life and I didn't mind – in fact, I loved my independence.'

'I know exactly what you mean.'

'It made me decide to take action. So I thought, in ten years' time, if I'm still single, where do I want to be?'

'Oh, please say here, in New York City, I'd hate to lose you as a friend.'

She smiled. 'Here in Manhattan, or New Jersey, or Connecticut, so still around. But as much as I thrive on my job, I couldn't see myself doing exactly the same thing for another decade. Which is where photography comes in.' She checked her watch. 'But staying at the magazine won't be an option if I miss my meeting, so I'd better go.'

'You sound like you've got a very good plan of action.' Darcy stood and hugged her friend.

'Actually, saying it out loud to you today makes it feel real.'

'Go book yourself on a photography course. I'll expect a full update in a couple of days.'

'I will.'

Darcy cupped a hand around the side of her mouth as her friend crossed the street. 'And let me know how Saturday goes!'

Holly waved away the request, a bit embarrassed, and when she disappeared into the crowds, Darcy sauntered back to the Inn for the afternoon shift. She didn't want to give up the sunshine but she had plenty to get through and after directing Mr and Mrs Miller to the New York City Fire Museum – Mr Miller was a retired fireman from Newcastle, England – she sat down with Rupert to review the menu choices for another corporate group in next week from Hong Kong. There were food preferences and allergies aplenty in the party that would be arriving so this would take careful planning.

Next it was on to general chores around the Inn – replenish the upstairs suite with more hand soap, fruit in the large bowl that sat on the counter in the kitchenette area, add more supplies as needed to the fridge, go down to the basement to fold sheets and towels after putting on another load of washing, which seemed never-ending at the Inn. She and Sofia had discussed outsourcing the laundry but for the extra cost and the admin, not to mention finding someone reliable and depending on them to be timely and do it as well as they would, they'd decided it wasn't worth it. At least not at this stage.

With a bit of jigging and a lot of hard work, Darcy grabbed a few free hours while Rupert managed dinnertime. She wanted to surprise Myles and go home to cook him dinner and so stopped at the Chelsea Market to grab everything she needed before she'd have to head back to work.

'Good afternoon, Mrs Tillman.' As she approached the stoop of the brownstone that housed Myles's apartment on the top floor, the old lady was coming down the steps. She'd seen Mrs Tillman's name on a mailbox in the mailroom and recognised the lady from last week when they'd been collecting their letters at the same time.

'Good afternoon, dear. Lovely day for a walk.'

'It certainly is. Where are you off to?'

'The usual,' she said as though it were obvious. 'Over to Shakespeare Garden, by Belvedere Castle, and then... well, we'll see how far my old legs will take me.'

'Enjoy the sunshine.' By now spring was definitely getting ready to merge into summer and the temperatures were increasing by the day.

As soon as Darcy opened the door to the apartment she took off her shoes, feeling the relief of the cool wooden boards in the hallway beneath her feet. She hooked her bag on the coat rack and took the groceries through to the kitchen, taking out her cell phone when she heard it bleep. It was Myles, asking what time she was coming home.

'I'm here!' she answered in a text, and he replied to say he was forty minutes away, they could talk about what to have for dinner when he got home.

That was one part of domesticity neither of them had mastered yet. They didn't seem to be able to plan much in advance. Whether it was their crazy work schedules or just them, she didn't know, but she figured they'd better sort it out if they were going to have a family one day.

She laughed as she thought about not being able to let the kids go hungry. What sort of dream world was she in? They hadn't properly moved in together yet, let alone started procreating.

She tied a ruby-red apron and got to work, chopping garlic, preparing the chicken pieces, putting water into a pan to boil ready for the rice. She drizzled another large pan with oil and added the chicken pieces that she'd seasoned with salt and pepper, pan frying them for a minute or so each side. She added the garlic, a nice dollop of honey, vinegar, water, soy sauce and measured out rice to add to the boiling water as she multitasked. She put broccoli into a microwave container and when everything else was almost ready she heard the door go and Myles calling her name.

'Surprise!' She took a beer from the fridge and thrust it into his hand the second he came through to the kitchen.

A smile spread wide across his face. 'You cooked?'

'I'm not that bad.'

He twisted off the top and looked beyond her shoulder. 'Watch the chicken.'

'You're distracting the cook,' she scolded as she turned the pan off completely.

Myles wrapped the arm that didn't have hold of the beer bottle around her waist. 'You smell good.' He nuzzled her neck and she was tempted to leave everything exactly as it was and take him into the bedroom.

'But not as good as the dinner, right?' She escaped his clutches and drained the rice. 'Now sit down, it's ready. I have to go back to the Inn later on but you've got me for a good two hours.'

'Wow, that's a nice long time.' He winked at her. 'Think of what we could do in two whole hours.'

She laughed and emptied the chicken into a serving bowl and took it over to the table where he'd finally sat down. 'We can eat.'

He reached across the table and put his hand over hers. 'You should cook more often. I should too. It's nice... this.'

'It is.' She leaned across the table and planted a kiss on his lips.

The glazed sticky chicken had enough sauce to coat some of the rice too and although Myles implied he'd rather be in the bedroom than sitting here, he didn't take long to scoff the lot.

'I spoke to Mrs Tillman today,' said Darcy, finishing her last piece of chicken.

'Our neighbour?'

Darcy smiled. 'I'm starting to feel a lot more at home here.' Was it her or did his eyes dart away from hers rather too quickly?

'That's good.' Focusing on the meal, he complemented her culinary skills once again and they launched into a conversation about what else they could cook.

'Chilli is a good one,' said Myles, 'I haven't made it in a long time. When you're cooking for one it's not quite the same, but I'll make an effort. I can freeze it in batches and if we're on different time schedules, it'll be easy enough.'

'You've been doing a lot of hours at the office.' She spoke tentatively, not wanting him to think of it as a criticism.

He rubbed a hand across the back of his neck.

They'd only been together six months but Darcy knew him well enough to realise something was going on. She'd had a feeling for weeks now and had ignored it. 'Myles, what aren't you telling me?' She put her own cutlery together, suddenly wishing she had a glass of wine to soften the blow of whatever was to come.

'I've been offered another position at work.'

So that's why he'd been working so hard. 'That's great.' She got up. 'I can't drink much because I have to get back to the Inn, but I know we've got a bottle of bubbly in the fridge.'

'The job's in Boston.'

She stopped still and then slumped down on her chair. The man she'd fallen in love with was driven, independent, handsome, strong. But with the first one of those adjectives came this, the inability to commit, not just to a relationship but to a place, a life.

'What have you told your boss?' She couldn't look at him. If she did, his face might tell her an answer she wasn't ready for.

'I haven't told them anything. Not yet. I wanted to talk to you.'

'How long have you known?'

'A while.'

'So why did you keep it quiet?'

'We've had enough going on as it is.'

'You mean the wedding.'

'Yes, the wedding.'

She picked up her plate, then his, and took them out to the kitchen. And when she sensed him behind her, she said, 'You're interested though.'

'Of course I am. It's how I've always been. It's why I came to New York. I was offered the next step up and I took it. Darcy... would you look at me?'

She stared at the white rectangular wall tiles with their thin rim of chrome running along to turn the kitchen into a sleeker version of itself.

'Darcy.'

She turned. 'So what happens now?'

'I think we need to sit down and talk about it properly.'

'It's your career, not mine.' She turned back to the sink and rinsed each plate, then the cutlery.

'Stop that.'

'I need to clear up. I need to get back to the Inn.'

'This is more important.'

'What, your job is more important than mine?' She stomped over to the table and picked up the serving bowl, which had one lonely piece of chicken left, the sauce beginning to congeal on the bottom. She found a Tupperware container out of the cupboard and dropped it in there.

'Darcy, stop.' This time he took the container out of her hands, set it on the countertop and gripped her hands firmly. 'I meant that this conversation was more important than the cleaning up, not that it was more important than the Inn.'

She leaned against his chest and inhaled the comforting warmth of him, the mixture of the laundered shirt and the under-tones of his aftershave that it had absorbed, giving her a sense of home.

They stayed that way, their arms around one another, until Darcy pulled back. 'You want the promotion, don't you?'

'It's not as simple as that.'

'If the new job were in New York, would you take it?'

'Of course.'

'Then it looks like we've got a problem on our hands.'

'Which is why I want to talk.'

'Do you even want to marry me?'

His eyebrows shot up. 'What?'

'If you're finding it difficult to choose, Myles, then maybe you're regretting us rushing into this relationship.' She was goading him, but she was tired of wondering whether or not one of them would snap and back out of this because it was all too hard.

'Darcy, of course I want to marry you. I've never been so sure of anything.'

She went out to the hallway and stepped into her shoes. 'I have to go. We'll talk later.'

'When?'

'Tomorrow. And, Myles... do me a favour, have a think about what you really want. I don't want to stand in your way.'

'Tell me,' he said, 'if you were offered your very own inn somewhere else, wouldn't you be even a little bit tempted?'

He had her there. She took a deep breath in and let it out slowly. 'Yes, I suppose I would.'

All that proved was that they were the same. And if they were too similar, did that mean they weren't really compatible long term?

She picked up her bag and, without looking back, shut the front door behind her.

It was the first time she'd left the apartment without either of them kissing the other goodbye. And it didn't feel good at all.

13

MYLES

Since the night he'd told her about Boston, Myles still hadn't managed to talk to Darcy properly. Every time he tried to lock her into a lengthy, detailed discussion, she always had something else to do and so far it had been a crazy month for the Inglenook Inn with corporate clients and tourists filling every apartment, making their usual guest demands. Ever since she'd challenged him about not wanting to marry her, or wanting his career above all else, plus admitting she'd be likely to do the same, he knew both of them were circling one another wondering where the hell they went to from here. And when they both had work to hide behind, avoidance became the best tactic in the world.

At the office now he stared out of the window, across at other skyscrapers filling the Financial District, at the smog that laced the blue skies of spring and told the tale of the busy city that swarmed below. Rufus had thankfully given Myles no cause for concern of late. He was working hard and pulling a couple of all-nighters but not taking on tasks he had no hope of doing well. It seemed the firm's newest employee was finally getting into the groove and after a successful breakfast meeting this morning with a client Rufus had managed to get on board with an incredibly well-researched presentation, Myles finally had the chance to think.

He turned and pressed the button on his telephone intercom to reach his secretary. 'Rhonda, can you mark me as out of the office from three o'clock today, please.'

'Consider it done,' she replied, her voice accompanied by the sound of keyboard clicks. Rhonda was good that way. She rarely asked many questions but always let him know the important stuff. And today she told him his boss, Neil, had booked an hour-long meeting with him at midday.

'I didn't see it in my diary when I looked first thing this morning.' He heard a few more keyboard clicks.

'Looks like he only just booked it.'

'Thanks, Rhonda.'

Myles resigned himself to the fact he'd get little thinking time now, with a meeting booked and leaving the office at 3 p.m. He wanted to head to the grocery store and then get back to the apartment well ahead of Darcy. Sometimes, by the time he got home she was either back at the Inn or had fallen into bed exhausted, ready to get up and do it all over again the next day. She was finishing around 8 p.m. tonight and usually he was still in the office at that time, especially over the last few nights since his newest client based in a different time zone had dictated his work schedule with conference calls most evenings to iron out the last parts of their agreement. But tonight, he wanted to surprise his wife to be in the same way she'd surprised him. They were both making the effort, and tonight it was time to talk.

Myles ploughed through paperwork, sifted through projections, and signed an agreement with a long-standing client he'd been responsible for bringing to the firm in the first place. He responded to client messages, checked pricing tables, and read over a credit agreement, until finally it was time for the meeting with his boss.

'Come in, sit.' Neil gestured to the chair in front of his desk when Myles knocked on his door at exactly 12 p.m.

Equally prompt was Neil's own secretary, Bea, who brought in a tray with coffees and a selection of cookies.

Neil waited for Bea to leave them to it and got straight to the point. 'So, any thoughts about the Boston move? We'd be sad to see you go, but I get it. I'd have done the same at your age, moved around whenever the opportunity arose. You've not been here long, Myles, but you're one of our strongest associates.' He reached for a chocolate-chip cookie and for some reason it made Myles want to laugh. His boss was a little kid at heart despite the bravado.

It was nice to hear when you were doing well at your job but Myles had different priorities now. As a single man he'd have been on the next plane over to Boston to talk to the management, discuss what his new role would be, meet some of the team, and decide on that basis whether he wanted the position.

'My circumstances have changed,' he said simply.

'You mean with Darcy,' Neil smiled.

'Exactly.'

'Is she happy to move to Boston, for a time?'

Myles's look said it all. 'We need to talk some more. But I'd say it's unlikely.'

'So that's why you've been dithering about giving me an answer.'

'I'm grateful to have been singled out,' Myles assured him, 'and not so long ago I would've jumped at the chance.'

'You know the same happened to me?' He brushed cookie crumbs from his suit jacket, belying his professionalism. 'My wife moved around a lot when it came to my job. For the first ten years we were deliriously happy, she loved the travel, but as soon as kids came along she put the brakes on and said it wasn't the way she wanted to raise a family. I hadn't thought about it until then, but it wasn't what I wanted either. There was always travel with my job, but we needed roots.'

'So you clipped your wings.' Myles had a feeling he'd be doing that too.

'I believe, Myles, that you can have both roots and wings. Home is here, in New Jersey for us, but I strap my wings on a few times a year and head to conferences, spend time in our other offices. My wife thinks it's glamorous – she still remembers our carefree travelling days from two or three decades ago – but in reality it's a lot of air miles, which is exhausting, staying in lonely hotel rooms, and saying goodnight to your family over an iPad rather than in person.'

'I feel that if I say no to this opportunity in Boston, then I'm freezing my career where it is.'

'Whatever makes you think that?'

'When I was a graduate, starting out as an analyst, I never said no to anything. I was hungry for it. But there was a guy I worked with, early forties he must've been, and I still remember him being offered another position, a promotion in Europe. He turned it down and even I noticed that after that he was bypassed on a lot of projects. In the end he upped and left and went to another firm but since then I've always been conscious to keep one step ahead when it comes to my career.'

'I wish I could offer you something here, Myles. But it'll be a good couple of years at least, possibly a few more, before we might be in the position to offer the equivalent of what Boston is offering. The question is, are you willing to wait?'

More confused than ever, Myles left the meeting and went to grab a sandwich from a café nearby. Only one thing was clear, and that was that whatever choice he made, he didn't want it to be to the detriment of either his career or his relationship.

Which left him with precisely the same problem he'd gone into Neil's office with in the first place.

* * *

'It's my turn to surprise you,' said Myles just after 8:30 p.m. when Darcy came through the door. He'd heard her keys in the lock, he'd grabbed the wine glass waiting for this very moment, and he'd filled it with her favourite pinot grigio, which he handed to her as she padded into the lounge.

'You're home early.' She took the glass and gave him a tentative kiss. This was how they'd been with each other lately, tiptoeing around, afraid to say anything that would end up in a full-blown row. 'What happened to those demanding clients of yours?'

'I've sorted everything this morning and anything else will have to wait.' Actually he'd warned Rufus to be on standby and Rufus had leapt at the chance to be his second-in-command.

When she tried to peer into the kitchen, he ushered her to the sofa. 'You wait here, don't touch anything, and I'll be back in a couple of minutes.'

She did as she was told and he disappeared into the bathroom, turned on the taps and poured in a generous capful of her favourite bath oil.

Back in the lounge he took her already half-drained glass. 'You go for a soak in the tub. I'll get you a top-up and bring it in.'

'Myles—'

He put a finger to her lips. 'Yes, we do need to talk, but we've got all night.' His heart sank. 'Unless you're due back at the Inn?'

She shook her head. 'Not until early tomorrow morning.'

'Then let's enjoy tonight.'

'Okay.' She answered without taking her eyes from his, a reminder that despite their disagreement, their relationship was still new.

'Go, you'd better turn off the taps, or faucet,' he said, attempting to fit in with Manhattan speak, 'before we have a flood and get to meet the tenant living below us. Who may not be as lovely as Mrs Tillman.'

She went off to the bathroom and he fetched her a top-up, and when he took her glass to her he had to force himself to ignore the curve of her bottom as she faced the bathtub and wiggled out of her dress. He'd give anything to take her in his arms right now, make love to her, and kiss away everything that needed to be said. As well as not talking properly for days, they hadn't been intimate since their confrontation, something that at less than a year into their relationship Myles knew was a bad sign.

'I'll leave your wine here.' He set it on the edge of the tub and when she unhooked her bra he left her alone before he couldn't resist temptation any longer.

'How long do I have?' she called after him.

'Take your time.'

Knowing Darcy she'd soak for at least twenty minutes, and he wanted to make sure everything else was ready. He'd found the email she sent him confirming the string quartet for the wedding and yesterday he'd sourced a playlist from them that he streamed through the docking station now, gently so she'd only hear it when she emerged from the bathroom. He went out through the doors in the lounge and now the sun had set, he switched on the festoon lights with the frosted bulbs that added bags of character to the terrace. He'd already set up the small round café table that usually sat at the edge and upon it he'd draped a white linen tablecloth he'd picked up from the discount store a couple of blocks away. On top of that he'd set out cloth napkins, polished cutlery, and an ice bucket. He went back to the kitchen to fill the bucket and pushed the bottle of champagne into it before heading out to the terrace again.

He stood back. The scene was set. And it was perfect. But there was one more touch to go. Back inside, he pulled out the flower garland from where it was stashed beneath the sofa and draped it over the inside of the doorway to the terrace, creating a replica arch. The bright pink roses and paler versions next to those added colour, and he hoped their wedding would be the first thing Darcy thought of when she saw it.

He chuckled to himself as he stood there and switched off the lights in the lounge. This was the most romantic thing he'd ever done in his life. He just hoped it worked.

When he heard water gurgling down the drain he hovered outside the bathroom door so he could steer Darcy to the bedroom to dress before she came to see what he'd been up to. And if she was surprised to find him waiting, she didn't show it.

'Shall I take that?' He held a hand out for her empty glass.

'Why thank you, sir.'

If they didn't need to talk so badly, his actions would be showing far more than his words right now.

With Darcy dressing, he turned the music up. The sounds of Bach filled the room and he waited at the entrance to the lounge until she emerged.

He laughed as Bach changed to the string quartet's rendition of 'Wonderful Tonight'. 'Kind of took the words right out of my mouth,' he grinned, looking at Darcy in a jaw-dropping red dress with a fitted top half and a bottom half that skimmed across her hips in just the right way. Her legs and feet were bare, her hair loose, curling around her collar bone.

'Which album is this?' She was almost as coy as when he'd met her that night to go to The Plaza for his firm's Christmas party last year.

'You don't recognise it?'

Her eyes held a sheen and he hoped it was a happy one. 'I guess that means you do read my emails about the wedding.'

He stepped forwards. 'I'm in this as much as you are. And, yes, I read every word.'

'But how did you get all this music? I didn't buy their CD – I meant to, but it was something else I hadn't got around to.'

'I called them, explained who I was, went to pick up a copy yesterday lunchtime. They're an eclectic bunch but jeez they can play.'

She nodded, enveloped by the gentle sounds of violins, a viola, and a cello, the three types of instruments he'd learnt made up the ensemble. And then she sniffed the air. 'I don't smell anything cooking yet.'

'It's all chopped and ready to go – it's pasta so it's quick.' He held out an arm for her to hook her hand into. 'Now if you'll come this way, madam, I'll show you to your table.'

Perplexed, she looped an arm into his and they went through into the lounge where they could see the double doors and the terrace beyond.

Darcy put a hand to her mouth. 'It's an archway.'

'I'm afraid the flowers aren't real, but it's the best I could do at the last minute.'

She beamed up at him. 'It's just like we'll have at our wedding.'

'I know you've selected white flowers for the day, so it's not quite the right colours I'm afraid.'

'Oh, Myles.' She stopped him moving on further to show her what was outside. 'I'm sorry I've been such a bitch.'

'What?' He held her upper arms and looked intently at her. 'You shouldn't be apologising.'

'I should. When you said Boston, I wanted to run. I thought it meant you didn't want me.' She hesitated. 'Wait, I'm assuming you still do if you've gone to all this trouble.'

'Of course I do, and we do need to talk. But most of all, we need some time together.' He took her by the hand, led the way through the arch, and out onto the terrace.

She took in the lighting, the table, the candle flickering away in a glass jar in the centre.

'Champagne?'

'Are we celebrating?'

'Only that we're together tonight,' he said.

'Well, in that case, go ahead.'

The cork made a satisfying pop and he poured it into the two awaiting champagne flutes. 'To us,' he said simply.

'To us,' she repeated.

Two very simple words but exactly what both of them needed to hear right now.

'Dinner won't be long, but you stay here,' he said before she made any effort to get up. 'I'll share my time between the terrace and the kitchen.'

'It's a gorgeous evening, I think I'll curl up on the day bed until dinner is served.'

When she smiled up at him he couldn't resist kissing her beneath the inky sky, her eyes twinkling as they reflected the lights strung along each side of the terrace.

She hooked her hair away from her face. 'Careful, or we'll never get to dinner if you kiss me like that again.'

She wasn't wrong there.

He grudgingly left her on the day bed and went to throw together the dinner he'd already prepared. He was serving shrimp pasta in a white wine sauce. The garlic was already finely chopped, the shallots cut into tiny pieces, the shrimps prepared and waiting.

Less than twenty minutes later and on their second glass of champagne, they sat down opposite each other as nightfall took Manhattan in its grasp. Darcy complimented the chef, they talked about her day and his, and when all that was left in their pasta bowls were a few leftover strands of linguine, Darcy asked whether they were ever going to talk about the elephant in the room.

'Or the elephant on the terrace,' said Myles, gazing across at the woman with whom he'd had a whirlwind romance. 'So... Boston.'

'Boston,' she repeated before sipping her champagne.

He held out his hand to take hers. 'Leave all this, let's sit down.'

They moved over to the day bed and she curled up and nestled into him so close he could smell her shampoo that always bowled him over. It was so Darcy. If ever he was walking through the Financial District and smelled something similar it made him want to call her, hear her voice, feel her in his arms.

'My boss says there aren't any similar positions in the New York office,' he told her.

'That's a shame.'

'I love it here, Darcy. I feel settled for the first time in my life and that's not because of the job for once, it's because of you. Over the years I've had offers to move sideways or upwards in my career and I haven't always taken them. You look surprised.'

'By what you've said, I thought you always moved when you're asked to.'

'Not always. I usually meet with the people who are interested in making me an offer, think about my options, make a decision. But it's different now.'

'Because of me,' she said, her eyes fixed on the bubbles in her glass as they battled their way to the top of the liquid before she tilted the vessel to get another sip and ruined their course.

'Because of you. Hey.' He put his fingers beneath her chin and tilted it up to him. 'I don't mean that in a negative way. Since you came into my life things have changed, but for the better. And I think we can both say it's taking a lot of getting used to, maintaining our careers and working on a relationship at the same time.'

'I didn't realise it would be this hard,' she said.

'It's not really though.'

'Isn't it? Boston has come calling and I haven't even asked you about the new position. We used to share details of our work days, talk them through. I'm assuming this is a step up the career ladder for you.'

'But that's the thing. I'm not sure I want to climb it alone.'

'You don't?'

He shook his head. 'Would you ever entertain the idea of moving anywhere else other than New York?'

'Boston is supposed to be beautiful,' she said.

'Not what I asked. Come on, Darcy, we've tiptoed around each other over the last few weeks and we can't keep doing it. Would you ever consider Boston?'

'I don't want to be selfish.'

'Darcy, I'm asking what you think and all I want is honesty.'

She took a deep breath. 'New York is my home, the Inn is just getting started with the corporate side, I'm loving being in charge a lot of the time. It's invaluable experience I couldn't get anywhere else.'

'Then it's a firm no.'

'Actually, it isn't.'

'Really?'

'It's a no right now, because at this stage I can't walk away, I think it would be detrimental to everything I've worked for. And Sofia relies on me. She's in Switzerland with Gabriella and if she had to come back here full time she'd miss out on the grandkids.' She turned the tables on him. 'Would you stay here for another couple of years if I asked you to? Gabriella won't be in Switzerland forever.'

'You mean you'd leave the Inn one day.'

She smiled. 'You know this has been our problem all along.

We've rarely had the chance to talk long into the night about the way we feel, our plans. I think we skipped a step.'

'I feel like someone hit the fast-forward button and is refusing to take their finger off.'

She turned so she was cross-legged and facing him, the material of her dress licking her knees as the breeze tried to lift it. 'I never thought I'd want to leave the city and I'm still not sure I do, but I think I would like to start my own business one day, you know, right from scratch. And with prices what they are in Manhattan, I could consider elsewhere if your job moved in the future.'

'You'd do that?'

'I would. I mean... if we had kids, it would be a different life for us anyway.' She took his hand in hers, her delicate fingers gripping tight. 'That's what we both want, isn't it?'

He held her gaze. 'It is, yes.' He reached out and twirled a strand of her hair, its silky length wrapping around his fingers. 'We just haven't really thought hard about it, or made any plans. I guess someday we'll have to.'

'What will it mean for you if you turn the job down?'

'It'll be a few years before I can get a similar opportunity here in New York.'

She pulled back enough that her hair fell from his fingers. 'You'll hate that.'

'Who says?'

'I know you, remember. I know the sort of man you are and you came to New York for a job you knew could propel you even further.'

'But I don't want to go to Boston without you.'

'Can you honestly tell me that a year or two down the line you won't regret it?'

'No, I can't.' When her face fell he said, 'But who knows how either of us will feel in a couple of years. It's not something we can predict, and I don't want to. And, Darcy, you know my family history. I have no intention of letting the past repeat itself. Mum and Dad are in a good place now, but they could've so easily split up and never sorted out the mess they were in when I was a kid. It's not the life I want for me, for you, for anyone else.'

They let his words fall on the air until Darcy said, 'We could make it work. Boston isn't all that far. You could come home, here, every weekend.'

He retrieved the champagne bucket from the table and set it down beside them before topping up both glasses. 'I could do that, but you're forgetting something. You work a lot of weekends.'

'Maybe I could arrange it so that I didn't have to.'

'Come on, you and I both know that would never happen.'

She smiled. 'No, it wouldn't, I'm just trying to see this from your point of view.'

'I think we're doing pretty well together if we can do that.' He clinked his glass against hers.

'The erratic hours and unpredictability of the job were something I once revelled in.'

'You don't any more?'

'I do, but it's the same as it is for you – I've found something other than my job and I want both. And I'm not sure it'll ever work when my home is on the other side of town to my work, and I'm working for someone else. One day I could get my own inn and run it alongside a family.'

He rubbed the bare skin on her knee. 'I never thought I'd talk about having kids with anyone. I'd have laughed if someone had told me I'd ever be having this conversation.'

'I never thought I would either.' She sipped her champagne. 'So, Mr Cunningham, what's it to be? Boston or here? It's your choice at the end of the day.'

'No, don't do that. It's a joint decision. From now on, our choices have to be. I would expect you to consult me about your work if it meant a change for me, and vice versa.'

'Things really have changed for the both of us.'

'And I'm glad they have.' He leaned forwards and planted a kiss on her lips. 'I'm saying no to Boston, Darcy.'

She took his face in her hands. 'Thank goodness for that. You'd have broken my heart if you'd taken it.'

'Then why didn't you tell me that in the first place?'

'I needed you to decide for yourself, rather than because I begged you to do something. And remember,' she said as he began to kiss her neck and moved lower to where her dress met her collar bone. 'Forever is a long time so it's not a permanent no. Let's see where we are in a couple of years' time. Deal?'

'Deal.' He took her champagne glass and set it on the ground next to his own and, arms either side of her, pushed her back onto the day bed.

'I'm hoping I'm right here,' she said as she wrapped her legs around him.

'Me too.'

* * *

They'd made love on the day bed. With nobody else able to see onto the terrace – at least he hoped there wasn't a hidden window somewhere – he'd taken her in his arms beneath the Manhattan skies and carried her inside for round two, and now, lying in bed with her snuggling lazily against his chest as he traced his fingers down her spine making goose pimples appear all up her arms, he knew Boston would never compare.

He gazed over at the wall hanging, the speech bubble that had changed both of their lives forever when he'd asked Darcy to marry him. 'Happy?' he asked.

'Of course.' She squeezed him tighter with the hand thrown across his bare skin.

'Not wishing you were still single and carefree?'

She laughed sleepily. 'No chance. Talking of being single, Holly had a date last Saturday.'

'Tell me more.'

'His name is Pierre.'

'French?'

'His family is, but he's American.'

'And is he good enough for our Holly?' He had mates whom he went way back with in the UK, but Myles enjoyed his friendships here just as much. It was another reason to look for other options apart from Boston. He'd never bothered much about his roots but maybe, with his woman in his arms now, it was time to.

'I love the way you call her *our* Holly.'

'She's a good friend.'

'Well I've yet to meet Pierre. I've seen a photo and he's gorgeous so that box is ticked, and apparently he was a gentleman on their date and they have a second arranged this Saturday.'

'Sounds promising.'

'Fingers crossed. She deserves to meet someone.'

When Darcy's cell phone rang, she groaned. 'I should check if it's the Inn.'

He held her back before reluctantly letting her go. He'd always thought his job was the most demanding but hers was on a par, not least because she liked to do things herself rather than outsource.

'It's Dylan. Sorry Dylan.' She put the cell phone back on the nightstand without answering it. 'Fiancé trumps website guru tonight.'

'Is he doing work for the Inn again? I thought the website was all sorted. And it's a bit late to be working isn't it?'

'I think he often gets things done in the evenings if Cleo is asleep as it frees up his mornings to sort the kids' breakfast and take them to school. I emailed him with a few more photographs and a really nice testimonial from a corporate guest. Sometimes I ask him to put an advert on the page for any special offers I might do in any quiet periods.'

'Do you have any of those?'

'Not lately, but I shouldn't complain.'

When her cell chimed again she said, 'I'd better get it. Perhaps it's not clear what I was asking for in my email.'

Myles kept his hand on her bare hip as she answered the call. 'Tell him he's got rubbish timing.' He trailed kisses from between her shoulder blades all the way down her back and felt her shudder beneath him. Dylan needed to be quick so he could have her attention back again. Whatever he was saying about his website design, it was taking him long enough.

'No, she's not here with us,' said Darcy into her cell phone.

Myles stopped, the mood completely altered.

'Let me know if you hear anything, Dylan. And keep me posted.'

'What's going on?' Myles asked after she hung up and grabbed her clothes from the floor.

'It's Cleo, she's gone off somewhere and Dylan has no idea where.'

'Shit. Given what Dylan said about her history with her mum, he must be going out of his mind.'

'He is.' She zipped up her dress and raked her fingers through her hair. 'Kaisha says she closed up the Little Knitting Box herself today, which is unheard of. Cleo always likes to do that – we joke that it's as though she's putting another child to bed.'

'Do the kids know?'

'Dylan's just about holding it together and pretending everything is normal.' She shook her head. 'He says she's been gone since eleven o'clock this morning. At first he thought she must've taken a

long walk, or he'd find her hanging around in a café drinking ho
chocolate, taking time out like he's been begging her to do. But he'
no idea where she is.'

Myles grabbed his jeans, tugged them on, and picked up a shirt
'She can't have gone far.' The first thing he did was to text Dylan
He'd become a good mate and he couldn't imagine what the man
was going through. 'Do you want to get a cab over to their house in
Stamford?' Funny how their own concerns had paled into insignifi
cance all of a sudden.

'We could. It might free Dylan up to go looking for her.'

Myles checked his cell. 'Then give him a call. He just sent me a
message to say he's close to calling the police, but I'm sure between
us we can find her before it comes to that. Can you think o
anywhere she'd go?'

Darcy clicked on Dylan's number in her contacts. 'I've no idea
apart from the store, and we know she isn't there.' Dylan must've
snatched the phone up. 'Hey, it's Darcy. I wondered if you'd like me
to come over to the house and watch the kids while you go looking
for her.' Pause. 'Okay, well let me know if you hear anything, and I'
rack my brains to think where she might've gone. I'm sure every
thing will be just fine.'

'He doesn't need us there?' Myles asked when she'd hung up.

'Apparently Prue happened to call and he told her what wa
going on. She's on her way to the house, then Dylan will go ou
searching.' She grabbed her purse.

'Where are you going?'

'I'm going to get a cab over to the Inn. And on my way I'm going
to call Holly and Isabella. They've had a few meetings with Cle
about my bachelorette party – don't ask,' she added when she saw
his raised eyebrows. 'They've seen her more recently than I have, s
maybe she said something.'

'I'll come with you.' As she pulled the door to the apartment shut behind them and locked it, he called a cab.

'God, I hope she's all right,' said Darcy as she impatiently pumped the button inside the elevator.

He took her hand and gave it a reassuring squeeze, because no words right now would be able to erase the worry Dylan must be feeling tenfold.

14

DARCY

The Inglenook Inn was the most central place Darcy could think of to get her friends together and brainstorm where Cleo may have taken off to.

'She was in good spirits last time we met up,' said Isabella when she joined them in the lounge at the Inn.

'I had no idea how hard she was taking this pregnancy,' Holly admitted after she'd slotted her umbrella into the stand by the door. The spring showers were out in full force tonight now that the skies had darkened. 'She always seems so capable, so superhuman.'

'Well that's just it,' said Darcy, hoping that wherever their friend was, she was sheltered and dry. 'She's trying her utmost to be super-human but it's not working and something must've finally snapped.'

'We'll find her.' Myles's voice fell on deaf ears. He had no more confidence in that claim than they did.

Darcy put her head in her hands. 'What happened with her mom has always terrified Cleo. She must be distraught, thinking the same could happen to her.'

'Am I missing something?' Isabella looked from one to the other.

'I think we must be,' said Holly.

'I know she doesn't talk about it with many people,' Darcy began, 'but I think everyone needs to know now that she's missing.' Darcy told the details of Cleo's past that she'd kept under wraps. Because of what happened with her mom, she never wanted to have children of her own.'

'The poor thing.' Holly perched on the arm of the sofa. Apart from one guest asking for restaurant recommendations tonight, the inn was quiet and Darcy was glad.

'But Tabitha is a little angel,' said Isabella, 'and Cleo is a great mom. I'm assuming she didn't suffer from depression the first time around, unless you're not telling us something.'

'That's it, you know as much as I do now.'

Myles offered to fetch coffees from the café across the street and the girls all put in their orders while he found the enormous golfing umbrella out from the closet. Darcy didn't know about anyone else but she doubted she'd be going to sleep tonight until Cleo was located safe and sound, so a caffeine hit would be just the ticket.

'Excuse me.' Darcy stood up to greet one of their more corporate guests who requested a scotch to take up to his suite, but before Darcy could do the honours, Rupert stepped in. 'Thanks, Rupert,' she whispered, getting back to her friends after the door of the Inn fell shut behind Myles, off on his coffee-seeking mission.

'Cleo believes that she was lucky with Tabitha, but she doesn't think she deserves to be so lucky twice.' Darcy opened the window in the lounge just enough to let the cool spring breeze in but keep the rain out, and sat down again.

'I wish she'd said something.' Holly toyed with the bracelet on her wrist. 'She didn't say a word when we met up a couple of nights ago.'

'Actually,' Isabella put in, 'she didn't say anything, but there was something going on. I knew she wasn't quite right.'

'In what way?' Darcy asked.

'I'm not sure how to describe it, and if she hadn't run off now I doubt I would've ever thought about it again. But I caught her staring into space more than once, and had to bring her back to the conversation. I laughed at the time, joked that it was her mommy brain not letting her multitask. She took it in good humour and we giggled about how she'd poured orange juice on her cereal that morning and then at the store she'd filled an order only for the customer to bring it back because it was completely wrong. She'd given her the wrong type of yarn, in bright orange rather than sea blue.'

'We all laughed along with her.' Holly shook her head. 'I teased her that you'd end up with one hell of a bachelorette party if we left her in charge.'

Darcy managed a smile. 'I don't even want to think about what you guys have planned.'

Holly thought some more. 'We moved on to talking about the worst bachelorette parties we'd been to, we cringed at some that were so tacky I wouldn't wish them on my worst enemy.'

'And where did you meet up?' Darcy grasped at the possibility of Cleo being at some venue nearby.

Myles returned and Holly helped him with the tray of coffees so he could wrestle the umbrella down and leave it to dry. 'We met at my place, and I already know she's not there.'

Darcy's heart sank. She concentrated on the taste and warmth of her caramel macchiato in an effort to stop herself worrying whether her friend was shivering somewhere, trying desperately to get home. Or, worse, whether she didn't care any more and was sitting out in the elements, all alone. 'Dylan texted to say he'd been

n touch with every person he could think of.' She checked her cell
for the umpteenth time to see if there was more news, but nothing.

Isabella was busy discussing the merits of the café across the
road and their ability to make a decent coffee when you needed it
most, when she suddenly turned to Darcy. 'She did talk a lot about
her mom at that planning meeting. Not how she'd died, and neither
of us asked, but she talked about how sad she was that her children
would never get to see their grandma. With Dylan's parents
deceased as well, the realisation seemed to have hit her particularly
hard.'

'That's right,' Holly recalled. 'Then we talked about Tabitha and
how good Ruby and Jacob are with their little sister, which turned
to talking about Dylan's ex-wife.'

'Talking of Prue,' Isabella pondered, 'do you think she could
have gone to hide out there?'

'She's not on the run,' said Holly with a frown. 'But good to
cover all bases.'

Darcy shook her head. 'Good theory, but I know Prue is over at
Dylan's as we speak, looking after the kids, while he drives around
everywhere he can think of.'

'That's that idea ruled out then,' Holly surmised.

'I guess she could've come to the city,' Myles speculated. 'But if
she had, I think she'd have come to the apartment.'

Isabella tried to continue piecing together clues about where
their friend might be. 'Talk in our meeting turned to how beautiful
Tabitha was, which prompted this one' – she indicated Holly – 'to
suggest Jake and I would have gorgeous children. What was it you
said? A cross between geeky and stunning?'

'Jake's got that whole geek look going on, with those thick-
framed glasses he wears – which I'm sure aren't prescription – and
you've got the striking blonde hair and cheek bones I wish I had.'

Coyly Isabella said, 'Well we're not ready to make babies just yet. And they are prescription.'

'Yeah? Huh... go figure.' Holly smiled. 'Anyway, back to the matter in hand, we then talked about Pierre and what sort of babies he and I would make. Don't go there,' she stopped Myles before he could say anything. 'And she was really happy, laughing about it all and winding me up a bit about my date, insisting she wanted details.'

'That's right, I remember,' said Isabella. 'And then she talked about her mom again. That was it. That was what made me think something was up. She'd talked about her already but it was as though as soon as the topic wandered off course, she wanted to get it right back there again.'

'What sort of thing was she saying?' asked Darcy.

Isabella thought hard. 'She told us about their time in England, how her mom loved the beach. Then she talked about her mom and dad when they'd first met, how her mom told her the story time and time again about the good times when they'd fallen in love. I think it was in Florida.'

'Let's hope she hasn't ventured there,' said Holly. 'No, don't panic, I'd say it's unlikely.'

'What else did she say?' Darcy wished they could come up with an answer as to where Cleo might have gone before they all went out of their minds with worry.

Holly took over the story. 'She told us all about how American her mom had stayed even though she'd moved to England. She talked about how her mom kept going with the Thanksgiving tradition, how her dad would always give his thanks for meeting Diana in the first place. And then Cleo told us some of the stories from her mom's university days.'

'She did,' Isabella confirmed. 'I remember it striking me as a bit out of place, made me think something was up, because she seemed troubled when she talked about how her mom's university days were the good times before anything had ever gone wrong.'

'That's right.' Holly was really getting going now. 'I said, "but she met your dad after that," and Cleo said something about him being the love of her life, but that with her happiness had come heartbreak.' She looked to Darcy. 'Now you've filled us in, I know she must've meant everything that happened to her mom.'

Darcy's cell buzzed. 'It's Dylan.' She took the call. 'Any news?'

'She hasn't turned up. But I think I may know what was on her mind. I could kick myself for not realising. Her grandpa Joe just called to talk with her and when he asked for her by her childhood nickname, I couldn't hide the truth from him. He called her Buttons when she was little and he often jokes around calling her that when other people are around, to embarrass her. And it just...' His voice cracked. 'It just reminded me of how fragile she is right now.'

'Oh, Dylan. She'll be all right, I know she will. She's probably gone somewhere for some space, I bet she's back soon. And what do you mean by you could kick yourself for not realising?'

'When I told Joe that she'd gone off and I was worried, he told me it's her mom's birthday today.'

The birthday, Cleo's pregnancy, and her utter exhaustion must've thrown Cleo's emotions into turmoil. Darcy shared what she knew with Dylan.

'Her friends saw it and I didn't.' He sounded crushed. 'I should've picked up on it. I've been so damn busy with the kids, Tabitha has kept everyone up the last few nights with a bit of a cold.'

'Don't be too hard on yourself. You're both crazy busy.'

'Darcy, I'm going out of my mind. I've driven all around Stamford, to every café we've ever been to, every store, the fields where the markets are held in Inglenook Falls, down Main Street near the Little Knitting Box. I just don't know what else to do. I wish I knew more about her mom, it might help me think of where she could be. She often talks about her, about the good things rather than the bad. Her grandpa has a photograph of him, Cleo's gran and Diana at her graduation, and Cleo always smiles fondly at it when we're at his place.'

'Remembering the best times,' Darcy said.

'Let's hope so.'

'She must miss her mom terribly.' She wanted to cry for her friend, for her loss, for the memories she carried around with her so heavily at times it had to be overwhelming. Throw pregnancy hormones, a busy career, and a hectic home life into the mix and it was no wonder she'd freaked out.

'You don't think she's gone to Yale, do you?'

'I suppose it's a possibility,' Darcy replied. 'Especially if her mom's on her mind.'

'I'll drive out and take a look.'

'Dylan, do you think it's time to involve the police?'

A deep sigh came down the phone. 'I'll do this last check, then yes, I'm going to have to call them.'

Darcy was about to tell him to let her know when he got to Yale and whether it came to anything when she heard Myles behind her and, looking round, saw him standing next to a bedraggled Cleo.

'Oh my God, Dylan. She's here.'

'Is she okay?' Panic rose in his voice.

'She's safe, don't worry. We've got her now.'

Darcy heard his breathing change, a sob built in as she delivered the overpowering news he'd been desperate to hear. 'I'll drive and get her.'

Darcy wanted to go to her friend, standing there in the hall of the Inn. 'How about she stays here tonight? I'll run her a bath, I'll make up the spare bed, I'll feed her too. And maybe she'll talk to me.' She looked over at Cleo, eyes sunken, drenched head to toe, staring at the floor as the others fussed around her.

'We don't want to be a burden.'

'Dylan, we're friends. This is what friends do. I'll text you later but try to get some sleep and we'll speak in the morning.'

'Are you sure she's okay?'

By now Myles had brought out towels, Isabella was squeezing out Cleo's wet hair, Holly had wrapped another around her body, and Myles had mouthed the word 'bath' at Darcy, to which she'd nodded.

After Dylan reluctantly hung up Darcy was at Cleo's side in seconds. 'You had us all worried sick.'

Wide eyes looked directly at her, the blue a paler version of their usual colour. Dark blonde wavy hair appeared brown and dead straight it was so soaked from the rain, and her turquoise cotton dress was stuck to her hips and thighs. 'I'm sorry.'

Darcy led her to her apartment, passing Myles on the way as he went back to the lounge, and it was only when they were the other side of the bathroom door that Cleo showed any emotion, fell into Darcy's arms and burst into tears.

* * *

'How are you feeling?' Darcy asked when Cleo polished off not only a healthy portion of lasagne but a generous helping of peach cobbler to finish. Darcy had popped her clothes in the washer and then the dryer, so now she was back in her dress with one of Darcy's cardigans to make sure she didn't catch a chill. They were sitting together in the dining room of the Inglenook Inn. With all the guests either in bed or out on the town, Myles now back at the apartment and Isabella and Holly having gone home themselves, it was just the two of them.

'I feel like I'm the size of a house after that meal. Although I guess I'm eating for two.' Cleo looked at her watch and frowned. 'It's gone midnight. I'm so sorry.'

'You've apologised far too many times already and there's no need.'

'Thank you for the food.'

'My pleasure.' They were dancing around the subject of why Cleo had done a runner but Darcy knew taking it slowly was the only way to go. 'Can I get you anything else?'

Cleo shook her head and toyed with her napkin, the only evidence left of her meal apart from a plate and a bowl. 'Is Dylan very angry?'

'Angry? I can think of a lot of adjectives to describe how he's feeling but not one of them includes angry. Worried, relieved, concerned… he's feeling all of those things, I'm sure. He's just glad you're somewhere safe.'

'I didn't think.'

'You've been gone for hours.'

'I know.'

'What made you take off?'

She looked up, eyes misting with tears. 'I had a really good morning, the baby was kicking so much and it made me feel connected in a way that told me everything would be okay.'

'So what changed?'

'It sounds so silly now.'

'Try me.'

'It was my grandma's sewing machine that did it.'

'I'm not sure I follow. Did it fall, hit you on the head?' Her comment at least raised a smile, albeit one accompanied by glassy eyes filled with unsure tears. 'That's better. Now tell me, I'll listen.' She moved next to Cleo rather than opposite and held her friend's hand.

'I was dusting it because it reminded me of happy times with mum. It was her birthday you know, and it's always a day I find so incredibly hard. But I could see her in my mind, so vividly, at her happiest in front of that machine. She'd sew for hours, almost like a therapy in the same way knitting could be, and Mum said everyone needs a thing or a place in their life where they can go to when things get too much. I asked her if the beach was her place where she could go and she thought about it, and said whilst the sea and the sand were beautiful, it wasn't where she'd go to escape.'

Darcy said nothing as her friend continued. Cleo's mum had taken her own life by walking into the sea and drowning, so the association of a beach and a happy place now must be hard for Cleo to talk about.

'She spent ages telling me about her time at Yale, her graduation day when my dad was with her, how happy she'd been and how perfect everything was. I remember she was sad because, living in England, we were too far away for her to visit there and she could only do it through photographs. She said she'd take me to see the university one day and that she was sure I'd fall in love with it as much as she had. She said, who knew – maybe I'd end up going to college there myself. It was the first time she'd mentioned returning to America, and... well...'

'And you can't help wondering whether if you had, she'd still be here now.'

Cleo put her head in her hands. 'I know it's crazy, but, yes, that's exactly what I thought.'

'Were you at Yale tonight?'

She shook her head. 'I went to Violet's place.'

'But Dylan called her and she said she hadn't heard from you.'

Violet was Cleo's very good friend and it was at her party one year that Cleo had first met Dylan.

'I didn't go in, I walked by and then I carried on to a tree.' Even

Cleo began to laugh. 'You're going to call the men in white coats in a minute. First I talk about a sewing machine sending me messages, now it's a tree.'

'I'll hold off for a minute,' Darcy assured her, 'I want to see what else you've got. And you probably don't know this but as a kid my favourite stories were by Enid Blyton, so of course I know all about strange things happening in trees.'

'Ruby is reading the Faraway Tree books.'

'Yeah? She'll love them.'

'She already does. She's a terror for not turning her light out, or last week I caught her reading by torchlight under the bedclothes.'

'I think that's amazing.'

'So did I. She'd usually get told off for ignoring the lights-out call at around eight thirty, but when I saw her all engrossed in the book, my heart melted just a little and there's no way I could reprimand her.'

'You're a good mom, Cleo.'

It was as though she suddenly remembered what had gone on in the last twelve hours. 'The tree is a sycamore and it's a couple of streets away from Violet's place. It's beautiful with a wide, gnarled trunk and a canopy of branches above. And it's where Dylan and I shared our first kiss.'

Darcy waited a moment and then said, 'You've been sitting under a tree for over six hours?'

'Don't be daft, I'm not that crazy. I went there first. I'd been on a high after feeling the baby kick and then when I thought of Mum again, everything crashed down like it always does and I got scared. Scared something will happen to the baby, scared something will click in my brain and make me think in the way my own mum did. I can't explain it, Darcy, but it's like a veil pulled over my eyes and whereas someone normal might swish it away, it's like I can't do that

– I can only wrestle with it, unable to get free. So I went to the tree first and then I drove out to Litchfield.'

'Why Litchfield?'

'Having Tabitha was like a whirlwind in our lives and there were moments, like I'm having now, where I thought I couldn't deal with it all and that it would all go to shit. But one day, in the fall, Dylan, Ruby, Jacob, Tabitha, and I drove out to go leaf peeping. The colours were spectacular, the yellows to reds, the orange, the bronze. It was almost magical. We had hot chocolates, the kids laughed, and Tabitha was settled. In fact, everything was perfect. I had a family of my own, something I doubted I would ever achieve. And this morning when I thought about Mum and how she said everyone needs a happy place, I knew I needed mine. I needed to be on my own, think, get some space, down time, remember that even when I feel overwhelmed, I've got a hell of a lot in my life and I won't quit.'

'You sound angry.'

'You know, sometimes I am. I'm in a constant battle and I'm angry my mum didn't try harder. I know, I sound like a complete bitch, but out in Litchfield as I walked around reminding myself of how lucky I really am, I wanted to scream.'

'Do it now if you think it'll help. Although we might scare some of the guests,' Darcy teased.

'I screamed in the car. When I got back in. I screamed so loud, Darcy.'

'And did it feel better?'

'I think so. But then I went on autopilot. I should've called Dylan, texted him or something, but I didn't see that. I got in the car, drove to the station and got on the train. I didn't want to go to Violet's place. She's so annoyingly perfect – and I mean that in the nicest possible way – and she has her own family to take care of. I didn't want to see my grandpa Joe because I didn't want him to worry, and I wasn't ready to go home. I came to the city and went to my favourite Italian in the Meatpacking District. Dylan goes there to buy me the puttanesca pasta – it's the best, you really need to try it – anyway, I bought myself a family-size portion. You probably saw the evidence on my dress when I dumped it on your bathroom floor.'

'Ah, so the stain was pasta sauce.' Darcy smiled kindly. 'I'm a little relieved. And it came out easily enough in the wash. I'm curious though. How did you manage to eat Rupert's lasagne and peach cobbler after a pasta meal?'

'Someone ran into me on the sidewalk as I was heading to an outside table and the whole lot went down me.'

Darcy covered her mouth with her hand and only when Cleo laughed did she realise it was all right to see the funny side. 'You poor thing.'

'I think the man offered to buy me more but I didn't hear him. I just wanted out of there. I went over to the West Village, back to where it all began in America for me.'

'But the store isn't there any more.'

'No, it isn't.'

'That must've been hard.'

'Actually it was exactly what I needed. To see change, the world around me getting on with its business. I stood there looking at where the front of the store once was, I stood back out of the way of pedestrians darting everywhere, too busy to look up, and it was the first time I realised that yes, life had taken me by surprise, and the surprises would keep on coming. And I decided I had a choice to make. I could either be in, or I could be out. And I choose to be in it, Darcy. And I'll fight to make it right.'

Darcy gripped her hand tighter. 'You're exhausted and you're stressed, and although you say you'll fight – and I hope I'm not speaking out of turn when I say this – sometimes you may not have control over it.'

'Over the depression you mean.'

Darcy hadn't wanted to say it, to make Cleo feel worse when she was being so strong.

'Darcy, I am getting help. When I was waiting for the train I called my doctor. I have an appointment scheduled for tomorrow afternoon, and I'm seeing a counsellor too. I realise now that I wasn't taking it seriously enough before, because part of me was in denial. I wanted to pretend I had it under control myself. So I threw myself into work hoping I'd sail through and out the other side without too many scars. But I've got a beautiful family and I owe it to myself and all of them to do whatever I can.'

'I'm sure your mom did her best too.'

A tear snaked down Cleo's cheek. 'I know she did. Sometimes when I'm angry it's just easier to lay the blame on someone else. But I don't blame her really, I just don't want the same to happen to me, to us.'

'You know you have friends who support you one hundred per cent, don't you?'

'Why do you think I turned up at the Inn?'

Darcy scrunched up her face in thought. 'Because you decided I would be easier to face than Dylan?'

'You're not wrong there. Can you thank everyone for me?'

'Sure I can.'

'And Myles was here.' She smiled. 'He's a keeper, Darcy. Not every man would help out when his fiancée's friend was having a hard time.'

'I'd better hang on to him them.' What had happened tonight made Darcy think about all the worry over the wedding arrangements, the stress over whether she and Myles could ever make this work. Cleo and Dylan were facing much tougher times and Darcy

knew that if she could have an ounce of Cleo's determination then
they stood every chance of making their own relationship work.

'Darcy, can I ask one more favour?'

'Sure.'

'Can I phone Dylan and the kids, to say goodnight?'

'Of course you can. I'll be in the lounge when you're done.'

15

DARCY

The hottest month of the year didn't disappoint and the rain stayed away in July, the humidity rose, the streets were packed with tourists and summer had well and truly arrived. The fireplace in the Inglenook Inn was underused, the air conditioning cranked up a notch, and Darcy managed her days on autopilot to get from one end to the next.

'It's so... hot...' She stood in front of the air conditioner in the lounge, fanning beneath her armpits to get any kind of air circulation.

'You should try being in the kitchen,' said Rupert. He filled a glass with ice and poured in a cold can of Coke at the bar. He downed the drink so fast that Darcy saw the fizz go to his eyes when he nodded to Miss Garcia as she came into the communal lounge and he went back to his job in the hottest room at the Inn right now.

'Our air conditioning unit seems to be having issues,' said Miss Garcia. 'I've had it on all morning and the apartment is still so hot.'

'Let me come and take a look.' Darcy followed her guest up the stairs, turned right on the landing and went into the apartment.

The heat almost knocked her sideways after being downstairs where it was warm, but nothing compared to this. The thermostat looked to be set at the right temperature but Darcy took off the front panel and removed the filter. She took it into the kitchenette and cleaned it off. She'd already done the same a few weeks ago, but with the soaring temperatures taking Manhattan over the last week, it had probably been working overtime. It was also in a sunny window and she seemed to remember Sofia mentioning this unit had issues most summers.

'I think the sunny window means the unit struggles,' Darcy explained. Miss Suzy Garcia was staying with her sister, Barbara, here in the city and they were the quietest guests Darcy had ever had, like two tiny church mice scurrying around up here. That was until the temperature of the apartment had sent them out into the wider world of the Inn. 'I know it's not desirable, but if you shut the curtains it should help. Do that for a couple of hours and it should start cooling down some more. May I?' She stepped towards the thick curtains, which had a thermal backing that Darcy hoped would go some way to stopping any more of the heat from outside coming in.

'Thank you, dear. I should've thought of that.'

No, she should've insisted to Sofia that the air-conditioning unit be moved to another window that wasn't in full sunlight. It was times like this, when Darcy was in charge but not fully in control, that she wished it were her own place. She'd have changed the unit over last summer when it became obvious there was an issue. But she understood Sofia's business stance. Everything in this city cost money, and a lot of it.

'If you need instant cooling,' Darcy went on, 'then I highly recommend the café across the street that serves the most delicious gelato.'

'Did you hear that, Barb?'

A hand cupped around her ear suggested Barb hadn't a clue what her sister just said and Suzy had to scream the word another couple of times to be heard.

'Come on, let's go.' Suzy grabbed her purse.

'Ask for Frankie when you go in,' Darcy smiled, closing the other set of curtains. 'Tell him I sent you and I can guarantee he'll give you extra-large scoops. With any luck this room will be cooler when you return.'

Barb and Suzy went on their way, Darcy escaped the heat of their apartment and returned to her desk downstairs, but her cell phone chimed the second her butt hit the seat as though it sensed she was back. It was a text from Gabriella:

Eight hours to go, girl! I'm sorry I won't be there for your bachelorette party but have a few drinks for me and we'll make up for lost time very soon.

Darcy smiled. She couldn't believe the time had gone so quickly. One minute they'd been planning the wedding, the next, here was her big send off – a few weeks before the day itself to give them plenty of time to recover and sort themselves out at work. It meant Winston couldn't make it from England for Myles's night and Gabriella's sister Sarah couldn't make it from San Francisco for Darcy's, but with their work schedules they didn't have a lot of choice. She texted Myles:

How's the golf game?

Neither Myles's brother, Winston, nor Myles's dad, Ian, would be around until right before the wedding and so Myles had collaborated with Dylan to make his bachelor party a pretty sedate affair, starting with a game of golf out in Greenwich. Darcy grinned when she saw his reply.

Terrible. I'm officially the worst and I doubt any of them will ever ask me to play again. I've lost my touch. Back to the city soon, and the winery... much more my style these days...

She replied to the text with a heart emoji and set her cell phone on the desk before closing her eyes against the air-conditioning unit, replenishing her energy as she wondered what the girls had in store for her later on.

* * *

'I thought tonight would never come,' Holly squealed when she turned up at Myles and Darcy's apartment on the Upper West Side and bustled through the door with a bottle of champagne. 'Is Isabella here yet?'

'You're the first,' said Darcy, winding her hair back up into its familiar chignon. It was far too hot for anything else. 'I can't believe we're going to be in a kitchen tonight.'

Holly stowed the champagne in Darcy's fridge, squeezed between a packet of butter and a sturdy wedge of watermelon. 'Relax, it'll be fun. And it's your fault. You said to Cleo a while back that you wished you knew how to make a decent pizza.'

'And so the seed was sown,' Darcy laughed.

'Talking of Cleo.' Holly successfully shut the fridge. 'How is she?'

'She's good. And not only that, she'll be here tonight.'

'That's amazing. I'm so happy. It wouldn't have been the same without her.'

Cleo had originally turned down the suggestion she join them for Darcy's bachelorette party but Dylan clearly had better persuasion techniques than any of them, because she'd called this morning to say she'd be there. And she was staying over so she didn't have to travel by train late at night.

'Dylan sorted extra childcare for her during the week too,' said Darcy.

Holly pulled a face. 'How did she take that?'

'Pretty well I think. And Kaisha is more than happy to put more hours in at the store. Cleo is finally admitting she can't do everything herself.'

'Sounds like someone you should be taking tips from.'

'Now, now. It's my party, you have to be nice.'

'How are *you*?'

'Good.'

'You know what I mean. How are you with all the arrangements, with work, with Myles?'

'I'm happy.' She wondered how much of her ups and downs were to do with the situation itself and how many were just because she'd always been wired to do things on her own and in her own way, and letting go of that wasn't as easy as it had first seemed. 'I can't wait to be married.'

Holly gave her a hug as the intercom buzzed again and Darcy pushed the button to release the security door downstairs. 'Then let's get this party started!'

'Nothing tacky!' Darcy yelled after her. 'I mean it, Holly, you promised!'

* * *

At the pizzeria a few blocks away from the apartment, Isabella, Holly, Cleo, and Darcy gathered in the small kitchen at the back of the restaurant watching the workings of the pizza kitchen as they waited to be taken through to the function room. The boss, Giovanni, was talking animatedly to his staff, giving orders in Italian, and the waft of garlic and bubbling cheese made the girls hungry to get started.

Before they'd left the apartment, Cleo had handed out cerise-pink tops with 'Bridal Support Team' written across the front and caricatures of a bride with her bridesmaids huddled together. Darcy had been ordered to put hers on with denim shorts rather than her floaty dress and off they'd set.

'It could've been worse,' said Isabella. 'She could've arranged for naked men to be cooking. Slice of pepperoni sausage anyone?'

Cleo almost snorted out the swig of water she'd just taken. She'd already ducked outside twice to escape the heat and had drunk a couple of bottles of the stuff claiming the baby was making her twice as hot as the rest of them.

'It's quite cute,' said Darcy, knotting her T-shirt at one side just like Holly had done with hers.

'Pierre certainly thought so,' Cleo grinned and looked over at Holly. 'He couldn't take his eyes off his woman.'

'I'm not surprised, with that far-too-toned midriff showing,' put in Isabella.

'Be quiet, the lot of you.' Holly had a golden tan from spending most of last weekend in Central Park with her new boyfriend.

'It's true, he can't stay away either.' Darcy was pleased her friend's relationship seemed to be blossoming.

'He came in on his way home from work. We hardly saw each other last week with me doing the intensive photography course.'

Isabella made kissing noises until Holly threatened to splatter pizza sauce all over her if she didn't keep quiet.

'In all seriousness,' Isabella began as she accepted another champagne from the owner of the restaurant, 'how's it going with him, Holly?'

Darcy took another glass too.

'Very well, thank you.' Holly had a hard time keeping her smile under control.

'How well?' asked Cleo. 'Are we talking first base, second base, third base or home-run spectacular?'

'Cleo!' Isabella scolded but then leaned closer to the group. 'Come on, tell us.'

'I will not.'

Darcy whispered to Isabella, 'Few more champagnes and she will.'

'I heard that,' said Holly, as the event organiser came to get them and take them through to the function room.

Inside there were work stations set up for each of them and they were welcomed to the pizza-making class. And for the first time in a long while Darcy realised how relaxed she was. Amongst friends she had hardly thought about the inn that she'd left in Rupert's capable hands, she'd barely thought about Myles's ambition and her own and whether it would be detrimental in the long run, and for once, she felt in a good place about the wedding. Since they talked that night and then pulled together over the worry about Cleo, they'd been closer than ever. And now it was countdown time, and in just under three weeks she would become the new Mrs Cunningham.

* * *

'You're a natural,' said the organiser, whose name was Kimberly. She'd put on a huge name badge and made all four of them do the same, although Cleo had already managed to splatter hers with tomato sauce. Marco, Giovanni's assistant, had taken them through the basics and now it was up to them to put theory into practice. It was pizza making time.

'Should I stretch it some more?' Darcy had thrown the dough up in the air for the first time and managed to catch it just fine.

'No, keep tossing it, and the shape will gradually increase as the dough stretches all by itself,' Marco advised.

Darcy almost lost it in a fit of laughter as she heard Holly say the F word rather too loudly then apologise profusely and blame the champagne. Her tossing hadn't gone so well and the dough had just plummeted to the floor.

Kimberly addressed the room. 'Ladies, make sure that when you toss you do it over the counter!'

Darcy concentrated hard and on the fifth toss the pizza diameter looked to be about right. She set the dough down and moved on to the next stage.

'Darcy wins the prize for the best toss!' Isabella chimed through uncontrollable laughter at her choice of words.

'They've had way too much champagne,' Darcy heard Cleo say from where she was working on her own pizza topping in between gulping back more water.

Marco grinned knowingly when Kimberly replied with, 'I've seen a lot worse, believe me.'

With the pizza dough ready and the toppings on, the pizzas themselves cooked in no time at all and the girls elected to take their creations back to the apartment to enjoy.

'I think we're much safer back here,' said Darcy as they filed through the front door armed with huge square pizza boxes. 'I'm starving after all that champagne.'

'Pace yourself,' Holly called from the bathroom. 'There's more champagne in the fridge.'

Darcy flicked on the air conditioning and then opened the cupboard in the kitchen but shut it when Cleo yelled, 'No plates, we'll eat from boxes.'

'Tastes better that way,' Isabella insisted, already pulling up a slice of pizza and weaving the stringy cheese into her mouth.

Conversation fell into a lull as they devoured their pizzas, and when Darcy couldn't eat another bite she handed round glasses of water and slumped onto the sofa.

'Thanks for tonight, girls. I loved it. I'm going to give pizza making a go here at the apartment, but it won't be the same not having it cook so fast in one of those pizza ovens.'

'You should install one on the terrace,' Holly suggested. 'I could see you out there, in your apron, making pizza when Myles comes home.'

'Or he could make it for her,' smiled Isabella. 'I bet there's nothing he wouldn't do for you.'

Darcy grinned. The feeling was mutual. 'What are you up to?' she asked Cleo, who was into something on her cell phone.

'Googling pizza ovens.'

'What, as a wedding present?'

'No, for Dylan and the kids.'

Darcy exchanged a look with Holly and again with Isabella. Cleo's disappearing act had scared them all, made them realise how fragile life was, and it was good to see her so present in the moment and back to her old self. The counselling session had gone well and she'd signed up for more without any persuasion from Dylan, which was a good sign.

'I wonder how the men are doing,' Holly mused.

'Has Dylan lined up any strip clubs?' asked Isabella.

'No he hasn't,' said Darcy. 'Right now they'll be at a winery and hopefully eating something to soak up the alcohol.' She looked at each of her very good friends. 'And I want to thank you all for not making this party too tacky. It's not me, and this... what's happening here... this is perfect.'

'I have a confession to make.' Cleo had stopped tapping away at her cell phone and was parked beneath the air conditioner, wafting her T-shirt to take in all the air she could.

'We all do,' Holly admitted. 'We all conspired in this.'

'Oh, don't tell me a stripper is going to turn up at any second. You risk sending Mrs Tillman into cardiac arrest if she found out.'

'No, nothing like that.' Isabella went off to the hallway and came back with a rucksack. 'I hid this under your bed when Holly distracted you.'

'What's in it?'

'The biggest load of tacky accessories you ever saw in your life!' Cleo beamed. 'But let's face it, at least it's in the privacy of your own apartment.'

Isabella giggled away and took out something very large, very pink and very bright.

Darcy tilted her head this way and that, taking in the colour, the shape. 'Oh! Is that what I think it is?'

'If you're thinking it's a penis, then you'd be right.' Cleo sounded so serious that all four of them fell about laughing.

'A giant penis piñata filled with tasty treats,' added Holly, silencing Isabella before she made a crass comment. 'Now, where can we hang it? The place where I bought it suggested using a tree.'

Darcy switched off the air conditioning and opened the doors to the terrace. 'I don't have many of those in here, but how about hanging it in the doorway?'

'What and have our candy disappear over the edge?' Holly frowned.

'It'll be like sweet missiles landing on the people on the street below,' said Cleo unhelpfully.

'I didn't think of that.' Darcy turned, looking at the inside of the apartment rather than the outside. 'We could move the dining table to one side, then the candy will only scatter into the room, and there's nothing breakable in the firing line.'

'Great idea.' Isabella took one end of the table, Holly the other, and Darcy pulled over a chair so she could tie the piñata on the hook that must've been left there by the previous owners for whatever reason.

Holly gazed upwards. 'It looks great.'

'It looks like a penis,' Darcy corrected.

'As long as Myles's doesn't look like that,' Isabella sniggered, 'I'd say you're good to go ahead and marry him.'

Darcy giggled. 'Right, what are we going to bash it with?'

Holly flexed her arms as Isabella disappeared out of the room and came back brandishing a very pink baseball bat with an even pinker bow tied around the handle.

Darcy shook her head until Holly yelled, 'Darcy, get going, girl! Happy bachelorette party!'

The others all cheered her on as she took her first swing, but it wasn't enough and she handed the bat over to Cleo.

'Is there anything more disturbing than seeing a pregnant woman whacking the crap out of something with a baseball bat?' Holly asked Darcy as they looked on.

Next it was Isabella, then Holly, and by her next turn Darcy was laughing so hard she barely had any strength in her arms. Suddenly the thought of clobbering a giant penis with a bat seemed quite funny.

They each had another go and then it was round to Darcy again. 'I almost broke it that time.'

'Heaven help Myles if he ever strays,' Holly laughed as she brought back the bat and gave it her all.

A collective roar echoed out onto the terrace as the contents of the piñata sprayed into the room and the girls ran to pick up the treats.

'I haven't had these in years.' Darcy picked up a packet of Cinnamon Disks, surprised the red, hard candy had survived its missile-like launch. 'Or these.' She crawled on her knees and retrieved a pack of Sour Patch Bunnies.

'My favourite! And the baby's,' Cleo grinned when she picked up the watermelon Pop Rocks.

Isabella was already shovelling a packet of Nerds into her mouth, one by one. 'Candy and pizza and champagne. Naughty but oh so nice.'

Darcy didn't have much candy before she declared she had to stop before she had no teeth left. She found a big plastic bowl from the kitchen and with Holly's help they picked up everything they could find, then divvied it up between them.

'I'll still be going with this lot come fall and Halloween,' said Holly, clutching her tummy. 'The champagne, pizza and candy are having a party right now in my stomach and I think it's telling me to stop.'

'Yes, stop before you puke. I'm sharing a taxi with you, remember,' said Isabella. 'Talking of which, I think it's time we were off. Cleo is almost asleep.' She moved closer to where Cleo had put her feet up on the sofa and was curled onto one side, baby bump protruding from the bottom of her bachelorette T-shirt.

'I'm not asleep yet,' came Cleo's voice as she opened her eyes. 'Sorry, don't mind me.'

'You get yourself to bed,' said Darcy. 'No arguments. These two are off, I'll clear up, you get some sleep, you need it.'

Cleo obliged, said goodbye to the others and headed to the bathroom to do her teeth.

'She looks so much better,' Isabella said the second Cleo was out of earshot. 'Her cheeks have colour, there's mischief back in her eyes, and the way she talked tonight, well, something is working, that's for sure.'

'I think it's a combination of her own determination, Dylan

being such a damn good husband, and those kids who she couldn't imagine ever being without.'

'I wonder what it's like.' Holly came over serious for a moment. 'Not being pregnant, I don't mean that, but having that life where you're with all these other people day in, day out, and they become a part of you.'

'Talking of parts of you,' said Isabella, 'you never answered our question earlier.'

'What question is that?'

'How far you've gone with Pierre.'

'That's for me to know, not you two. But let's just say we're off to Vermont next weekend and yes, we will be sharing a room.'

Isabella had so many more questions and as they put on their shoes, picked up their bags and said goodnight to her, Darcy knew Holly would get the rest of the grilling in the taxi tonight. And she didn't envy her. When Isabella wanted to know something, she didn't give up very easily.

Darcy picked up another couple of pieces of candy that had escaped her radar earlier and dropped them into the bowl. The summer breeze filtering through the terrace doors was bliss and she left them wide open. She checked on Cleo, who was out for the count in the spare room, and after a shower to freshen up she went back to the lounge, far too wired for sleep yet.

She'd just settled down outside on the day bed with a glass of water, hoping their antics hadn't disturbed any of the neighbours, when Myles came home.

'Where's Cleo?' He stepped onto the terrace and came over to kiss his wife-to-be.

'Sleeping.'

'Already? How did she cope with tonight?'

'Really well, she's in a good place. Is Dylan worrying?'

'Dylan wouldn't be Dylan if he wasn't. But he managed to have a good time.'

Darcy reached for her cell and tapped out a message, pressing send. 'Just messaged him. He'll appreciate it. She was back to herself tonight and there was no pretence. He'll sleep better knowing that.'

'You're a good woman, Darcy Spencer.'

'And you're a good man. Anyway, tell me about your day. You don't seem too worse for wear.'

'Neither do you.'

'Does this mean we're old before our time?'

'Who cares?'

She leaned forwards and kissed him. 'You taste of wine. What was the winery like?'

'A good end to a crappy golf game,' he laughed.

'I never knew you played.'

'I haven't for a while, and I'm rusty. I might play again or I might just accept that running is more my thing.'

'Did you eat already?'

He patted a taut stomach. 'Steak.'

'No strippers or surprise lap dancers?'

He pulled a face. 'Well…' When she thumped him on the arm he added, 'Just kidding. None of that, no. It's not really my thing. Although…'

'Oh no, don't get any ideas. And besides, Cleo is in the spare room.'

'Shame.' He raised his eyebrows. 'Seriously though, we had a very good time, just Dylan and me, your brother, and a couple of my work colleagues. It was a good balance. Without Dylan or Tate the others would've talked shop but this kept it away from anything about the stock exchange. How was your night? What did you get up to?'

'Pizza-making classes.'

'Huh. Now that I approve of.'

She told him all about the dough, the tossing, the super-duper ovens that cooked the pizza so quickly. 'We could put one on the terrace.'

'Really?'

'Maybe not.' She breathed in the New York air. There weren't many places to avoid the smog but up here, so high above the streets on the Upper West Side, Darcy liked to think it was the best level of fresh air they could get. 'But we could get a pizza stone for our oven, it'll help the pizza cook better.'

'Worth a try.'

'Shame your brother wasn't with you for the bachelor party. But thanks for including Tate, I know he appreciated it. Although, he's a pretty good golfer.'

'I know. Thanks for the heads up.' He squeezed the top of her knee. 'You weren't too upset your sister couldn't make it were you?'

'No, and we'll see plenty of our families when they're over for the wedding.'

'True. We'll probably get fed up with them by the end of it. Does Sarah have many plans for her visit?'

'Sarah and her family are coming to Manhattan a couple of days before, then they'll be off to Connecticut to stay with my parents before heading to Cape Cod, the lucky things. I'm beginning to feel jealous – it's as though they're all having the honeymoon we have to delay because of work. I'm not complaining,' she added before he thought otherwise. 'Are your parents going to travel anywhere else when they come, or how about Winston? He and Victoria could take the kids on some real adventures.'

His smile disappeared. 'Damn.'

'What's up?'

'I haven't booked their accommodation.'

'Whose?'

'Winston and Victoria's. I said I would and it went clean out of my mind.' He put a hand to his head. 'How could I be so stupid?'

'Well there's no room at the Inn, it's fully booked with other guests, but we'll find somewhere. Between us, Myles, we can do it.'

He smiled, relieved. 'That's why I love you, Darcy.'

'For saving your ass?' She picked up her cell and fired off an email to three hoteliers she knew who had boutique premises in the city, and to whom she'd sent guests before and vice versa. They were all on a first-name, very familiar basis and it felt good having built up some loyalty along the way. 'By morning, I bet we'll have a family apartment sorted.'

'Why thank you, Mrs Cunningham.'

'I'll take payment in kind,' she told him.

'Is that so?' He scooped her up from the day bed and walked across the terrace with her in his arms. 'I'm taking you to bed to say thank you.'

'Suits me. As long as we're quiet; we don't want to give Cleo nightmares.'

But just before he stepped into the lounge he looked up to see the remains of the piñata. 'Darcy, is that a penis hanging from my ceiling?'

* * *

Darcy was up early the next morning to make Cleo breakfast, insisting she had to take better care of herself and the baby she was carrying. And after she'd seen Cleo on her way to the station to head back to Inglenook Falls, full up from the mushroom omelette and freshly squeezed orange juice, Darcy climbed back into the rumpled sheets of her bed. Myles would be back any second – he'd forgotten his cell phone, which lay on the nightstand, and she wondered how many blocks he would go before he retraced his steps to pick it up.

Beneath the sheets and with the sheer curtain billowing at the window, allowing the summer breeze to freshen up the apartment, Darcy looked over at the caricature picture and smiled at the thought of Myles getting down on one knee that day in Central Park. Her gaze turned to her ring now ensconced on the fourth finger of her left hand, the diamond sparkling as the morning sunshine met the jewel. She wished she could laze here all day, maybe entice Myles back to bed, but looking at the clock she knew she had to start getting ready before too long because today she had a meeting with a pharmaceutical firm from out of town. She'd only got the email late last night and had confirmed a time for today, wanting to strike while the iron was very much red hot. This corporate client was interested in holding Thanksgiving for his employees at the Inn with accommodation as well as a celebratory dinner all thrown in. Darcy had explained that the Inn had a few bookings this year already; she'd asked if he'd be interested in next year and surprisingly he'd agreed to view the Inn and, if he liked it, secure a booking for next year with a deposit. This was a major coup for the business, Sofia would be thrilled to bits, and Darcy hoped that by the end of the day she'd seal the deal.

She picked up her paperback – a romantic comedy set in a remote English Cotswold village – and lost herself in the pages for the next thirty minutes, a rare treat she'd not been able to enjoy for a while. She swore the paperback had gathered dust it had been sitting waiting for her for so long. She looked forward to more of this, more relaxing and taking time for herself and Myles, when they finally went on honeymoon.

When the time ticked around to almost nine thirty she reluctantly swung her legs out of bed. The apartment had cooled down from the heat of yesterday but she shut the window now to keep it that way.

Myles's cell phone pinged to indicate a text coming through and she was about to head to the bathroom when she wondered if he'd made it to the office, used someone else's cell and messaged her on his device. There was no way he'd be able to get the message to her own cell – the numbers were imprinted in the phone's memory rather than his. They'd joked the other day that maybe they should exercise their brains by learning phone numbers like they did once upon a time, starting with each other's.

Darcy picked up his cell phone to see a message not from Myles but from someone stored in his contacts as Monica – Manager.

Darcy slumped on the edge of the bed, device in hand. It wasn't the female name that had her discombobulated, but the words that accompanied it.

She attempted to take it all in, understand what she was reading:

We look forward to welcoming you to Boston in the middle of August. If you need any local recommendations prior to then, please contact me at any time. I look forward to meeting you soon.

When the door to the apartment went, she heard Myles rummaging through the debris on the hall table, probably looking beneath the pile of mail, the jumble of bits and bobs that had been dumped there. Usually they both kept the place spotless but the shenanigans of yesterday had left them lazy.

'Have you seen my cell?' Myles came into the bedroom next. His chocolate-brown eyes roamed the room, little flecks of grey danced in the shaft of sun that highlighted dust motes.

Darcy still had the cell phone in her hand and as much as she

vanted to throw it in his face, she was restrained enough to sling it
across the bed closer to where he stood.

'Hangover that bad?' His teasing smile did little to quell her
temper.

'When were you going to tell me?' Her anger bubbled right up
to the surface. This gorgeous man, her gorgeous man. This man
who'd hidden the truth.

'Tell you what?'

'About Boston.'

'What about Boston?' He sighed as though he simply didn't
have time for any of her fuss and nonsense.

'Stop playing the innocent!' She stood up and hoped he could
take her seriously even though she was only wearing one of his
shirts she'd grabbed from the back of the chair this morning along
with her undies. He'd always said he couldn't resist her when she
dressed that way, showing teasing glimpses of the tops of her legs,
enough skin below her neck that he wanted to kiss her. Darcy
wished she had a suit on instead, a work outfit that said she meant
business, she was in control, she wasn't about to be taken for a ride.

'Darcy, my head is still delicate from yesterday. I'm late for work.
Whatever this is, either spit it out now or put a pin in it until later.
Quit playing games.'

It was the last comment that got to her the most. 'You think I'm
playing games? I tell you what' – she gestured to his cell phone
lying helplessly in his hand – 'why don't you check your text
messages and then we'll see who's playing games.' And with that
she pushed past him and headed for the bathroom to do her teeth.

So much for a relaxing morning. She couldn't be bothered with
any of it right now. She didn't want to dwell on how her fiancé had
kept something so monumental like a job relocation under wraps
from her. What, was he going to spring it on her as a wedding
present? Did he think she'd go along with whatever he wanted

when they were married? Where was the trust? All she could see were lies. And what had happened to the claims he's made on the terrace the other night, saying he was turning Boston down?

Liar!

She'd been right to stay independent all these years. When other people came into the mix, that was where things went wrong. Maybe his involvement in ending her job in London and then the email he'd sent in anger when he was a guest at her inn had been warning signs she'd been blinkered to because of her attraction. Perhaps she should've been more careful.

She spat out the excess toothpaste. Her poor gums had taken a battering from sheer frustration. And when the bathroom door opened she didn't even turn her head.

'You've got it all wrong,' was all he said.

Maybe, maybe not. But perhaps this had given them both an out.

She unbuttoned the shirt and let it drop to the floor. 'Whatever, Myles.'

'Now you're being childish.'

She stepped into the shower and turned the water on. 'I need to get to the Inn. I'm putting work first, just like you appear to do. Of all the selfish, unfair—'

'Darcy!' He yelled now but then winced. Clearly it had hurt his head. Good. 'Why don't you ever listen to me? Why won't you give me the benefit of the doubt?'

She shut her eyes against the jets and let the water cascade over her face, and when she turned around he was still standing there.

'We'll talk tonight,' he said.

She wiped the steam from the shower screen so she could see him properly. 'Is there much point?'

'What's that supposed to mean?' The realisation dawned. 'Are you serious? So as far as you're concerned, this is it?'

'Starting married life on a lie doesn't seem like the best thing to do.'

'So you're giving up? You know what, Darcy, I think you've been looking for an excuse to pull out of this relationship and now you have one. Or rather, you *think* you have one.' He went out of the bathroom but came back less than a minute later. He threw something down, which floated to the floor and landed near the shower recess. 'I don't suppose we'll be needing this any more either.'

'What is it?'

But he didn't answer. Face like thunder, he left.

She opened the shower door and peered at a piece of paper, and as water dripped onto the ink, she saw what it was. Staring back at her was confirmation of flights and a luxury hotel in Marrakesh, Morocco. In October. Their honeymoon.

What had she done? He'd planned the surprise of a lifetime and she'd more or less thrown it in his face.

But wait... he'd wronged *her*, not the other way around. And a honeymoon booking wasn't going to make up for the lies either. It wasn't the fact he was going to Boston, it was that he hadn't told her. It was that he'd done it without factoring her into the equation. If this relationship had a hope of working then decisions needed to be made as a couple, not with one of them changing the game and the other simply falling into line.

She leaned against the cool tiles of the shower and for the first time in a long time, Darcy lost control, and let the tears fall until there were none left.

16

MYLES

Myles was miserable. At home. At work. When he ate, when he slept. Full-on miserable. He'd called his parents in England after hearing nothing from Darcy since their row, and told them the wedding was off. He couldn't face being the one to tell the other guests so he'd asked them to contact everyone on the list and do it for him. His mum had said she'd take care of it all and to call her any time, day or night. She probably knew he wouldn't. They'd never been that close and were only just on their way to repairing a fragile relationship as it was.

'Knock knock.' It was Rufus at the office door. 'Do you have a minute to go through the Wilkinson presentation?'

Myles frowned. 'I thought you were ready.'

'I am,' he answered confidently. 'You gave me a few revisions yesterday, remember.'

It had gone clean out of his mind.

'I want to double-check them if you have the time, don't worry if not.'

Myles eased up on the frown that was threatening to leave a permanent crease in between his eyebrows. 'Yes, of course. Come in.' He'd gone off at the newest analyst on his team for jumping in too soon, for taking on too much responsibility, so he could hardly reprimand him for being cautious. If Myles knew him, he wouldn't check his work with his boss many more times, but for now it was a good thing.

Myles ended up appreciating the distraction. He lost himself in talk of expense projections and it was almost like therapy, but when Rufus left, Myles was back to where he'd started, thinking about the wedding that was never going to happen, how maybe he was no different now from the man who'd come to New York in the first place, formidable and driven solely by work. He'd thought he'd known where his life was headed.

Until he'd met Darcy.

He buzzed Rhonda. 'Cancel my afternoon meeting, I'll be gone the rest of the day.' He didn't wait for an answer, just picked up his cell and his bag and left the office. He had to get out of here.

He battled his way through the crowds of the Financial District to the subway along with the hordes of other people in Manhattan. He'd done it so many times now that he knew where he was going as well as any native New Yorker.

He waited below ground level on the bleak, black-walled platform until the train reliably trundled alongside, its steady rhythm the same as yesterday, the same as it had been the day before. He was on autopilot. If he'd stayed at work any longer, his distraction would've got the better of him and he'd have made more mistakes than Rufus had made in a long time, something his boss wouldn't have appreciated he felt sure.

Back on the Upper West Side he trudged back to his apartment, the heat of the day sapping him of his energy. He went through the door hoping at least a little bit that Darcy had come back and that he'd be sitting in the lounge or the bedroom ready to talk about this rationally. There were little signs of her all around: the pillow next to his that still smelt of her perfume, a pair of heels she'd left in the bottom of the wardrobe, the lipstick on the table in the hall.

But the apartment was empty. Since their row she hadn't come here, hadn't texted, hadn't been in contact at all. And so much for surprising her with an all-inclusive, luxury honeymoon in Marrakesh. He wondered, was she busy cancelling the arrangements right now, or had she wiped her hands of it? All because of a crazy misunderstanding. As soon as she'd said the word Boston he knew the conclusion she'd jumped to but she was wrong.

Myles showered and made a strong coffee to take out onto the terrace. He needed something to knock sense into him, let him think, work out where he went to from here. Yesterday he'd been tempted to take the Boston offer – to hell with it, Darcy thought the worst of him anyway – and this morning he'd even dialled the number of the boss over there, but had hung up before it clicked through.

He settled his coffee on the table next to the day bed when the rude buzz of the intercom interrupted the peace and quiet. He knew it wasn't Darcy. She'd have used her key. He wasn't in the mood for visitors and so he sat on the day bed, put his bare feet up on the table and ignored it when it buzzed a second time and then a third.

The only thing that got Myles's attention was when there was a thumping at the actual door to his apartment. He got to his feet prepared to reprimand whoever it was, but when he flung open the door his jaw dropped. 'Mum, what are you doing here?'

Hot and uncomfortable, with a suitcase at her heels, she said 'Well, are you going to invite me in?'

'Of course, of course.' He grabbed the case, brought it inside and shut the door behind them. 'How did you get inside the building?'

'After you ignored the buzzer, you mean?' He felt like a young boy caught doing something wrong. 'Mrs Tillman, lovely lady. And I've only got a couple of hours because I'll be taking a walk in Central Park with her later. Said she'd show me around. Do you know she's never lived anywhere else?'

'You work fast. You'll have more friends in this city than me soon.'

'Life's too short not to. I should know that more than anyone, Myles. Now do I get a hug?'

He obligingly stepped forwards and when he wrapped her in his arms – she was too slight for it to be the other way around – he felt a strange sense of calm.

'Right, now that's done,' she said, 'it's time for this.' And she lifted up a hand and swiped him across the top of the head with it.

'Ouch, whatever was that for?' It was the first time he'd laughed since his bachelor party.

'For throwing away the best thing that's ever happened to you. Now, do you mind if I take a quick shower before we talk? The New York summer makes England's look weak and feeble and I've battled the crush of something called the AirTrain from JFK, then the Long Island Rail Road, plus a sea of people who all seemed to know where they're going. I also faced a very questionable young man at Penn Station who kept insisting he could take my suitcase and show me where the elevator was.'

'Did you let him?'

'I wasn't born yesterday, Myles.' She adopted what he could only describe as the parent-tone-of-voice. 'Although I think he was just trying to make a bit of cash from tips, you never know people's circumstances, do you? But I stayed on my guard. It's the first time I've travelled so far without your father.' A wide smile spread across her face. 'I'm quite proud of myself.'

'You're looking well.'

She touched a hand to his face. 'And you look like crap.'

He laughed. 'Thanks, Mum.'

She shrugged, enjoying the shared joke with her son. 'Do me a favour, would you?'

'Of course.' He pulled some towels from the closet in the hallway and handed them to her.

'While I take a shower, could you fix me a cold drink?'

'Of course, what would you like?'

'I'd love one of those virgin mojitos you made for me last time was here.'

'I'm afraid that'll be pushing it. I think the only ingredient I have is ice.'

She opened her handbag, which was perched against the wall in the hallway, and took out a bottle of sparkling water, a lime, a bag containing what looked like mint leaves and handed everything to him. 'I stopped at a convenience store on my way,' she said, using the American terminology he was sure was all part of her doing this on her own, an accomplishment for someone who had shied away from the world once upon a time. 'I'm assuming you have water and sugar for the syrup.'

'Now those I do have. But I have no idea how to make it.'

She smiled. 'Let me do that part and it can cool while I shower. It won't take long – pop it in the fridge to speed it up. Your father tells me off when I do that at home, but everyone needs to be a little rebellious in their lives, don't they?'

He followed her into the kitchen where she took out a pan, he found the sugar, and she made a simple syrup in next to no time at all. When it was in the fridge and cooling she disappeared off for her shower while he tried to tidy up a bit. She'd been nice enough not to mention the mess but his head was in such a state that cleaning up after himself hadn't been a priority. Last night's takeout containers were still lined up on one side of the kitchen, his plate still sitting in the sink and dregs of this morning's cereal were stuck fast to his breakfast bowl. He tackled the crockery first, embarrassed she'd seen it this way but not sorry that she hadn't taken him to task or even mentioned Darcy so far. It had been enough to see her at the door and get his head around the fact she was here.

Once the kitchen was sorted and the ingredients for the mojito ready to go, he took her suitcase into the spare room. He stripped the bed, which hadn't been changed since Cleo stayed the night, and put on fresh sheets, opening the window to let the summer fall inside the apartment. His mind on Cleo and their other friends, he wondered, had Darcy told anyone what had happened? He'd only been able to face telling his mum, the person he never would've confided in up until recently. Who had Darcy told to help her cope? Or was she so focused on work that she was blocking out everything else?

Back in the kitchen the syrup had cooled quickly and Myles went through the motions of making enough virgin mojito for two. It was a stinking-hot day and an ice-cold drink out on the terrace suddenly seemed a much better idea than the black coffee that was still sitting out there waiting for him.

He'd just added the ice to the glasses and was pouring in the sparkling water when his mum appeared in the kitchen. He handed her a glass.

'Shall we go out on the terrace?'

His heart beat harder, he knew the discussion was coming and he had to face it but it didn't make it any easier.

'Why are you here, Mum?' he asked after he'd taken the coffee cup away and put it in the sink before returning to the day bed to sit at the opposite end.

'Because my son needs me.' She looked right at him.

And for the first time in his whole life it was time to admit that he really did.

* * *

Settled outside with their drinks, Myles told her everything. About the stresses of the last few months, how Darcy wanted total control with the wedding, about how they'd looked after Tabitha that day in the park – although he hadn't admitted the responsibility had made him and Darcy realise how much they'd have to juggle if they wanted a family of their own. He told her about the offer from Boston, the step up the career ladder that at one time he would've taken without much hesitation.

And then he told her about the text message and the giant misunderstanding.

'So why didn't you tell her the message wasn't what she thought it was? Why not set her straight?' Martha put her glass down, the drink gone, just the mint leaves and lime gathered at the bottom waiting to be emptied.

'She never gave me a chance. And why should I? She should trust me, believe what I said about not taking the job. She chose to think the worst without letting me explain.'

'Oh, Myles, trust isn't something that magically comes in a relationship.'

'I know, but I thought we had it by now.'

'It takes time to build and you two haven't been together long.'

'You think we rushed into it.' It wasn't a question.

'You probably did.' She put up a hand to indicate she wasn't finished. 'But, sometimes, when you know, you just know. Then it becomes a whole different thing.'

'That's just it, I don't know why she doesn't want to work on this. On us.'

'Because in the beginning relationships aren't supposed to be hard work. They're supposed to be all about the fun, the sex—'

'Mum!'

'Sorry. But you get where I'm going with this. You and Darcy fell in love in quite the whirlwind romance but you cheated yourselves out of the days where responsibility should've been the last thing on your mind. But you know what? I don't think either of you could have ever done it differently. It's the way you, and Darcy, operate. And both of you went into the relationship when you had your own lives mapped out just fine. Neither of you was looking for anyone, neither of you felt you needed anything else other than career in your life.'

'Darcy always resisted relationships.'

'Do you know why?'

'Because she never wanted to give up her independence.' He briefly recapped what Darcy had told him about other women she knew who'd depended on a man only to have the relationship and their lives completely fall apart. 'She never wanted to leave herself open to that.'

'Until she found you,' Martha smiled. 'Until she fell in love. I expect it will take some adjusting for her.'

'Yeah, well I feel like she's been fighting this all the way. I couldn't see it until now, but every obstacle we've come up against… well, I feel as though she's been looking for an out. And I'm not sure I want to battle my way into someone's life if they don't want me here.'

'Why do you think she doesn't want you?'

'Because she let me walk away and she's made no attempt to contact me since. And it's her who's in the wrong here, Darcy who jumped to a conclusion without waiting to hear my side of it.'

'That's another thing about relationships, Myles. There's a lot of work to do to keep one on track – I should know because I nearly lost one with your father. And part of that work is about building trust but other parts are about learning not to lay blame without trying to see the other side of the story or being able to forgive and

move forwards. People make mistakes, they say things they don't
mean. It's happening to you both early on in your relationship but
it won't be the last time. Ask anyone who's been married for a while.
Ask Winston.'

'He and Victoria don't argue.'

Martha's head tipped back against the sun as she let a laugh
escape. 'Only last week he was moaning about her, something to do
with her not being able to decide on an outfit for your wedding so
she'd bought three different dresses. You know how careful he is
with money. Anyway, I don't know the nitty-gritty of it, I don't need
to, and it'll sort itself out. Last week I went to my friend Maureen's
place for afternoon tea and she'd had a row with her husband
about his muddy wellies after a visit to the allotment. He hadn't
spoke to her for a week!'

'That's a bit harsh.' Even Myles saw the funny side of that one.

'You see my point,' said Martha. 'It's not all hearts and flowers in
the world of relationships or marriage. They take work. But what
you do need are two people who are fully committed to each other.
Who aren't going to throw in the towel when the going gets tough.'

'That's the thing,' he said, 'I get the impression Darcy will run
whenever the slightest thing goes wrong. I don't want that for me, I
don't want it for the family we want one day.'

A smile spread across her face. 'You two want kids?'

'Well, yeah. Why are you surprised?'

'I'm not. Okay,' she admitted, 'I am a little. Darcy hinted at it
once, but I know you're both career-focused. And I've never heard
you talk this way.'

Myles frowned. 'I think meeting Darcy has changed me.'

'It's a good thing, Myles.' She moved right next to him now and
took his hands. 'You can have jobs and a personal life, plenty of
people do. And if your relationship is strong, you'll find out how to
make it work. Just don't muddle along on different tracks like I did.

with your father. We were lucky, we found each other again, but so many marriages don't survive. Sort it now before it's too late.'

'I don't think Darcy wants to. For all I know she's cancelled the entire wedding, especially if she found out I had you tell all the guests via email.' He put his head in his hands. 'God, she must hate me.'

'She won't because I didn't follow through.'

He looked up at her.

'I never emailed anybody. I simply got onto the airline, booked the first flight here to come and talk sense into you. There are times when a boy needs his mother, and that time is now. I know I'm not the best person to hand out advice on relationships, but hopefully some of what I've said makes sense. And there's only one way to find out how Darcy feels. Go to her, Myles. Don't mess this up. Don't let the best thing that's happened to you slip away.'

It was her choice of phrase that did it. Because Darcy was the best thing that had ever happened to him. And he'd never been one to back out of a challenge.

He stood and picked up his cell phone.

'What are you doing?' Martha asked, on her feet too.

'I'm texting a few friends and calling the Moonlight Loft & Terrace. If Darcy hasn't told any of them we're cancelling, then the wedding is still on.'

In a few clicks and with a short phone call plus two replies, one from Dylan, the other from Holly, he knew that they had heard nothing about an argument as the responses to his out-of-the-blue and apparently last-minute query about food allergies before the wedding were only filled with sarcastic comments suggesting he probably should've already checked these things before the wedding was just around the corner.

'Looks like we're still on,' he said.

'Then go get her, Myles.'

He scooped his mum up in his arms. 'I'm getting married!' he said. And then louder, so anyone on the Upper West Side would hear him across the rooftops, yelled it again. He was a different man to the one who'd arrived all the way from England. And Darcy wa the reason for that.

They moved from the terrace to the inside. All he needed wa his keys and wallet and the practised skill of hailing a cab outside and he'd be on his way to the Inglenook Inn. And this time he'd make Darcy listen.

Martha stopped him at the doorway to the lounge and pointed up above. 'Is that what I think it is? I've been staring at it since I go here and it seems awfully like a man's—'

'Don't say it,' he grinned. 'But yes it is, it's the remains of Darcy' bachelorette party.'

'Now I wish I'd been here for that,' said Martha.

17

DARCY

'You didn't have to come all the way to the city. Facing summer in New York in your condition can't be much fun.' Darcy brought Cleo a glass of water with plenty of ice cubes. When Darcy had spoken on the phone with her this morning Cleo hadn't missed a thing, and when she'd asked what was going on Darcy had burst into tears, which was something new for her. She wasn't a cry baby, far from it, but this situation with Myles had taken its toll. And so Cleo had caught the next train from Inglenook Falls and, arriving in Manhattan, had trekked all the way from Penn Station in this summer heat, with her pregnancy thermostat facing overload.

'Plenty of women do it every day,' she insisted between gulps of water. 'And you're doing me a favour. I'm feeling lost with all the rest I'm getting, my lack of responsibility with the store.'

'It's your store, Cleo.' Darcy knew from Dylan that it had taken a lot to persuade her to loosen the reins. 'And you're feeling okay now, aren't you?'

Cleo smiled. 'If by "okay" you mean not anxious or depressed, then yes, I'm okay.'

'Good.'

'Dylan is fussing around me like a mother hen, it's driving me crazy.'

Darcy laughed as she put the pile of mail on the desk in the lounge. 'He's probably more anxious than you now. You do look relaxed.'

'It's the heat.' She made herself more comfortable on the sofa, using a cushion to support her back.

When the door to the Inn went and Darcy saw Jill, she excused herself.

'Take your time,' said Cleo, 'I'm far too blissed out to mind.'

With no guests booked for lunch, Darcy asked Jill to tackle the dining room this morning, paying particular attention to cleaning the area around the door leading to the outside. 'We've been opening it most days and it's pretty dirty around the edges,' she explained as they stood on the compact balcony just off the dining room.

'Well, I'm here for a couple of hours so I'll do this and then the hallway and stairs.'

'Thanks, Jill.'

'Where are all the guests?' she asked. 'If I was staying here I'd be sitting down there.' She pointed to the small courtyard garden reached by a set of steps leading down from the balcony. Sofia had put two white, cast-iron tables with a vintage patina, along with three chairs around each, beside a flowerbed filled with a riot of colour now it was the end of July.

'I think my guests are too busy enjoying Manhattan but I'm sure they'll be out here later.'

'Not if I get there first,' Jill smiled. 'I've got my book in my bag. When I've finished the clean I might ask Rupert to fix me one of his famous mocktails.'

'Go ahead, enjoy every second,' Darcy smiled. She loved this job, everything about it from choosing a menu for guests to intericting with the staff. How could Myles assume she'd be happy to ust give it all up at a moment's notice and move to another city?

Back in the lounge, Cleo was waiting for her. It had worked out vell that it was such a beautiful day because it meant that, now all he guests were out, Darcy could talk to Cleo, although she'd ilready redone her make-up once after crying on the phone earlier ind she didn't want to fall apart a second time.

'Refill?' Darcy spied the empty water glass.

'No thanks. Now come and sit.'

Darcy did as she was told.

'Now, are you going to tell me what is going on? Or do I have to orce it out of you like we forced the candy out of the piñata the other night?'

And so Darcy told her everything, about the last few months, he pressure she felt, Myles's job offer, the dream honeymoon he'd booked, the text from Boston, how they'd argued and she'd walked iway from the apartment and never gone back.

'And I thought I was the only one with problems,' said Cleo.

Darcy was glad she wasn't crying now. If anything, she was ingry. Angry that she hadn't stayed with Myles and talked this hing through. She'd walked away and thrown herself into work because it had been the easier thing to do, and she wasn't proud of herself.

'He'll probably go to Boston glad I'm no longer a part of his life.'

'Since when are you not a part of his life?'

'Didn't you listen to the story? I've never seen him so angry it me.'

'And upset, don't forget. Myles loves you so there'll be anger here but I'll bet he's also gutted things aren't going right at the noment.'

'We shouldn't have rushed into this wedding.'

'Are you saying you want to call it off?'

'I may not have any choice, Cleo. Myles may already have decided that for me. I haven't heard from him. Maybe he's waiting for me to cancel everything and hoping this whole mess just goes away.'

'I haven't known Myles for long but he doesn't seem like the type of guy to simply wash his hands of you without sitting down and working through what's happened.'

'Then why Boston, Cleo? Tell me that. Why accept a job, set up a date to go, and not tell your fiancée?'

Cleo hesitated. 'Okay, that's a bit out of character.'

'A bit? It makes me feel like I never knew him at all.'

'But you do. Forget about all the other stuff right now, the work schedules, Boston, and think about Myles. Just Myles. Do you love him?'

Her hands gripped the hem of her dress above her knees, fiddling with the material. 'Of course I do.'

'Can you imagine ever being with anyone else?'

'I don't think I have the energy, Cleo. There's a reason I fill my life with work. It's always been easier that way. I know where I'm at.'

'From what Dylan told me, Myles was pretty much of the same mind before he met you. But meeting each other has changed you both – and, I think, for the better. Life's too damn short, Darcy, to work all the hours and neglect everything else in your life.'

'Myles's dad said the same to him, back when they were repairing their relationship, sorting through their family issues.'

'Then learn from it. I don't tell many people this, but I was married once before.'

'You were? When?'

'A long time ago now, in a different life, back in the UK. To cut a long story short my ex cheated on me, but I'd pushed him away time and again so he wasn't entirely to blame. For a long while wondered whether I'd screwed up the only decent thing I had going n in my life apart from work, and it made me realise how much we eed a balance, how none of us is a one-man, or one-woman, band.' he grinned at her descriptive terms. 'What I'm trying to say is we on't get an endless number of chances, Darcy, and I think Myles is our chance, your opportunity to have it all. He's your Dylan.'

'But Boston, Cleo. Boston.'

'Boston's not so bad.'

'And how would you feel if Dylan took a job in another city ithout telling you?'

She pulled a face. 'Fair point. But talk to him, Darcy. If you two re going to get married and make your relationship work, you eed to come up with a plan. Neither of you is a stranger to hard ork, so this can be your new project. Think of it like bridesmaid resses.'

'Not sure where you're going with this,' Darcy smiled.

'I went to have another fitting and my baby bump is increasing y the day. I stood there feeling frumpy compared to Isabella and olly and no doubt Gabriella will look stunning when she arrives.' he held up a hand to stop Darcy interrupting. 'But you know hat, as well as carrying a baby, I'm voluptuous. I always have een. I have curves. Once I accepted my shape and thought about ringing another human being into the world, I didn't feel quite so ad. I saw the positive. And it's the same with you and Myles. You on't need to fight to change yourselves, either of you, but you do eed to adapt. Serenity and Alexis had gorgeous ready-made resses but, at the end of the day, they were just a load of loose bric. It took time for them to hem, pin and sew and dedicate emselves to the craft to make the dresses fit perfectly and compli-ent the person wearing them. And it's the same with your rela-onship.'

Darcy hugged her friend. 'That's an amazing analogy.'

'I'm exhausted thinking that one up.'

'I don't know what I'd do without you. Any of you. I feel so lucky to have so many special friends.'

'So you're glad I came over?'

'Of course.'

When the door to the Inglenook Inn went and let in a blast of summer heat, Darcy stood, straightened her dress, and took a deep breath, ready to turn into hotelier mode.

But she froze on the spot. 'Myles.'

Cleo looked at him, then at her. 'I'll be in the dining room. I need some more water.'

Neither of them said anything until Cleo left and the room fell silent once again. Aside from the street noise that filtered in no matter the season or the hour, it was just the two of them.

'You know,' Myles began, 'I fell in love with you back in London. I didn't realise it at the time because I was angry. I'd had itching powder put in my bed, barely any sleep, but then there was this unbelievably sexy woman, hands on hips, defending her employee and not willing to back down an inch.'

Darcy wasn't sure how this was going to go. He commanded attention standing here in front of her and she didn't dare say anything. She couldn't work out if he was here to break up with her or make her see reason.

'I fell in love with you that little bit more when I stayed here as a guest last year.'

'But?'

'There is no "but", Darcy.'

'You still love me?'

'You drive me crazy, but I figure that's part of any relationship.' He wasn't close enough to touch her, not yet.

'I suppose it is.'

'I know that for me, I've never been with anyone long enough to see it before.'

'Me neither.'

'I need you to be entirely honest with me now.'

'Go on,' she encouraged.

'Do you still think we can build a life together?'

She was about to reply that yes, she did. She wanted to fall into his arms, have him kiss her and take away the pain of the last few days, but she couldn't. 'You didn't tell me about Boston, Myles. I can't get my head around that at all.'

'And you...' He stepped forwards and took both of her hands in his. 'You didn't give me a chance to explain.' When she tried to move away he was ready and tightened his grip, persuading her to stay where she was, in front of him, looking up into eyes that spoke of the same angst she'd had since that morning at his apartment.

'I'm listening now.' In the corner of her eye she saw a guest come in but instead of lingering they marched straight on up the stairs.

'That text, about Boston, was nothing to do with work. And it was supposed to be a surprise.' He grinned. 'Which, I suppose, technically you did get when you read it.' Her face told him this wasn't the time for jokes. 'We both agreed not to take a long honeymoon straight after the wedding because of work commitments and family visiting, but I wanted to do something. And so I started looking into somewhere to take you that wasn't so far away that travel takes up valuable honeymoon time, but remote enough that we get some together time, away from jobs, away from Manhattan. And it'll fit nicely with a trip to Cape Cod, where I've found us a beautiful beach house I know you'll love. I've squared the trip with Sofia so we'll have five nights to be together, no distractions, apart from each other. I wanted it to be a surprise, I was going to tell you at the wedding. And about the trip to Marrakesh too.

'You see, we missed a big step along the way, Darcy. We didn't take the time to get to know each other. That's why you jump to conclusions. We both need to invest time in this, in us.'

'So you haven't taken a job?'

'No.' He shook his head and his grip lessened on her as his fingers rubbed hers gently. 'My job is here, in Manhattan, and will continue to be until you or I decide to relocate. But whatever happens, we'll be making the choice together. Our lives have run in parallel before now but we need to find a way to follow the same track.' He took out his cell phone. 'Check out the pictures, Darcy. First stop is a luxury hotel in Boston where I've already taken the liberty of booking you some spa treatments – Holly helped me out with that one – then it's on to Cape Cod and a cottage within walking distance to the ocean. We can sit on the sun deck, cook dinner on the grill.'

'It sounds and looks unbelievable.'

'And then there's Marrakesh to look forward to, where we'll be on our own again, spending time getting to know one another some more. What do you say?'

'To the holiday? To you spending a fortune on a surprise honey-moon?' But when he dropped to one knee in the same way he had that day in Central Park she knew full well that wasn't what he was talking about at all.

'Darcy Spencer, for the second, and hopefully final, time... will you marry me?'

She made him sweat, just a little, before a huge grin took over. 'Yes, yes I will.'

When he stood up tall and she leaned in to him and lost herself in his kiss, she felt at home. This was right where she wanted to be. With him. Wherever in the world they may end up, as long as they were together, she didn't care.

18

DARCY

It was a whirlwind couple of weeks. Darcy and Myles had spent three days juggling work and seeing Martha on her impromptu visit to New York, and they'd spent the rest of their free time – or at least what little they managed to grab – preparing for the wedding. But rather than the exhaustion and feelings of being overwhelmed that she'd experienced before, Darcy rode the wave of excitement. She had her final dress fitting with Alexis and Serenity, which the girls, including Gabriella who had arrived from Switzerland, insisted on being present for. The bridesmaids were good to go, each with her dress in her own possession. The cake was ready, the catering and venue confirmed for the millionth time – all part of Darcy's checklist – yesterday the photographer had confirmed what time she'd arrive at the Moonlight Loft & Terrace, and everyone who needed accommodation was sorted.

And now, on the morning of the wedding, Darcy emerged from her bedroom into the kitchen of the apartment at the Inglenook Inn.

'Good morning, sleepyhead.' Isabella was in the kitchen with Gabriella and Sofia, and the smell of toast drifted towards Darcy.

'I'm hungry.'

'I'm not surprised.' Gabriella, a breath of fresh air all the way from Switzerland, cut another two generous slices from the loaf on the board and slotted them into the toaster. 'You must've had over eight hours sleep.'

'Anyone would think she wasn't a bride,' put in Sofia. 'She doesn't look nervous at all.'

'Actually, I'm really not.' Darcy nodded to the offer of fresh orange juice and pushed an empty glass towards Sofia for her to fill from the jug on the table. 'I'm excited. Is Rupert coping upstairs?'

Sofia shook her head and set the jug back down. 'Uh-uh... you're well and truly off duty. The Inn is not your concern today, I've got everything under control. And even if I didn't, it's not for you to worry about.' Darcy opened her mouth to protest that she still cared but she knew she needed to accept that today her words would fall on deaf ears.

When there was a knock at the door, Isabella went to answer it and in came Darcy's sister, Sarah. She gave Darcy a hug, almost knocking her juice flying.

'All the people I love, back in Manhattan,' claimed Darcy. 'I should get married more often.'

Sarah pointed a finger at her. 'Don't say that. Once is enough and it'll be all you need. And I have something for you. Close your eyes.'

'What is it?'

'Just close your eyes.'

She did as she was told and felt something soft in her hand. When she was at last allowed to look she saw an ivory and blue lace silk garter in her palm. 'I seem to remember buying this for you, for your wedding.'

Sarah hugged her. 'And now it's your something old, something blue and your something borrowed. And you've got plenty of new lready. That engagement ring is damn gorgeous by the way.' Darcy extended her hand so her sister could admire it some more. 'Looking at it over FaceTime just didn't do it justice.' She pulled her ister into yet another hug, clasping her tight. 'I'm so pleased for ou, little sis.'

'And you're happy with your dress?'

'It's gorgeous. And Serenity and Alexis couldn't be any nicer, ould they?'

'Aren't they wonderful?'

'They gave us champagne at the final fitting,' Gabriella related, and we didn't feel at all rushed. As a matter of fact, I almost wanted o stay in there for longer.'

'Well, I'm glad you're happy. You're all going to look wonderful.'

'Not as wonderful as you,' Sofia winked across the table.

'How's the groom?' Isabella spread butter onto the toast ollowed by raspberry jelly. 'Have you heard from him, Darcy?'

'He texted this morning.'

When she saw Darcy's grin Isabella quizzed her friend. 'Dare we sk what he said or is it too explicit to share?'

'It's not that sort of text.' She wondered if he was worried her erves would get the better of her today, but so far so good. Letting o of her complete independence was going to take time, and Darcy new she had to keep reminding herself of the bigger picture: a ong-term future with a wonderful man who'd stepped into her life uite unexpectedly.

'This is good.' She bit down on the second piece of toast.

'I can't believe you have an appetite,' said Sarah. 'I was so ervous on my wedding day that I couldn't eat. I almost passed out uring hair and make-up.'

'I remember! I bought some candy from the store across from he hotel we were in and force-fed you until you could stand on our own two feet.'

'I was terrified at mine,' Gabriella admitted. 'I was convinced Trent was going to stand me up at the altar.'

'What?' Sofia put down her own glass of juice. 'You never told me that.'

'I never told anyone.' She swished away the thought. 'I don't think that deep down I believed it but a little voice in my head kept niggling at me. I was so relieved when I saw him standing there at the end of the aisle.'

'Aren't you nervous at all?' Sofia watched Darcy demolish her toast, her juice, and start on the fresh fruit from the bowl on the countertop.

'A little.' But now she was here and everyone was asking, her emotions seemed to be creeping up on her and all she wanted was to stop them from being too overwhelming. She took out a list from her pocket. Being organised always helped her feel in control.

'You had that in your PJs?' Sarah pointed to the piece of paper. 'You slept with it?'

'I may have run over my checklists last night, right before I fell asleep,' she admitted.

'I should never have expected anything less.' Gabriella mussed Darcy's hair as she walked past to make herself a cup of camomile tea.

'Come on then, let's get this over with,' said Sarah.

Clutching the list, Darcy asked, 'Get what over with?'

'You're going to run through that list, aren't you? Check everything off... again.'

Sheepish, Darcy unfolded the paper and handed it to her sister. 'Do it with me?'

'I'd love to.'

And as they ran through everything from the plush car coming in four hours to take them to the grand hotel not far from the Moonlight Loft & Terrace on Madison Avenue, the exact where abouts of her dress as well as any products she wanted to take with her, to the time the cake would be delivered to the venue and when to expect the photographer for pre-wedding photos, Darcy felt at ease.

In six hours' time she would be married. And she couldn't wait.

* * *

'We sound like a gang of schoolgirls,' Sarah remarked as she, Gabriella, Isabella, Cleo, Holly and Darcy failed to keep their excitement under wraps in the stretch limo as it travelled uptown until they reached the hotel where Darcy would get ready and where she and Myles would spend their wedding night.

They bundled out of the vehicle amidst laughter and bossiness about taking care of the dresses they were holding. Darcy held her precious cargo in her right arm. Sunglasses pulled across her eyes, she looked back down the street – the most fashionable address in Manhattan – with its enormous apartments overlooking Central Park. Today the sun made it look all the more spectacular, and tonight she'd be staying in this luxury hotel they walked into now, with its spotless shine on the glass doors, the impeccably dressed concierge. Strange to think this street held so many memories of shopping with girlfriends, taking in festive lights and Christmas windows every holiday season, and now it would set the scene for the next stage in her life.

Up in Darcy's suite, which was so much more than just a hotel room with its super-king-size bed, a bathroom to die for, and a lounge with floor-to-ceiling windows taking in the park and the traffic down below that seemed miles away when you were up here in the quiet, the girls congregated, voices rising an octave a minute along with their enthusiasm.

'You always were a giggler,' Gabriella told Isabella.

'Hey, don't blame me, we're all as bad as each other.'

'I think she's right.' Cleo stood near the air-conditioning vent while she admired the view. 'It's lucky the men aren't here. They'd find us far too annoying.'

'I know my dad would,' Sarah agreed. 'He hated us giggling when we were kids.'

Darcy grinned. 'No, he hated not being in on the joke.'

'Are you looking forward to Boston?' Gabriella looked around for somewhere to hang her dress.

'I really am.'

'And Marrakesh, you lucky thing. All that sun in October, what a lovely escape.'

'I hope you're turning your cell off both times you're away.' Cleo still hadn't moved away from the vent.

'I will, don't worry.'

'Is Mum joining us here?' Sarah claimed a hook for her dress.

Darcy shook her head. 'Mum and Dad are with Myles's parents. I think they were going out for brunch near the apartment, then getting ready back at our place, then making their way to the Moonlight Loft & Terrace, dropping Dad off here on the way. He gets to ride with me,' she smiled, 'before he gives me away.'

'Throws you away more like,' Sarah teased.

'Enough of that,' grinned Darcy.

'Ah, sibling rivalry,' said Cleo. 'You're not too dissimilar to Ruby and Jacob.'

'Aren't they still little?' Sarah asked.

'Exactly,' said Cleo.

Darcy rolled her eyes. 'That's enough out of you, sis.' But she smiled at her. 'Is Tate organised to make the wedding on time?'

'If he's not,' said Sarah, 'he'll have Dad to answer to. Our brother,' she elaborated to Holly, 'is not the most organised of people. Used to drive Darcy up the wall.'

'I can imagine,' said Holly.

Darcy felt relaxed with the banter, with just being here, another step closer to the wedding. She was showered and dressed in a silk robe with her underwear in place and so comfortable – it should be, it was expensive enough. Her dress was hanging on the other side of the bathroom door, asking to be put on. The bridesmaid dresses were hanging at various points around the room – Cleo's was on the hook on the back of the main door, Isabella and Gabriella had claimed a hook each at the panelled end of the wardrobe in the bedroom, and Holly had hung hers on the back of the bedroom door.

Holly was busy humming the 'Wedding March' when a knock at the door announced the next stage of getting ready. It would be Susan, the freelance make-up artist who'd come to do the girls' hair and make-up, starting with Darcy. They'd had a practice run in May and it had been another item to check off her to-do list.

Darcy clutched Isabella's hand. 'I'm so excited.'

'I never thought you'd get down the aisle, you know. You always seemed to be talking yourself out of it. But now, well, I'm so happy for you.'

'Darcy?' Holly's voice travelled from the other side of the room.

'What's up?' She went towards the door expecting to see Susan and Susan was indeed who she saw, but not quite as she'd expected. This Susan had her arm in a sling, bruised fingers and a look of terror on her face. 'What happened?'

'I only went and fainted, didn't I. This morning on my way to the subway. Luckily I was with a friend and she helped me up, took me to the doctor.' She lifted her arm slightly to show more of her fingers but winced.

'Don't move it,' said Holly. She looked at Darcy.

'I can do make-up with one hand, easy,' Susan claimed. 'I won't let you down. Well, I will. I can't do hair.'

'You should have called,' said Gabriella, her mom voice well and truly taking over. 'We could've found a hairdresser.'

'At this short notice?' Susan asked. 'I knew you'd have a job doing that so that's why I didn't want you to panic. And I won't charge for today. Honestly, I'm so, so sorry. I really am.'

Darcy squeezed the arm that wasn't injured. 'You didn't do this on purpose.'

'Your hair is reasonably easy, Darcy.' Susan looked about to cry and Darcy didn't want her falling apart. 'I'm so sorry.'

'What's done is done, enough apologising.' Darcy addressed her friends, taking control. 'Girls, here is where I need you all. I'm going for a natural, wavy look, and it's all washed and ready, so I'm sure Susan can help you lot get the placement of the veil right. No need to panic.' Was she trying to convince them or herself?

'What about the rollers?' Susan asked, already fishing in the bag she'd brought with her.

'I'll have to go without. My hair has some wave anyway.'

'Rubbish,' said Holly, 'I've heard Myles talk about your hair and how sexy it is when it's super wavy. You're having the rollers.'

'I don't think Susan is up to it,' said Darcy. 'One-handed rolling would be a challenge too far.'

'I know how to use Velcro rollers.' Cleo jumped up. 'If my expanding girth allows me to reach your hair, that is.' She patted her stomach. 'Seriously, Darcy. I use them on Ruby's hair all the time.'

'That's true, she does,' said Gabriella. 'She put those photos on Facebook, remember, of Ruby going off to a friend's birthday party last fall.'

'I'll guide her through,' Susan assured Darcy, 'then once the rollers are in we can do your make-up while we wait for them to set.'

'She should've told us,' Isabella whispered to Darcy as Susan pulled more things from her bag.

'Let's just hope between us our make-up skills are good enough,' said Sarah, as Cleo lined up the rollers and ushered Darcy into the chair.

Within thirty minutes and under Susan's expert guidance, Darcy's hair had been wound into the Velcro rollers and left to set. Her make-up had been done in another thirty, with Cleo at the helm and Susan dictating the colours she'd already picked out after their initial consultation, and by the time Darcy's hair was sprayed before the rollers came out she was confident she was wedding-ready, happy this little upset hadn't turned out to be a major one. Sarah had held a mirror in front of her at all times so she could see the gradual transformation and, now, Darcy was thrilled to see it was as natural and flawless as it had been in the practice run.

Susan used her good arm to tease the waves in Darcy's hair ever so gently so they fell sexily around her shoulders. 'There, perfect. Thanks to all of you for totally saving the day. I owe you all big time.' She grabbed a portable mirror and showed Darcy the back of her hair.

'I love it, thank you. It almost seems a shame to put the veil on and cover it.'

'Nonsense. Once the veil is on you'll feel like this is all real. You'll really feel like a bride then... trust me.'

'Where's the veil, Darcy?' Isabella asked.

'It's in the wardrobe. I hung it there ready to grab.'

Isabella went off and returned with the garment in its see-through cover. 'Darcy, it's beautiful.'

All the girls stood around admiring it until Darcy got too impatient. She needed to keep things moving before nerves got the better of her. The day they'd argued about Boston, Myles had told her she'd been looking for an excuse to back out, and since she'd

had a chance to think about it, she knew that was true. 'Come on
put it in my hair, please.'

Cleo handled the veil as gently as she could and, under Susan'
guidance, found the right position to push in the stunning pear
and diamanté hair comb with its flowers surrounded by a scattering
of shimmering pearls. She secured it with a couple of discreet clip
in the same shade as Darcy's hair.

'They'll keep it in place the whole time,' Susan assured her.

Darcy took a deep breath in and let it out slowly. 'I really look
like a bride.'

'You really look like a bride,' echoed Holly, a tear in the corne
of her eye. 'And to think, this time last year we hadn't even met, and
now, well, you're one of my best friends, and I'm at your wedding.'

Cleo whipped a tissue from the box on the cabinet at the side o
the room. 'Don't cry, Holly. Or you'll make her start, or one of us
and we've still got to finish our own make-up. Time is marching on.

'Yes, ma'am,' she said kindly, flashing Darcy a smile.

Darcy was under no illusions as to how strong their friendshi
was despite it being so new. Just like with Myles, it was one of thos
bonds she couldn't ignore.

'Pierre won't want a snivelling wreck either,' said Gabriella.

Holly ignored the ribbing and instead picked up her cell t
make a call.

'Oh yes, the famous Pierre,' added Isabella. 'I'll bet he look
good in a suit.'

'Your Jake certainly does,' said Darcy.

'I know, he looks hot.'

'I'd watch her at the wedding,' said Gabriella, 'no shenanigan
in the restrooms.'

'I think I can control myself,' Isabella batted back. 'Okay, make
up time, girls.'

When there was a knock at the door it was Holly who went t

answer it and in came room service with two buckets filled with ice, each with a bottle protruding from the top. 'What?' she said innocently. 'I thought we all might need to relax.'

'I always knew she was a good judge of character,' said Gabriella, lining up the accompanying glasses with Sarah's help.

* * *

Hair and make-up complete, and relaxed from the bubbles, Darcy stood in the bedroom of the suite. 'I can't wait to put it on.' She looked at the dress as Gabriella, the tallest out of the lot of them, held it up high and unzipped its protective cover.

Sarah gasped and squeezed Darcy's arm. 'It's just gorgeous.'

Susan had gone on her way and it was just the six of them now, ready for the final stages of getting ready.

Isabella looked at her watch. 'The photographer should be here by now. I thought we could get some fun photos of us in our robes, before we're dressed. I took a few pictures using my cell phone, you know, when you were in rollers, Darcy.'

'Thanks... I think.' She looked at the clock herself. The photographer was more than half an hour late. 'I'll give her a call, find out what's going on.' But just as she picked up her cell, it rang. 'This is her, I hope she's not stuck in traffic. Hello.' Her face fell. 'Right... right... but we paid a deposit.' She swished away comments in the room that weren't helping her to hear what the photographer had to say. 'Well that doesn't help me much, does it? No, no, I know there's nothing we can do. I'll expect a full refund and if you're looking for a review from me, you've got one, but don't expect it to be nice!' Heart pounding, she jabbed a finger at the screen to end the call.

'What the hell just happened?' Sarah was by her side in seconds.

'She's only gone and double-booked.'

'What?' Holly was incredulous. 'And she only realised now? When you've been confirming and re-confirming all along! That's insane. Who does that? I've a good mind to go get her and drag her here myself.' She looked at Darcy. 'Oh no, do not cry! DO NOT CRY!'

Isabella handed Darcy a tissue. 'Hold this beneath your lower lashes, it'll stop any tears spoiling your make-up. But Holly's right, don't start crying. Myles will never marry you with a red nose and a face full of snot.'

'What the hell am I going to do?' Darcy asked. 'We have no wedding photographer.' Was this a sign? A bad omen?

'You'd think she'd suggest someone else and have sorted it for you,' cried Cleo.

'She did. She was about to tell me and I... well, you heard, I just lost it.'

'I'll do it,' said Holly. 'That's right.' She looked around the room. 'I'm not a bad photographer, Darcy should know.'

'You're good, you really are. Myles suggested asking you in the first place.' Darcy was on her feet. 'But I wanted you to enjoy the day.'

'I'll enjoy it all the more now.' Holly grabbed her cell and her keys. 'My place isn't far. I'll be half an hour tops. I'm off to get my camera.'

'Thanks so much, Holly!' she called after her, and just like that her friend was gone. Darcy sat down again, reminding herself to breath in and out slowly, not to panic, that everything was going to be just fine.

'Darcy,' Gabriella prompted, holding the dress up again. 'Are you ready to put this on? Because I get the feeling as soon as you're in this, you're going to forget about everything else.'

Was she right? Would putting on the dress make her feel as though she was still in control?

'Time to lose the robe,' Gabriella joked.

A collection of admiring gasps and exclamations about Darcy's underwear had her blushing and worked wonders for distraction as she stepped into the dress.

'Myles is a lucky man.' Isabella was on to another glass of champagne, but she could handle it. After her first half glass of bubbly, Darcy had opted for water until the ceremony. She didn't want to risk being tipsy and stumble or have any more bad luck on her big day.

Gabriella and Sarah helped her put her arms through the delicate lace bodice.

'Darcy...' Tears sprang to her sister's eyes.

'Don't, Sarah. Or I'll cry.' She felt close to tears now her hair was done, her make-up ready, and she stood in an ivory gown with the most intricate, romantic lace she'd ever touched. She told herself that everything that could go wrong had already done so, and it was time to pull herself together and do this.

'That must be your dad,' said Cleo when there was a knock on the door. 'I'll let him in.'

'Thanks.' Darcy stood looking at her reflection, contemplating the life-altering event she was about to embark on. And when her dad appeared in the doorway, she turned to face him. 'What do you think?' She did a little twirl, the same way she'd done when he bought her a fairy dress with more lace than she'd ever seen for her eighth birthday. She remembered every detail of that day because she'd been sick with the flu and hadn't thought she'd make the party let alone choose something to wear, and he'd gone from store to store until he found his little girl something suitable.

'Wow.' His voice croaked as he moved forwards and kissed her lightly on the cheek. 'My darling daughter. My beautiful Darcy.'

'I've just stopped the tears forming,' she told him, wagging a finger, 'don't start me off again.'

'No, don't, Mr Spencer,' added Isabella as she passed by the doorway with a waft of perfume.

'You look very handsome, Dad.' Darcy didn't get to see him in a suit much now he was retired, but the navy-blue material along with a crisp, white shirt and lavender tie looked good on him. She knew from her mum that he'd insisted on choosing it himself, too and for that she was very proud.

He fiddled with the collar. 'I'd forgotten what it's like to dress so smart. Darned suit isn't very comfortable, especially with a tie in the height of summer. Mind you, I've been sitting in the air-conditioned restaurant downstairs for the last half an hour.'

'Why didn't you come up?'

'I'm giving away my youngest daughter.' He took both of her hands in his. 'A man needs a bit of time to get used to that.'

'Dad...' Her voice threatened to break. 'Were you this emotional when Sarah got married?'

'Worse!' came Sarah's voice from the other room.

'I was terrible,' he admitted. 'With her, she was my first born – always hard. And with you, you're the last daughter to marry and... well, that's difficult in a different way.' He fiddled with his collar again until Darcy stilled his hands. 'I was driving your mom crazy this morning... another reason to come to the hotel early.' He checked his watch. 'Are we leaving soon?'

'Just waiting for Holly.'

'One of your bridesmaids? She's not here yet?'

Darcy giggled. It was almost calming having to keep his emotions in check rather than her own. 'Relax, Dad. She's gone to get her camera. The photographer double-booked,' she explained when his face begged the question. He began to ramble on about customer service and complaints procedures but Darcy put an end o it. 'Holly is fabulous, and it'll be nice having a friend. Save any of those stiff poses you get when people aren't relaxed.'

Isabella plucked a clean glass from the tray on the trolley that had been brought in earlier. 'Mr Spencer, a glass of bubbly while we wait?'

'Don't mind if I do. But only if you call me Paul.'

It wasn't long before Holly returned, camera at the ready and even a case with a tripod.

'She's quite the professional,' her dad observed.

Once Holly had her own dress on and added a gorgeous pair of diamond stud earrings, she set the tripod in the lounge area.

'We're going to be late,' Paul whispered to Darcy.

But for once she didn't panic. She'd spent her whole life working hard, making sure she was on time for everything and never let anyone down. And today, she wanted to savour the moment. 'Bride's prerogative,' she said as Holly ushered them all into position.

'I've set a timer so once I press the button, I'll jump in beside Isabella and we're good to go.' Holly moved Cleo over slightly, asked Darcy to turn her body a little, straightened Paul's tie. 'I think we're ready.' She fiddled with the camera and at the last minute jumped into the group in the position she'd allocated for herself.

Holly called out, 'Everyone say wedding!'

'Wedding!' they chorused.

Once Holly had taken a few shots and packed away the camera, was all systems go. A text from the car service pinged onto Paul's cell phone to say there were two cars waiting downstairs at the front of the building.

Paul turned to his daughter. 'Are you ready for this?'

'I'm ready,' said Darcy.

'Then come on, let's not keep Myles waiting.'

They bustled out of the hotel room, into the elevator, drawing admiring glances along the way. It whisked them down to the ground floor and they all filed out, the bridesmaids giggling ahead.

Darcy concentrated on putting one foot after the other. She had the loop of her built-in train over one wrist and with the other she linked her dad's arm, a moment of serenity before she faced the excitement of the rest of the day.

'Darcy.' It was Holly, who had reached the door to the hotel but turned back. 'I don't want to alarm you but have you seen the weather outside?'

Darcy tried to look past her friend but the others were huddled behind and she couldn't see. She dropped her dad's arm and stepped forwards. 'Oh no.' The balmy Manhattan summer day had spilled over into a downpour, as though someone had turned on a giant rainfall shower overhead in the time it had taken for the party to leave the suite upstairs and head down to ground level in the elevator. None of them had noticed the clouds creeping up on them as they'd jollied around getting dressed, having photographs taken.

'Does someone have a cell phone?' She held out her hand.

Sarah took hers out from her purse. 'Who are you calling?'

'The venue. We'll have to have the ceremony inside.'

'Darcy.' It was her dad. 'They'll have it under control. I was there, remember, at the food tasting when we met with Lisa.' The sound of him referring to the events coordinator calmed her a little. 'She explained plan B so there's no need to call. Let's just get there.'

Maybe he could sense her rising panic. It was another thing gone wrong and she was close to tears this time. It was like taking a giant step forwards and then being shunted back farther than before.

'Hey,' came Isabella's voice from beside her. 'In some cultures rain on your wedding day is believed to bring good luck.'

Not from where she was standing. She'd picked the venue for it rooftop terrace, the beauty of being able to see Manhattan and Central Park, feel New York as part of them, part of their ceremony.

Her dad tightened his grip on her arm. 'Let's go.'

Her legs felt heavy, her spirits damp. Her friends' voices were beside her, a concierge had dished out umbrellas and staff were fussing around her to make sure she would stay completely dry on her journey from the hotel lobby to the car door that was mere metres away.

Inside the car, Darcy felt her dress. It had survived a soaking. She was completely unscathed, at least on the outside.

'It's only around the corner,' said Paul. 'Mind you, I couldn't imagine walking in this.'

Darcy hadn't seen rain this heavy for weeks. It had been glorious this morning when she woke up, boiling hot as they arrived at the hotel, and in the suite they'd got so busy she hadn't noticed it change.

'Are the others following?' She realised she'd barely said a word since she got in the car.

'Relax, they're right behind us.'

Darcy looked up at the tall buildings surrounding them. Madison Avenue was home to some of the most extravagant stores, littered with fashion designers: Givenchy, Gaultier, Ralph Lauren. Darcy and Gabriella had done a lot of window shopping here back when they'd left education behind and were out making their mark in the real world. They spent many a day walking along amongst glamorous women walking their groomed Maltese or cocker spaniel, dreaming about one day when they might be able to afford to buy the sophisticated dresses, the shoes that cost more than their rent, and bags they'd be frightened to actually use.

Her dad whistled. 'I'd forgotten what New York traffic was like. The venue may only be round the corner but we're bumper to bumper. Myles might start to think you're not coming.' He stopped laughing when he saw her face. 'Darcy, what's wrong?'

She felt the colour disappear from her cheeks. 'What if I'm jinxed?'

'I haven't heard you use that word since you were little and you, Sarah, and Tate used to fight and jinx one another. I seem to remember Tate cut his fingers when he was chopping up an apple after you'd jinxed him for snipping off your Barbie doll's hair, then an hour later he fell off a ladder. I tell you, a tiny bit of me started to believe in this jinx thing.'

'You're not helping, Dad.'

'I'm trying to distract you. I think it'll work,' he added confidently.

'How so?'

'I'll keep jabbering on until we get there, then we'll get you upstairs to the Moonlight Loft & Terrace, and then once you see everyone, you'll know it's all going to be just fine.'

Darcy retold the story of the hair and make-up lady hurting herself, the double-booking with the photographer. 'And now it's raining.'

The car pulled up outside the venue and her dad told Darcy to stay put. The driver went around with an enormous umbrella, staff came out the front of the building and between them they got the bride inside and to safety. They did the same with the bridesmaids and finally they all congregated in the lobby.

'Wait up, Darcy.' Sarah stopped her before she walked into the elevator. 'The bow at the back of your dress has come undone. I can just about see it under your veil.'

Darcy stopped where she was. 'Thank you.'

'Are you wearing the garter?' her sister whispered as she fastened the bow again.

'I sure am.' She couldn't wait to show Myles, he'd love it. He'd asked her what underwear she was wearing for her big day but she'd refused to elaborate, saying it was unlucky. He'd insisted that only went for the dress but she'd been adamant. Maybe she'd let him discover the garter all by himself tonight in the honeymoon suite.

Inside the elevator they all chatted away, Darcy unsure as to who was the most excited. The only stoic one among them was her dad and it was grounding, it kept her in control.

'Check Myles isn't around,' she insisted before they stepped out in front of the doors leading through to the venue.

'He knows not to be anywhere near the elevator as of 3 p.m., and we're well past that.' Holly poked her head out, camera tripod in one hand, accessories bag in the other. 'Can't see him. There are loads of people inside. And the room looks amazing, Darcy.'

'Will one of you go and check he isn't there,' she pleaded.

Sarah and Gabriella went to do the honours and Lisa appeared. 'You look beautiful,' she said. 'Absolutely stunning.'

'It's raining.'

'Doesn't matter. The set-up is perfect, the aisle runs right down the middle, we've brought the arch inside. All the flowers arrived on time, the baby's breath and white freesias smell gorgeous and look amazing. Your bouquet is in the dressing room. The cake came first thing and looks spectacular. Your groom is waiting in there with a best man who has definitely remembered the rings. All we need is you, so let me show you to the powder room. Come on, he won't see, he's hidden on the other side of the bar under strict instructions to stay there until he gets the nod.'

The words were pouring out of Lisa but Darcy couldn't take any of them in as she and her procession of bridesmaids including Sarah and Gabriella, who had re-joined the ranks after confirming that Lisa's claims were indeed true, filed through to the powder room.

Sarah adjusted some of the waves of her sister's hair, smiling fondly at her as she did so. 'You okay?'

'Yep. I'm all set.' She sounded convincing enough.

Cleo moved her veil slightly to ensure it fell just right. 'Not long now.'

Darcy smiled but said nothing. She couldn't.

Holly went out with her camera ready to capture the ceremony the second Darcy and her father emerged to take that walk towards a different future.

Sarah, Cleo, Isabella, and Gabriella left Darcy in the powder room. Lisa came in to confirm they were good to go. She could faintly hear the rain on the skylight up above, murmurings of voices from a crowd of people who she knew would be a sea of faces as she walked towards Myles. She could hear the gentle sounds of the string quartet running through some of the songs they'd added to their list for this part.

And she could feel her dress, the waistband squeezing her tighter and tighter, the sleeves digging in to each shoulder, her palms clammy, the heat rising from her feet to the top of her head.

'Darcy... Darcy...' It was her dad. He'd opened the door to the powder room and was standing behind her. 'Darcy, sit down.' He led her over to the chaise longue. 'Now breathe. Come on, my girl. You're getting yourself into a state.'

'I don't think I can do this.'

'Yes, you can. You love Myles, he loves you, and he's willing to take you off my hands,' he joked, putting a finger to the tip of her nose in the same way he'd done when she was in junior high. 'That's my girl, that smile tells me I'm right.' He held out a hand and helped her to her feet.

'Oh no.'

'What's up?'

She turned and looked down at the floor. She'd felt something oosen, and sure enough, in the plush carpet pile was a button, from her dress. It must've come off as she tried to get her breathing under control, when the material felt as though it was far too tight.

Her dad picked up the button. 'Nobody will even see under the veil, honestly.'

She shook her head. 'I'll know.'

'Darcy, you're being ridiculous.'

She looked up at him with wide, innocent eyes.

Cleo poked her head around the doorjamb. 'Are we almost ready to go? Oh.' She saw the look on Darcy's face.

'We just need a minute,' said Paul, his eyes not leaving his daughter.

Cleo went off into the melee and left them alone. Darcy sat down again. 'What's wrong with me, Dad?'

'Nothing as far as I know.'

'It's as though I want to sabotage something that could be my own happy ever after.'

'Bit dramatic, Darce.'

She smiled at the name he used. He rarely shortened Darcy, hated it when others did, but it kind of fitted right now.

'I'm scared.'

'I was too.'

'When you married Mom? No, I don't believe you, you're just saying it to reason with me.'

'Honestly, I was a mess. I took off the day before the wedding.'

'You did not.'

'I did. I went and stayed with a friend in Brooklyn and told him I couldn't do it. He was my best man.'

'Hal?'

'That's right. And he never breathed a word of it. Not to Sandy, not to anyone.'

'So what happened?'

'I drank a lot of beer.'

'Dad.'

'I won't tell you how many bottles we got through, but what w
also did was talked. Hal was single, he didn't meet Donna unti
much later when we joked I'd need to be there for when he did
runner. Men don't talk like you women do, but going over t
Brooklyn was the best thing I ever did.'

'What did he say to you?'

'He basically told me to get over myself.'

Darcy's laughter filled the dressing room. 'I was waiting for yo
to tell me something deep and meaningful.'

'We're men, and it's Hal,' he shrugged.

'Good point.'

'But if I'd gone somewhere on my own I might have done some
thing silly like run out on your mom. I'm just grateful Hal told m
to take it one step at a time. First, shower and clean my teeth, have
shave, pretend it's a normal day, he said. After I'd done those thing
he told me to put on the suit, just like I did for work every da
While I did that he called a cab and told me to pretend we wer
going out for Friday night drinks like we'd done a million time
before. And when we arrived at the hotel he told me to pretend w
were going into the bar and I was going to hook up with the mo
beautiful woman I'd ever laid eyes on. When he patted me on th
shoulder as I went into the ballroom to wait for your mother,
knew I was doing the right thing.'

Her dad held her hand, his warm skin instilling a sense of calr
in her. 'Thank you.'

'For what?'

'For sharing that story with me.'

'Don't tell your mom.'

'I won't,' she grinned.

'Did it help?'

'A little.'

It was Sarah's turn to check on them now. She poked her head around the door. 'What's going on?'

Again, Darcy's dad said, 'Give us a minute.'

'You've already had quite a few of those,' said Sarah, the only one of Darcy's bridesmaids who would dare reprimand the man.

'Sarah, I said not now.'

When she left them to it Darcy asked, 'How do I know we can make it work?'

'You and Myles?'

'His family history isn't great, I told you about his parents. Even he worries about how we'll manage between our jobs and our relationship. My job has been the only thing I've ever been sure of. Even when it wasn't going so great, I've always known I could turn it around with hard work.'

Her dad started to laugh. 'It sounds a lot like a marriage to me. You have to work at those too. But the work needn't be hard. It can be fun, and well worth it in the long run.'

'What if we fall apart a few years from now?'

'Then you'll pick yourselves up and deal with whatever shit life throws at you.'

She grinned at his choice of words. He was always so careful in front of his kids. Even when their former neighbour cut down part of Paul's apple tree that was hanging over the dividing fence, her dad didn't curse, he simply went over to talk it through with the man. Although come to think of it, they had heard raised voices and perhaps it was just ignorance that made her think they'd kept their language respectable.

'Life isn't always easy,' he said. 'Look at when you were fired in London.'

'Not my finest career moment.'

'You forgave Myles for his part in it though.'

'It wasn't really his fault. I should've kept my mouth shut and been more professional.'

'It doesn't matter. You dealt with the fallout of a situation that had gone bad. And you can do it again.'

'I want to believe that.'

'Myles's parents' relationship is probably a good one to keep in mind, Darcy.'

'But it was terrible on so many levels.'

He held a finger up in the air. 'Exactly. It *was* terrible, and now it's pretty great from what I understand. They've got past everything that went wrong, there have been apologies, there's been forgiveness, each member of that family has faced up to his or her part and worked through it.'

'Mom really does tell you everything.' Darcy had confided in her mom and told her about Myles's background not long after she and Myles got together.

There was a firm knock at the door. And this time it was Myles with a hand across his eyes.

'No! Out!' Darcy ran inside the toilet stall, tucking her dress around her and pushing the door shut. 'You can't see me! It's bad luck!'

'Then I'll talk to you from this side.'

Darcy didn't hear her dad say anything but she heard the other door go again and she knew he'd left them to it.

'Darcy, are you listening to me?' It was Myles. He didn't sound angry or upset, just resigned.

'I'm listening.'

'I've been getting periodic updates out there in the bar. First from Cleo, then Sarah. And I know what's going on.'

'You do?'

'You're having second thoughts.'

'I... I...'

'I get it, Darcy, I really do.'

'I'm worried we won't make this work.'

'Me too.'

She leaned back against the closed door and heard his body do the same on the other side. She tried to imagine what he looked like in his navy suit, the dark tie with its white pattern against a shirt the same colour as her ivory gown, the cream rose he'd be wearing on his lapel and the tiniest hint of a handkerchief poking out of his breast pocket. She'd seen the outfit on a male model online – Myles had wanted her opinion, although she'd known already that the one he'd chosen would be the one he'd wear. Once he'd made his mind up about something, it usually stuck.

'Why are you worried?' she asked.

'For the same reasons you are, Darcy.'

The sound of her name on his lips made her shut her eyes and savour the moment.

'I also think you're reading too much into everything that's happened today.'

'What do you mean?'

'I heard about the hair and make-up lady's accident. I heard about the photographer – you should see Holly, bossing everyone around out here.'

Darcy managed a smile, she could just see it. Holly was never backwards in coming forwards.

'I even know about the button on your dress.'

Tears pricked at her eyes but she would not let them fall, absolutely not. 'You can't see the button, it's hidden by my veil, and this dress isn't going anywhere, I feel like I've been sewn into it.'

'I also know about the rain, I saw that part with my own eyes,' he told her through the closed door.

'I wanted to marry you on the rooftop.'

'I wanted it too.'

'I feel as though they're all signs, Myles, telling me we're crazy to think this will work.'

'Here's what I think,' he said. 'You're panicking because you're not in control like you usually are. You won't be completely independent like you've always been so determined to be. Life will throw things out of left field, it always does, with everyone.'

Hearing his voice was all she'd needed. She should've had him come in here sooner.

'I have a different proposal for you,' he said through the door.

'And what's that?'

'How about when today is over, we make another commitment. Once a week we have a date night, we pretend we're not even married, and we just have some fun.'

He was saying everything right. Things had been full speed ahead since they met, the fun had been missing because of it, and it was no way to start their lives together.

'What do you say, Darcy? We got things a little out of sync, that's all.' He sounded deflated.

'No more keeping things from me, promotion offers and possibilities of moving. I need you to tell me everything, Myles.'

'I will, I swear. And promise me you'll let me help now and again, with whatever life throws at us. Because there will be ups and downs, everyone has them. There'll always be the little things like photographers cancelling, make-up artists hurting themselves or it raining when we've planned an outside occasion. As long as me and you stay constant, we'll handle everything else.'

She wished she could fling open the door right now and fall into his arms, she wanted it to be him and her, nothing else to think or worry about, just their path to the future that she felt ready to follow.

'Come on, Darcy, tell me what you're thinking.'

'Myles... could you go and get my dad and the bridesmaids?'

19

DARCY

Ready?' Her dad put his hand on his hip, the proud father, waiting or his daughter to take his arm.

'I really am.' With Holly taking the photographs today, there vere only four bridesmaids leading the procession when they left he dressing room.

Gathered in the foyer outside the bar, Isabella handed Darcy er bouquet with the same baby's breath and white freesias they'd ad put around the wedding arch, delicate lilies the same shade estled in between. Fresh white ranunculus added another touch of legance with their cup-shaped blooms and delicate paper-thin ayered petals.

'See you out there.' Cleo smiled.

Darcy breathed in the heady floral scent and said to her dad, 'I ıink she means *in* there.'

'No, she means *out* there,' Gabriella winked.

Darcy was too nervous to think about their mistake as she heard ıe string quartet playing 'First Day of My Life', waiting for her to ppear and begin her walk down the aisle.

She returned her dad's smile. 'Let's do this.' And for the first time today she could honestly say she was one hundred per cent sure about this, excited, looking forward to the future, whatever came their way.

The doors to the bar area opened and in they walked, but instead of seeing chairs on either side, an arch at the end, Myles waiting for her, the bar area was clear and the sounds of the string quartet echoed through from the terrace. The sun was out in full force, she could see the ground from where they were standing; it was as though the rain hadn't really been there at all.

'Looks like a good sign,' her dad whispered.

'How... how did...'

'It was all Myles.' Cleo turned to her before they moved on. 'When he realised you were in panic mode he said there was no way he was letting this happen. The skies had cleared, the heat had already begun to dry the puddles outside, and so he had everyone – old, young, weak or strong – help shift everything back to the way you wanted it. He said he didn't care if the heavens opened again. If they did, you'd both get wet.' She took Darcy's free hand. 'He's a keeper, Darcy. Don't you ever dare let him go.'

Cleo took her position and off they set and when they passed through the doors to the outside, the string quartet started to play the 'Wedding March' as Darcy followed the aisle all the way to the end where Myles was waiting in front of an arch bedecked with so many flowers the scent on the air drifted right for her. On either side was a blur of faces, people she knew but couldn't focus on now. She only had eyes for one man, standing in front of her, his gaze never leaving hers once. There was no sign of rain, no indication of last-minute nerves, and only a vague awareness of the music that carried her along towards her future.

* * *

Darcy buzzed on the euphoria of her special day. She spoke to every one of their guests, laughed with Rupert and Sofia about her inability to have a conversation and not mention the Inn, met Myles's relatives and tried to remember all their names, chatted with people young and old who'd all come together to make this day what it really was: perfect. She enjoyed time with Winston and Myles's niece and nephew, she admired Victoria's lilac silk dress before her now sister-in-law whispered that her expenditure on dress options was a sore subject and so they'd changed the topic to Manhattan and all the sightseeing the family were going to do during their stay.

'I'd love to see Boston someday,' Victoria told her as the round tables were shifted out of the way so guests had more space to mingle. 'Come to think of it, I wouldn't mind going to Marrakesh either. Myles has chosen well.' She kissed Darcy on the cheek. 'With his holidays and his bride. Welcome to the family.'

'I'm happy to be a part of it,' Darcy replied. A fresh breeze surrounded them up so high and away from all the noise at street level. Darcy moved her hair back across her shoulder and Victoria adjusted the end of her veil that had curled in the wind. 'Myles might have an opportunity to move to Boston with work, so a few days there will be a chance to see what it's like.'

'You guys wouldn't leave New York, would you?'

'Not for a long time yet.' But rather than sending her head into a spin, it was as though the wedding band now in place on her finger along with her engagement ring solidified their promise to make decisions together. Which, she supposed, was what it was there to do. They were in a partnership all of their own now, and the world was set to be very different.

Talk moved to the Inn and what Darcy had been doing with the place. Winston joined them and Darcy found out more about his business, got to know this extension of family. Darcy danced with

Ian, Myles danced with his mum, Dylan and Cleo cuddled together chatting as they watched the sun begin to set on the far side of the terrace.

Darcy found Holly taking shots of their friends without them noticing.

'If I'm ever half as happy as those two...' Holly looked over at Dylan and Cleo, in the moment, as though they weren't at a wedding but in their own private universe.

'You have Pierre,' Darcy smiled, 'he's pretty dreamy.'

Holly sighed as they looked over his way. 'You're not wrong.'

'I don't know how to thank you, Holly.'

'It's been my pleasure.' Not only had she taken shots of the ceremony, the wedding breakfast, the official posed pictures afterwards, but she was continuously darting around taking natural shots that the other photographer hadn't even suggested. 'I'm loving every minute.'

'You saved the day.'

'Well actually I should be thanking you,' said Holly.

'How?'

'I just got asked to photograph this place for a Christmas feature, and they're paying me a pretty good whack, let me tell you. Lisa said she'd watched the way I photographed, the way I put people at ease, she looked at some of the shots on my camera and just said she wasn't interested in anyone else.'

'I'm thrilled for you,' Darcy beamed. 'Your first photography gig.'

'I know, pretty amazing, huh? Looks like that intensive photography course has already paid off.'

'I think it also has a lot to do with your natural talent,' Darcy smiled.

Cleo came along next but by the look on her face she wasn't completely happy. 'It was a beautiful wedding, Darcy,' she said through gritted teeth as Dylan came hurrying over with her purse. 'The baby loved it so much it decided it wanted to see for itself.' She didn't get any more words out because she doubled over in pain.

'Oh my God! Is she...'

Dylan grinned. 'Looks like we're having a baby. There's a car waiting outside to take us to the hospital.'

'What can we do?' Darcy had hold of her friend's hand, and the way she was squeezing it threatened to imprint her wedding and engagement ring in her skin forever.

'I'll take it from here.' Dylan congratulated her again but accepted Myles's help to the elevator and downstairs.

'Is she...' Sarah was at her side now.

'In labour, yes.'

'I should've got a photograph of her,' said Holly.

'In pain?' Gabriella asked.

'It's all about capturing the moment,' Holly insisted.

They chatted about their friend, speculating as to the sex of the baby, and when Darcy noticed Pierre she said, 'He seems to be fitting in.' If you didn't know, you'd never have put the two of them together tonight. He was doing his thing and she was doing hers, but Darcy should know – some couples simply worked that way.

'He's enjoying himself,' Holly agreed, waving over at her boyfriend. 'Did you hear, he's in charge of some new hotel complex opening up out in Inglenook Falls?'

'Cleo was telling me about that.' Darcy could see Myles making his way back over to them. 'It sounds like it'll be amazing. I hear there'll be a spa. I might be up for a weekend away.'

'Good thinking. I'll let him know.'

When Myles reached her side she asked about Cleo.

'She's in good spirits,' he told them. 'She and Dylan went off to the hospital and said they'd send updates. I think she was panicking she'd ruin the wedding because people would want to be there when the baby comes, that's why she didn't want too much fuss here.'

'She'd never spoil the wedding,' said Darcy.

'See, capturing the moment,' said Holly and showed them both the camera's display. She had taken a photograph of Darcy and Myles in conversation, both smiling, the moonlight high up above them on the terrace now the sun had gone down over Manhattan. 'Perfect.' And with that, off she went to capture more of their wedding moments.

'I'm almost glad the other photographer bailed,' said Myles.

'She's pretty good, isn't she?' They watched her pass by Pierre and squeeze his arm. 'I wonder if it'll last between her and Pierre.'

'Only time will tell.' Myles wrapped his arms around her waist. 'Happy?'

'Couldn't be happier.' She leaned into him.

'I feel as though I've barely seen you tonight.'

'We need to keep our guests happy.'

'The story of my life, I'll always be second to your guests.'

'I think we both know that's not true.' She squeezed his hands. 'Would you look at Mrs Tillman!' She nodded in the direction of their neighbour, whom they'd invited just yesterday. It seemed the right thing to do and Myles's great uncle Douglas seemed to think so too.

'Good for them. But I'm surprised she's interested. Great Uncle Doug has been going on and on about how I'm responsible for putting his back out moving all the furniture from the inside to out here.'

'Doesn't look like he has many back issues now.' Darcy giggled as they watched the man take Mrs Tillman's hand so she could twirl beneath it as they moved in time with the music.

'I'm glad everyone is having such a good time.'

'I can't wait for Boston, just the two of us,' she said.

'You know it's supposed to rain, don't you?'

'Shame... we'll have to spend our time in the bedroom.'

'Rumour has it you're wearing a garter,' he whispered into her ear.

'Who told you?'

'Your sister. I think she's letting her hair down tonight.' They looked over at her dancing away with Darcy's dad, swaying in time to the string quartet's version of Katy Perry's 'Firework'. They were an amazing group of musicians and Darcy knew they couldn't have asked for anything else. What's more, they all seemed to be enjoying themselves, especially since Myles kept sending free drinks their way.

'Do you think it's time?' Myles asked. 'We haven't given the guests the showpiece dessert yet.'

Her eyes lit up. The sky had darkened and the terrace felt alive with the tiny globes strung along each edge, their white lights highlighting the faces of happy guests, excited relatives, and a very happy bride and groom. 'It's definitely time.'

Myles grabbed a microphone. 'Ladies and gentlemen. May I have your attention please.' His voice certainly commanded respect and for that she loved him just a little bit more.

He waited for their guests to face him and stood up on a wooden platform so he was above the level of everyone else. Lisa had had staff set up the makeshift bar at the side of the terrace but everything was still under wraps. 'As most of you know,' he said into the microphone, I fell in love with Darcy when I was a guest at the Inglenook Inn. I was new to Manhattan, America even, but it didn't take long to be introduced to some of your traditions.' Sounds of intrigue peppered the night sky. 'And anyone who knows Darcy will now that her favourite winter dessert is...'

'S'mores!' her brother Tate yelled from the crowd.

'That's right. So, without further ado – and I sincerely apologise to all the English guests here and ask that you follow what the Americans do – I'd like to say, off you go.' The waitstaff pulled the black tablecloths off of the displays to reveal long tables with everything you needed to make the American delicacy. 'And be warned it can get very messy!'

Darcy loved the way everyone went straight to the tables and formed an orderly line, Mrs Tillman and Great Uncle Doug at the front. 'I'll bet Mrs Tillman is going to show him how it's done.'

Myles spun her around so she was facing him. 'I thought while nobody was watching, I could kiss you again. I did it after I put the ring on your finger, but now I want to do it properly.' He took her face in his hands and looked deep into her eyes and then she heard nothing of the giggles and voices around them as Americans enjoyed a familiar dessert and the Brits made a fantastic discovery. All she heard, felt and knew was that this was the man she wanted to kiss for the rest of her life.

'Now where are we off to?' he asked when she grabbed his hand.

'I'm going to get me some s'mores!'

'In a wedding dress? Darcy... don't.' But she wasn't stopping. She was heading right for their novelty wedding dessert. 'What if you spill chocolate?'

'Then I spill chocolate!' she beamed. 'Life is full of unexpected surprises, Myles, some good, some bad. And for once, I'm just going to let it unfold in front of me.'

'Now that sounds like the best plan I've heard all day.'

And with that they raced to the table, each grabbed a skewer and held marshmallows over an open flame as they shared another kiss to start their married life.

MORE FROM HELEN ROLFE

We hope you enjoyed reading *Wedding Bells on Madison Avenue*. If you did, please leave a review.

If you'd like to gift a copy, this book is also available as an ebook, digital audio download and audiobook CD.

Sign up to Helen Rolfe's mailing list for news, competitions and updates on future books.

https://bit.ly/HelenRolfeNews

Christmas Miracles at the Little Log Cabin, the next book in the New York Ever After series, is available now.

ABOUT THE AUTHOR

Helen Rolfe is the author of many bestselling contemporary women's fiction titles, set in different locations from the Cotswolds to New York. Most recently published by Orion, she is bringing sixteen titles to Boldwood - a mixture of new series and well- established backlist. She lives in Hertfordshire with her husband and children.

Follow Helen on social media:

twitter.com/hjrolfe
facebook.com/helenjrolfewriter
instagram.com/helen_j_rolfe

Boldwood

Boldwood Books is an award-winning fiction publishing company seeking out the best stories from around the world.

Find out more at www.boldwoodbooks.com

Join our reader community for brilliant books, competitions and offers!

Follow us
@BoldwoodBooks
@BookandTonic

Sign up to our weekly deals newsletter

https://bit.ly/BoldwoodBNewsletter